The wind kicked up
feeding the flames

The angry red glow
winking on in the
trees farther away, j
south, heading up the mountainsides.

The wind, shifting almost wildly, blew smoke their
way, blinding them, causing Mary to cough as it
burned her throat.

Huge tongues of flames leapt upward, more than
twice the height of the trees. And on the wind they
could hear the distant roar, like that of a hungry
beast.

A shoulder brushed Mary's, and she looked to her
side. Elijah Canfield stood there, staring at the fire.
"Where's Sam?" he asked.

"I think he's still down with the crew building the
firebreak. He didn't come back after he took food
down."

His eyes, intense even in the dull red glow that was
lighting the night, fixed on her. "Doesn't anyone
know for sure?"

Mary felt a stirring of impatience, accentuated by
her growing anxiety. "That's the last we heard from
him." She paused, then asked skeptically, "Why? Are
you worried about him?"

A January Chill "is an entertaining romantic
suspense that stars two wonderful lead characters."
—*Midwest Book Review*

RACHEL LEE

July Thunder

MIRA®

ISBN 1-55166-885-8

JULY THUNDER

Visit us at www.mirabooks.com

Printed in U.S.A.

July
Thunder

Prologue

Lightning struck the same day Elijah Canfield arrived in Whisper Creek, Colorado. It struck at precisely the same hour, and within a few minutes of Elijah's arrival. No one took note. Not then.

The lightning struck a forest as dry as tinder. It hadn't rained in months, and the snowfall of the past winter had been light.

Had anyone been around just beforehand, they would have known it was coming. The charge built in the ground until boulders hummed like angry beehives. Animals scurried away, their coats prickling and trying to stand on end, racing through charged air that felt as if it were full of cobwebs. It was as if the mountain came alive with anger, as if its very spirit rose to the heavens in outrage. The world hummed and buzzed with fury.

No one saw it happen. The bolt came out of a nearly cloudless sky, unexpected, unlikely.

In an instant, with a single thunderous clap, the

lightning struck, picking as its target a tall, dead pine. The pine rent with another crack, lost in the rolling explosion that echoed off surrounding mountains, then burst into flame. Thin wisps of black smoke rose from the burning pitch, blown away immediately by a brisk breeze, concealing the evidence that otherwise would have been visible for miles.

But the wind did more than conceal. It lifted and carried tongues of flame with it, scattering them almost merrily among the other trees. Some died before they found sustenance. A few licked happily at dry branches and grew.

But no one was there to see.

Just as no one was there to see when Elijah Canfield pulled his car up to The Little Church in the Woods some forty miles away. Elijah was a minister, and the church was to be his new home. It was a small congregation and a small church, but it was a congregation that thirsted for the message that Elijah brought with him, the same way the flames thirsted for the dry limbs and needles of the pines. Elijah brought thunder and hoped his words would strike as lightning.

And flames began to devour the mountain.

1

Sam Canfield regarded the beautiful day with disfavor, then wondered if that wasn't just getting to be a bad habit. It had been three years since his wife's death, and common sense told him he should be getting past his dislike of beautiful sunny days. Especially beautiful sunny days when there was no snow on the ground.

After three years, he told himself, it should no longer seem like a personal affront when the sky wasn't filled with low, leaden clouds that wept. So maybe he had just developed some bad habits.

Still, he wasn't happy to see a sky so blue it hurt to look at it or feel the warmth of a summer day, a day the locals would call "hot," even though they would be lucky to see eighty.

He locked the door of his snug little house behind him, closing it on the memories within that had haunted his nights for a long time. This morning, for some reason, closing that door didn't feel like a betrayal. At once, the realization filled him with guilt.

Was he healing? Part of him thought it was about time, and part of him wondered how he could even think of letting go.

Sighing, he got into his patrol car and headed for his job as a sheriff's deputy in Whisper Creek. Another day, another dollar, he told himself. But this morning the words didn't sound quite so... despairing. This morning they just sounded cynical.

It occurred to him to wonder if he would even like the man he had become, assuming he bothered to look closely, then he dismissed the question. When life dealt you lemons, you made lemonade. He wasn't at the lemonade stage yet, though. He wondered if he would ever be.

And he wondered why he should even bother.

Morning roll call, such as it was, was quiet as usual. A dozen deputies, just waking up, got ready to go out to their cars and patrol the remote byways of the county and the quiet streets of the town. The kinds of crimes that plagued major cities were rare here. Domestic violence and brawls topped the list of problems, followed by relatively rare robberies and burglaries. That was one of the reasons Sam had moved here from Boulder. A quieter life. A less dangerous job. Because he and Beth had planned to start a family.

The thought darkened his soul, but he was making a decent effort at shaking the mood off when Earl Sanders, the sheriff, stopped him on his way to the car.

"Hey, Sam," Earl said. "How's it going?"

"Great," Sam replied. He wouldn't admit to anything else. Earl had held his hand through some of the darkest nights of his life, a friend at every turning, and Sam was determined not to lean on him any longer.

"We're still on for dinner tomorrow night, right? Maggie's swearing she'll kidnap you if you don't show up under your own steam."

Sam summoned a smile to his stiff face. "I'll be there." He couldn't blame Earl for checking. He'd accepted more than one invitation to dinner with the Sanders family only to beg off at the last minute because he couldn't bear the thought of being immersed in their happiness for several hours. "I promise."

"No excuses."

"Not a one."

"Good." Earl's smile suggested doubt, but he wasn't going to say so. "I wanted to ask you.... Didn't you say your dad was a minister?"

Sam wondered which of his drunken binges had caused those words to tumble out of his mouth. He never talked about his family, made a policy of pretending he had none. Which he didn't, not really. But more than once in the last few years he'd gotten in a mood and drowned his sorrows in beer, and he had probably babbled unwisely.

He didn't drink like that anymore. A sign of healing, maybe, or a sign of despair. He didn't know which. Something inside him had begun a painful dying when Beth was killed, and maybe it had finally given up the ghost, leaving him dead inside. Which was fine with him. Feelings weren't all they were cracked up to be.

"Yeah," he said reluctantly. "Why?"

Earl shrugged, but the sharpness of his gaze belied his seeming indifference. "There's a new minister over at The Little Church in the Woods. He arrived in town yesterday. I wondered, because his name is Elijah Canfield."

Elijah Canfield. Recognition hit Sam like an explosion in his head, and for an instant he couldn't even see. And he had thought he was dead?

Life poured into him, painful life, with an anger so pure it burned in him like a white flame, with a hurt so deep it filled his gut with molten lead. Holding himself in became a nearly impossible act of will.

He could barely see Earl's face. Between clenched teeth, he said, "He's my father."

Then he turned and walked out of the station, his limbs as stiff as ice.

In his patrol car, he sat for long minutes trying to calm himself. Nothing had changed, he told himself. The old bastard was just closer than he had been before. It didn't make any difference. Elijah would still treat his son as dead, and Sam would continue to ignore the existence of his father. They might see each other on the street or in a store from time to time, but what would that change?

Walls of ice could be opaque. Elijah had built those walls block by block, and finally, when the anguish surpassed bearing, Sam had sprayed water over them, sealing even the tiniest chink. The anger that burned in him now was dangerous because it might melt that wall.

He couldn't allow that. By sheer force of will, he tamped it down. Ice. He had to maintain the ice. It was the only protection he had.

Mary McKinney was driving to the store for her week's groceries, puttering along Main Street, thinking about nothing in particular. She was good at that when she didn't have something to occupy both her hands and her mind. Often she wasn't quite sure where she drifted to, but things popped in and out of her head. Safe things. Simple things. Like whether she should drive down to Denver to visit her aunt this weekend.

The cat darted out from between two cars, directly into her path. It was as if time slowed down and her entire universe suddenly focused on that cat. Orange, tiger-striped. Big. Ratty looking. And right behind it there would be a little boy. She could almost see the dark top of his head as he ran after the cat.

She jammed on her brakes, tires squealing. An instant later there was a loud crunch and she was slammed back in her seat, her head banging against the headrest.

The cat paused to look at her, then darted away across the street. The little boy—oh, God, there was no little boy. She started to shake, her hands so tight on the steering wheel that it shook with her.

Deputy Sam Canfield was suddenly beside her, looking in the passenger window. "Mary? Mary, are you okay?"

Still shaking, she turned her head, speaking through stiff, bloodless lips. "The little boy..."

"What little boy?"

"Did I hit him?"

His rugged face changed. At once he straightened and walked around to the front of her car. There were some passersby standing there, and they spoke with Sam, but Mary couldn't hear what they said. Her mind was spiraling downward into a dark, terrible place, a place she couldn't let herself go again.

"Mary?" Sam was back, leaning down to her, his face now concerned. "Mary, there's no little boy. You didn't hit anything. Nobody saw a little boy. Just a cat."

"Oh, God..." Tremors shook her so hard that her teeth chattered. No little boy. *No little boy.* The words whirled around in her head, almost incomprehensible. She'd seen...no, she hadn't seen. She hadn't really. She'd just expected to see.

"Mary, are you okay?"

Licking her dry lips, she made herself look at him again. "I'm fine," she managed to say. "Just shaken."

"You got rear-ended pretty hard. Can you put the car in neutral? I want to push you over to the curb."

She nodded and reached for the stick shift. The car had stalled when she jammed on the brakes, and she didn't try to start it. Sam opened the driver's door and leaned against the post, pushing the car with deceptive ease to the curb just ahead. Mary managed to steer, even though her hands felt welded to the wheel.

"There," he said, when the car bumped gently against the curb. "Set the brake and take it easy."

But her tremors were easing somewhat, and she couldn't just sit in the car and think. She needed to be active. Immediately. Before the pit swallowed her again. Climbing out, she stood on rubbery knees and looked at the vehicle that had hit her.

It was a pickup truck that had probably been young about the time Elvis had been in the Army. It was driven by an eighteen-year-old boy who was claiming the Subaru had stopped too soon.

Mary recognized him. He'd been one of her students last year in senior English class. He was a good student and pretty much a good kid, she thought. Just careless, the way many of his age group were.

"It wasn't my fault," Jim Wysocki said. "Honest

it wasn't, Deputy Canfield. She shouldn't have stopped there.''

Sam wasn't looking too forgiving, Mary noticed. That surprised her, and she clung to the surprise, because it kept her from thinking about anything else. Still feeling wobbly, she walked to where they were standing between the vehicles. Cars eased past them, people craning their necks to look.

Oh, God. The pit of memory yawned, opened by the familiarity of the scene. Mary leaned against the side of her car, looking down at her crumpled rear fender without seeing it. No sirens, she told herself. There were no sirens. Nobody was hurt. Nobody.

But nightmare images hovered at the edges of her mind like the fluttering black wings of bats, waiting to pounce. She closed her eyes and bit her lip until it hurt, then tasted blood. ''It was my fault,'' she heard herself say hoarsely. She didn't know whether she spoke to the memories or to the present.

''Like hell it was,'' Sam snapped.

It was such a shock to hear the mild-mannered Sam Canfield bark that Mary was shocked out of her memories. ''Sam?'' she said questioningly. She didn't know him that well; he liked to keep to himself. But she'd come to think of him as a gentle, kind man, albeit withdrawn and sorrowful.

But Sam didn't seem to hear her. He jabbed his finger at Jim Wysocki. ''You've had two speeding tickets just this year. You're hell-bent on getting yourself or somebody else killed.''

Mary's instinct was to protect Jim, her student, barely more than a child. "Sam, please. I did stop suddenly."

Sam shook his head, his gray eyes as frigid as the tundra. "If he hadn't been following too close, he wouldn't have rammed you. Careless driving, that's what it was. At a higher speed, he could have killed you."

His gaze swung back to Jim, who had stopped protesting. The young man's head drooped. "I'm sorry."

"Sorry ain't good enough," Sam snapped again. "Sorry isn't going to fix Ms. McKinney's car. Sorry wouldn't resurrect her if you killed her."

Jim shrank even more, and Mary felt compelled to intervene again. "Sam..."

He shook his head at her, silencing her. "This young fool needs to understand that a car is a deadly weapon that has to be handled with care. Maybe he doesn't care about his own life, but he should care about other people's." He turned on Jim again. "How would you feel if you had to attend Ms. McKinney's funeral in a couple of days because you were being reckless?"

Mary knew how he would feel. Knew it like the beating of her own heart. The pit yawned beneath her feet again, and she could feel herself teetering, ready to fall over the brink.

Struggling to hang on to the here and now, she

reached out and gripped Jim's forearm. "Listen to him, Jim," she said hoarsely. "Before it's too late."

She felt Sam's curious gaze settle on her, as if he wondered why the change of heart, but she never took her gaze from Jim's. It was crucial that he hear her, that he *listen* to her.

Slowly the young man nodded. "I'm sorry, Ms. McKinney. Really. I *was* following too close. Deputy Canfield's right. And I'll pay to have your car fixed. Every dime, I promise."

Mary searched his face. Satisfied with what she read there, she let go of his arm. "Don't give him a ticket, Sam. Please. He won't do anything silly again."

"I wish I believed that," Sam said gruffly.

Mary looked at him, knowing she could never in a million years explain why she felt it was so important to protect Jim from the consequences of his own actions. Knowing that she must, believing the boy understood.

"Oh, what the hell," Sam said after a few moments. "No ticket. But I'll tell you, boy, I'm gonna have my eye on you. If I see you doing *anything* the least bit reckless or stupid, I'm pulling you over. I'm gonna be on you like white on rice, you hear?"

Jim nodded. "I hear."

"All right. Ms. McKinney's going to get an estimate on her car and give it to you. See that you take care of it."

"I will, I swear."

"Get out of here."

Jim didn't argue. He hurried to climb into his truck and drove away considerably more slowly than was his wont.

"Thank you," Mary said to Sam. Her voice sounded distant, even to her own ears.

"You don't look good," Sam said. "I'm taking you home. I'll get Taylor's to tow your car."

"I need to go grocery shopping," she protested, but the words were automatic, almost inaudible over the buzz in her ears.

"Not in that car. Not when you're shaking like a leaf. Let me take you home. I get off at three. I'll take you shopping then."

She nodded, past arguing. The cat. The child. There was no child. But in her heart there would *always* be a child. Always and forever.

"Come on," Sam said, his voice suddenly softening. He took her arm and guided her to his cruiser.

That was closer to her nightmare than he would ever know.

2

Sam was concerned about Mary McKinney. When he dropped her off at her home, she was still shaking and pale. Extreme reaction to the shock of the accident? Or something more?

He didn't know how to ask. There were secrets in those deep green Irish eyes of hers. As a man with secrets of his own, he figured it was better not to pry.

Besides, he didn't like the way he was noticing her. Damn it, he'd known the woman for years. Why was he suddenly noticing the way the sun struck fire in her red hair, or the way her green eyes seemed to be layered with both darkness and light? Worse, why was he noticing her tidy breasts and lush hips? Or the delicate shape of her ankle?

He wasn't ready to notice those things about a woman. He didn't know if he would ever be ready. Or if he would ever want to be.

But he noticed anyway. Noticed the faint scent of

her perfume, a gentle hint of lilac. Noticed her delicate, pale hands with their slender fingers and short nails. Wondered if her skin was as soft as it looked.

Wondered what it would feel like to touch her.

Forgive me, Beth.

But Beth wasn't there anymore to ease his heart with a touch or a smile, and somehow that only made him feel more guilty.

He set his jaw and walked Mary McKinney to her door. "I'll be back a little after three to pick you up," he said.

Before she could say anything and he could discover the pain that lay behind her mossy-green eyes, he turned and went back to duty. The boring hours spent cruising the streets and nearby environs of Whisper Creek were a blessed escape from temptation.

He didn't want to be tempted. He didn't want to be unfaithful to Beth, gone though she was, and he didn't want to risk that kind of pain again. Two good reasons to avoid Mary McKinney.

But the world was apparently in no mood to leave him in his icy prison. Summer heat dogged him, making him aware of the smell of the grass and the pines, of the sound of buzzing insects, though at this altitude there weren't all that many. Memories teased him, memories of lying in the grass beneath the summer sun while clouds drifted overhead painting fantastic pictures in white and gray. The bark of a dog in someone's backyard reminded him of

Buddy, his golden retriever, already old when Sam married Beth, who departed in his sleep one dark night.

He missed Buddy, too, missed the friendship and companionship of his warm, furry body and soft brown eyes. Maybe it was time to get another dog. Maybe that would settle his heart down again.

A dog he could risk. A woman, never.

But God was not done with him, either. She reached out her hand and turned his day upside down.

There was a battered old car pulled over on the county road about a mile out of town, sitting forlornly on the grassy shoulder, just inches from a drainage ditch. Behind it was a large orange rental trailer, one tire flattened.

The sun was playing tricks, and Sam could barely make out that there was a figure behind the wheel. Hurt? Man or woman? He couldn't see anything except the silhouette of a head.

The driver probably had everything he owned in that trailer and didn't want to abandon it beside the road, not even long enough to drive to town for help. Sam keyed his radio and notified dispatch of the problem. They promised to call for a tow.

Leaving his roof lights flashing, Sam climbed out of his car and went to tell the motorist help was coming. It was not until he stood right beside the open driver's window of the car that he realized who he was looking at.

A fist seemed to slam him in the solar plexus as he looked at a man he hadn't seen in nearly fifteen years.

"You!" he said.

Icy-blue eyes met his, set in an austere, deeply lined face that was surrounded by the snow-white mane of long hair and a beard. The man looked like a prophet of old, and his gaze held the same fanatical zeal. He pushed open the door of his car and climbed out, standing tall and straight.

But Elijah Canfield didn't say a word. He hadn't spoken to his son but once in all these years, and that once had been to strike the deepest wound he had ever given Sam.

Sam couldn't speak, either.

The two men stood staring at each other, strangers with an old, anguished history between them. Sam felt hatred simmering on the hot pavement between them, buzzing in his head like angry bees. But it wasn't his hate; despite everything, he had never hated his father. But his father had hated him. Still hated him.

In response, Sam felt despair rising in him, a choking, agonizing hopelessness. For a few seconds he thought he was going to lose the battle. Then, in an instant, all the painfully constructed defense mechanisms slammed into place. Distancing him. Turning this old man into just another stranded motorist.

"There's a tow truck on the way," Sam said.

Elijah nodded once, briefly, a bare acknowledgment. But still he didn't speak.

Of course not, Sam thought, looking past his father to the mountains beyond. Elijah hadn't spoken to him in so many years other than to condemn him that he probably couldn't even manage a civil word anymore. Simple human courtesies such as "how are you?" and "thank you" could no longer fill the silence between them. It was too late.

It had been too late for a long, long time. Sam bowed his head for a moment, battering down a surge of feeling, then looked at Elijah again with the chilly gaze of a stranger. "I'll wait until it gets here."

Then he turned and went back to his car, slipping inside behind the wheel, grateful that his suddenly unsteady legs didn't need to support him any longer.

Sometimes, he said silently to God, you have a nasty sense of humor.

And for a few moments, he almost thought the hills laughed back at him.

"Mary?"

Mary McKinney held the phone closer to her ear. "Yes?"

"Fred Taylor, Taylor's Auto Body."

"Oh, hi, Fred. What's the bad news?" But she didn't care. At least *this* bad news would distract her from her other unhappy thoughts. Funny how the past could sometimes be more vivid than the present. She'd spent all day since the accident trying to put it back where it belonged.

"Are you *sure* you don't want me to call your insurance?" Fred said hesitantly.

"That bad?"

"The bumper has to be replaced, and the tailgate is really bent. I don't think we can straighten it, so we'll probably have to get a whole new door assembly. Taillight assemblies, paint...well, you're not gonna like it. But the car's almost new. You ought to have it fixed the way it was or it's worthless. The bank wouldn't like that."

"How much?" she asked.

He quoted a price that caused her to straighten abruptly.

"That much?" she said, appalled. No way was Jim going to be able to pay for that, not after working at the mine for little more than a month. But neither could she afford it herself. A schoolteacher's salary didn't stretch *that* far.

"Let me call your insurance," Fred said. "They'll work it out with the other insurer and it won't cost you a dime."

She was tempted, sorely tempted. But it might cost Jim Wysocki his insurance, and without insurance, he wouldn't be able to drive, even to get to work. Biting her lip, she fought down a sense of panic. What was she going to do without a car? "Is it drivable?"

"Not now."

"How long would it take to get it drivable?"

"At a minimum, five days. I have to order parts, and there's a lot of work to do just to get that far, never mind the paint."

Well, of course, she thought miserably. It was only what she deserved. "Let me get back to you, Fred, okay?"

After she hung up the phone, she sat staring out the window. Across the street, someone was moving into the small house, a man with incredible white hair. A couple of people were helping him. It crossed her mind that she ought to wander over and offer to help, too, but she felt too stunned. Too...depressed.

Jim wouldn't be able to pay for the repairs. She wouldn't have a car to drive, which meant she wouldn't be able to go visit her aunt this weekend. That troubled her, because Nessa was seriously ill, undergoing chemotherapy for cancer. But it was no more than she deserved, she reminded herself. No reason her life should be easy when she had destroyed someone else's.

With a heavy sigh and a heavier heart, she picked up the phone and called Jim Wysocki. He was just getting ready to go on his shift at the mine.

"Oh, jeez, Ms. McKinney," he said when she told him the bad news. "Oh, jeez. I can't pay for the whole thing at once. Half. I could do half. And maybe pay the rest in installments over the next couple of months?"

Paying half would wipe out her savings. But apparently it would wipe out Jim's, too. Her shoulders sagged. She could have insisted on going to the insurance company, but she couldn't bring herself to do that. She would manage somehow. She had to.

"All right," she said. "Take the money over to Taylor's. You can pay me the rest when you're able. And tell Fred Taylor to give me a call after you stop in, will you?"

"Sure, Ms. McKinney. Thank you! I mean..."

But she didn't want to hear his gratitude. As quickly and gently as she could, she ended the conversation. He was a good kid. But like most eighteen-year-olds, he still had some growing up to do.

And she had to stop spending so much of her own money on classroom materials. Like all too many teachers, she was always finding things that she thought would stimulate interest in her students, things the school system didn't provide. And of course there were always the students from poorer families who needed the most basic supplies, from pens to notebooks. She never regretted those purchases, but she *did* need to be more careful about them, if her savings could be wiped out by a single car accident.

Forcing herself to shake off the mood that had been plaguing her since the accident, she went to freshen up a little. Sam would arrive to get her soon. And there was the neighbor across the street. She needed to at least welcome him.

The past needed to return to the dungeon where it belonged.

Which of course it didn't want to. But after all these years, Mary had some experience of twisting her mind away from it by playing tricks with herself. She rewrote her shopping list, telling herself she needed to forgo a few extravagances she had planned. Crossing these things off the list simply wouldn't do.

And finally she went across the street to welcome her new neighbor, sure that a few minutes of conversation until Sam arrived would be just the distraction she needed.

He was a beautiful man, she thought as she approached him. Tall, lean, with the thickest, whitest hair she had ever seen, and piercing eyes as blue as ice. His very presence seemed to command, and something about him struck her as familiar.

"Hi," she said brightly. "I'm Mary McKinney, your neighbor across the street."

He smiled. "Reverend Elijah Canfield," he said in a deep voice that hinted at thunder. "I'm the new pastor at The Little Church in the Woods."

"Oh, it's a lovely little church," Mary said warmly.

"You'll join us sometime for worship?"

"I'll think about it," Mary replied, though she had no intention of that. She belonged to another church with which she was quite content, thank you very much. "Canfield? I know a deputy named Sam

Canfield.'' It was a casual remark, something to mention to a stranger when she didn't know what else to say. She didn't expect the answer she got.

"I know him," said Reverend Canfield.

"Are you related?" The thought surprised her. While she didn't know Sam all that well, she suddenly realized that she'd been under the impression he didn't have any family at all.

"I know him," Elijah repeated.

"Oh." Mary felt uncomfortable suddenly, as if she'd trod somewhere she shouldn't have. A strange feeling for a first, casual encounter with a stranger. "Well, I hope you enjoy your time in Whisper Creek, Reverend. It's a lovely, friendly little town. And if there's anything you need, don't hesitate to let me know. I'm always good for a cup of sugar."

He laughed, and the uneasiness was dispelled as if the sun had come out from behind a cloud.

"I'll remember that, Mary McKinney. Is that missus?"

"Ms."

"Miss McKinney," he said with a little bow.

Mary, who was quite opposed to "miss" because she didn't feel her marital status was anybody's business but her own, realized she had just run into an old-time preacher who thought women had their proper place. However, out of common courtesy she said nothing. Some old dogs couldn't learn new tricks, anyway.

"So, what do you do, Miss McKinney?"

Was she imagining it, or did he emphasize the "miss"? Down, girl, she told herself. It was not time to get on her feminist soapbox. "I'm a teacher at the high school," she answered. "Creative writing and literature."

At that moment two of the helpers came out of the house, and with a suddenly sinking heart, Mary recognized them. They were parents who had last year attempted to get some of the books on her reading list banned.

"Literature," Elijah Canfield said. "That wouldn't be *The Catcher in the Rye* and *The Adventures of Tom Sawyer,* would it?"

It would be. It also included *The Return of the Native, Pride and Prejudice, Captain Blood* (for the boys) and a lot of other classics, like *Catch-22* and *The Old Man and the Sea.* She'd had to go to the mat over some of them last year before the school board, and she was prepared to do it again.

But now she found herself looking into the eyes of a new enemy, one who could be considerably more powerful than the handful of parents who had complained last year.

She felt her dander rising but tried to remain civil. "Among other books," she said pleasantly. "I always feel it's best to introduce young people to a wide variety of the greatest works of literature. It tends to be instructive in ways that help them better avoid some of the errors and temptations of life, not to mention exposing them to powerful writing."

So take that, she thought almost childishly.

"The Bible is powerful writing."

"Indeed," she agreed with a smile. "Very powerful. But it's wisest to leave that in the hands of ministers, don't you think? I'm sure you'd be very unhappy with me if I pointed out the apocryphal nature of some of the Biblical stories."

And thank goodness Sam's patrol car pulled up across the street just then. Escape was at hand. But then she noticed that Sam didn't get out and come join them. Why not, if he knew this preacher?

"There's nothing apocryphal about the Bible," Elijah said sternly.

"Not about its message, no," she agreed, clinging to her smile. "However, I'm sure some of the stories are more illustrative than factual. But I have to go now, Reverend, so I'll leave the Bible in your capable hands. Let me know if I can help with anything."

Except banning books in my school, she thought irritably as she crossed the street and climbed into the patrol car beside Sam. Then it struck her as odd that Sam hadn't even climbed out to open the car door for her. That didn't seem like him. What was going on here?

"That man," she said as Sam pulled away from the curb, "is going to be a major thorn in my side, I know it."

"He enjoys being a thorn," Sam said levelly.

"It's his stock-in-trade. Don't get into it with him, Mary. You'll regret it."

"I have a feeling he's going to want to ban books."

"Probably. He has everywhere else he's been, as far as I know."

She turned in her seat and looked at him. "Sam, what's going on? Who is he? Do you know him?"

"I *used* to know him," Sam said after a moment.

"Friends? Relatives?"

They were almost at the store before he responded. "He's my father."

A million questions occurred to Mary, but she didn't voice them. The store simply wasn't the place to have such a discussion.

Sam pushed the cart for her while she selected items and dropped them into it. He seemed preoccupied, which gave her the opportunity to look his way frequently without being detected. He was a strong man in his mid-thirties, with a face attractively lined by exposure to the harsh mountain elements. His gray eyes, so unlike the icy-blue of his father's, were warm, even now when he seemed low. And never, not once, had she ever found him to be anything but kind.

A remarkable man. A handsome man. One who would give women little heart flutters simply by smiling. As well she knew.

She remembered his late wife only slightly, a petite dark-haired woman with a thousand-watt smile who always seemed to be laughing. Sam must sorely miss her. Which, she told herself sternly, was one of the best reasons to ignore those little flutters.

Besides, marriage wasn't for her. She didn't deserve such happiness.

But she owed Sam something for going out of his way, so she picked up extra for dinner, determined that he was going to eat with her tonight. No matter what he said. No reason for him to go back to his empty house, and no reason for her to spend the evening alone, worrying about that preacher across the street. Besides, it would give her an opportunity to ask one or two of those millions of questions that kept popping up in her mind.

At the very least, learning about Sam Canfield would keep her mind off her own problems.

Which, she told herself, was a very selfish way to think. Okay, so she was selfish. Maybe it would be good for both of them to talk a little.

But nothing more than that. Not ever.

3

Sam helped carry Mary's groceries in for her. From across the street, where the moving activity had ended, leaving only a locked-up trailer in the driveway and a battered Oldsmobile parked out front, he could almost feel his father's eyes boring into his back.

Elijah wasn't in sight and might not even have been there, but Sam could still feel his presence and had to steel himself not to dart any looks in that direction. For all he knew, the old man was staring out a window at him.

Although why Elijah would do that, he couldn't imagine. He hadn't cared to look on Sam's face in fifteen years, and he hadn't seemed any happier to see him on the road today.

But the feeling persisted anyway, and he was glad when he carried the last bag into Mary's kitchen.

"You'll stay for dinner, of course," she said to him as he set it on the counter.

Part of him just wanted to escape to his safe hermitage, but another part of him couldn't resist the warm friendliness of her smile. He stood there, torn, and realized that his social graces had apparently gone the way of the dodo, because as his silence grew longer, her face began to fall.

He couldn't allow that. "Sure," he said. "I'd like to." Then he added, so she wouldn't misunderstand, "Eating alone is the pits." Then it struck him that that had been an ungracious thing to say. Damn, he sounded like he'd been raised in a stable.

The corners of her mouth lifted, however, letting him know she hadn't taken his words amiss. "It sure is," she said. "And it's absolutely no fun to cook alone. What we need to do is start a singles dining club. Get a group of us lonelyhearts together to cook for each other once in a while."

"That might not be a bad idea," he allowed, although in truth he had no intention of socializing that way. He'd avoided all the singles clubs in town because he was convinced that whatever they claimed was their purpose, their members were all after the same thing: marriage. And he didn't want that ever again.

He unpacked the grocery bags for Mary, handing her each item so she could put it away. The way he'd once done for Beth, because she'd been convinced he would screw up her pantry organization if he put things away himself. His heart squeezed painfully at the memory.

"Are you all right, Sam?"

Mary's voice, quiet and sweet, drew him back to the present. "Uh, yeah. I'm fine."

Her brow knitted with concern and maybe a bit of disbelief, but she didn't press him about it. He handed her a container of grated Parmesan cheese, and she turned away to tuck it into the cupboard.

Then she gave him another kick in the heart. "So that's your father moving in across the street?"

He couldn't blame her; her curiosity was natural. But he wished she would talk about the weather, the upcoming school year, or even his job. Anything but this. On the other hand, he couldn't be rude.

"Yeah," he said, and pulled some cans of soup out of a bag.

"I take it you don't have a good relationship?"

He gave a harsh crack of laughter. "That's an understatement."

"I'm sorry."

For a minute he thought she was going to leave it there. But women never left anything there. A man would have, but a woman always wanted to pry into a guy's heart. Hadn't he learned that with Beth? Secrets were anathema to women. Particularly secrets of the heart and soul.

"What happened between you?" she asked, her voice as gentle as gentle could be. That gentleness was going to kill him.

"He disowned me fifteen years ago," Sam said flatly. "Threw me out and disowned me." His tone was meant to be a bar to further questions, but that didn't work, either.

"Oh, Sam," she said, groceries forgotten, her gaze sorrowful. "Why in the world would he do such a thing?"

"He said it was because I refused to become a preacher." Although, in his heart of hearts, Sam believed it was more. As far back as he could remember, he and his father had disagreed on basic religious beliefs. Sam had challenged Elijah more than once with the brashness of youth. And even now that maturity had mellowed him somewhat and made him more tolerant, Sam still couldn't buy into a lot of his father's notions. Or at least the notions Elijah had tried to raise him with.

"I'm sorry," Mary said. "That's terrible."

"It was a long time ago. It's just better that we don't speak. More peaceful for everybody."

Mary nodded and resumed putting the groceries away. "Well, it's going to be awkward for you, living in the same town."

Sam shrugged and passed her a box of crackers. "I'll deal with it."

Yeah, he thought. The way he was dealing with it right now? Feeling the pressure of his father's presence like a dark cloud? Entertaining fleeting thoughts of taking a job elsewhere? Cripes, he had to quit running.

He helped Mary make their dinner, a simple meal of salad, bakery rolls and two porterhouse steaks, which he was sure had been a big splurge for her. He felt bad about that, knowing that schoolteachers made about the same as cops.

"How's your car?" he asked when they sat to eat at the dinette in her kitchen.

"Bad." She tried to smile. "Jim can only pay for half of it right now, so I'm anteing up the rest until he can pay me back."

"You should have made him take responsibility for it, Mary."

"He *is* taking responsibility. And I don't want to be responsible for making him lose his insurance, because if he can't drive, he can't get to work."

"That's true. But that kid seems to need a lesson."

"He's eighteen. He's getting his lessons. But sometimes it's necessary for adults to provide a bit of a safety net so these kids don't crash and burn while they learn."

He nodded slowly. "You're a kind woman, Mary."

She shook her head. "I'm a teacher. I haven't had a chance to forget all the stupid things *I* did at that age."

Sam nodded, admitting to himself he was coming down harshly on Jim, more harshly than was his wont. Maybe he was just getting sick of human stupidity. He sure saw enough of it.

"You know," Mary said, "I've never known a preacher's kid before. Well, other than one I taught.

Is it true that you guys cut up more than usual as kids?''

"I don't know about anybody else. I think I was just average.'' Actually less than average, because his father would have put him through hell for even minor misbehavior, but he didn't want to get into that.

"That seemed to be true of my student, too. Just the average sort of stuff. He seemed like a normal kid to me.''

"An interesting concept, normal.''

She smiled. "Isn't it?''

Her smile, he realized, was warm enough to make his toes tingle. Why had he never before noticed her? And why was he noticing her now? Both questions left him feeling uncomfortable, and he began to develop an urgent desire to get away from her. She was disturbing him, and he didn't like that.

But she was a beautiful woman, and he had plenty of opportunity to notice that while they did the dishes. Her movements were inherently graceful, as if she were comfortable inside her own body. What was more, she didn't have that boyish look that seemed to be so popular in women these days. Her hips were well rounded, looking as if they could cradle a man in perfect comfort. And her breasts, while not overly large, were full and inviting. He couldn't understand why some man hadn't snatched her up long since.

Which was, surely, a damn good reason to get the hell out of there.

"Do you have any other family?" she asked as he washed and she dried.

"Not a soul."

"I'm not blessed that way, either," she admitted. "My aunt is still alive, but right now she's getting chemotherapy."

"I'm sorry. How bad is it?"

"I don't know. The doctors seem hopeful, but...I'm not sure they're not lying to us."

"Where does she live?"

"In Denver."

He reached for another towel and dried his hands. "If you want to go down and visit her before your car gets fixed, let me know. I'll be glad to take you. In fact, if you need to get anywhere between now and then, just let me know."

"Thanks, Sam." She smiled. "You're a kind man."

Hah, he thought as he stepped out into the night. Kind? Not hardly.

He paused in the driveway beside his patrol car and stared at his father's house across the street. The long mountain twilight had erased the shadows, making the evening strangely flat. A light had come on over there. The old man was home.

Sam stood for a few minutes, trying to deal with the reality of his father moving to town. All day long he'd stewed in discomfort, but he hadn't allowed himself to really think about it. He supposed it was something he needed to do, and the sooner the better.

It kind of surprised him, though, that fifteen years of separation didn't seem to have given him any real emotional distance. The instant he'd laid eyes on his father this morning, all those old feelings had been there, as fresh as they'd ever been. That wasn't going to make the situation easy.

Just then he thought he smelled a whiff of smoke. Instinctively he scanned the area, looking for signs of a fire. Nothing. He supposed that someone must be burning a log in their woodstove to take off the chill of the evening, even if it did seem warm enough to him.

Another whiff and then it was gone. Nothing.

Sighing, he climbed into his patrol car and headed home.

Elijah Canfield had seen Sam help Mary in with her groceries, but he hadn't seen him leave. He hadn't intended to watch, but he was getting older and had collapsed into his easy chair, surrounded by the boxes that held the residue of his life, too tired to do any more today. It just happened that his chair had been put in position to see out the front window.

He wandered briefly into the kitchen, where everything was still in boxes, and helped himself to the dinner his new congregation had brought him: cold sliced turkey, salad and slabs of homemade bread. For dessert there was a generous square of crumb cake.

When he returned to his easy chair and settled in the only position that would ease his stiff back, he resumed his absent contemplation. That was when he saw Sam come out of the McKinney woman's house.

So they were dating.

That was inconvenient, he thought. When he'd accepted the pastorship here, it had never occurred to him that Sam would still be living in this town. Sam was a runner. He'd run away from Elijah more than once in his younger days, and Elijah had just somehow figured that Sam would have moved on when his wife had died.

Regardless, it hadn't been a possibility that had entered into his decision one way or the other. He'd long since buried his son, emotionally speaking.

Or he thought he had. Judging by the way he was reacting, things weren't quite as dead as he'd believed.

He felt angry. Of course, anger wasn't unfamiliar to Elijah Canfield. He routinely got angry at sin. Anger was, in fact, his stock-in-trade. Sometimes he even let his anger spill over from the sin to the sinner, if he thought it might do any good.

But when he thought of his son, he wasn't angry at sin. He was angry at waste. Sam had wasted himself and his God-given talents. The Spirit had been upon him, but Sam had refused the call.

Belle, his late wife, hadn't seen it that way. They'd fought bitterly over their son on many occasions, especially after Elijah had disowned the boy. Belle had thought it wasn't Elijah's place to determine their son's calling. Elijah felt that, as a preacher, he was better able to judge that matter than anyone else.

But whatever the arguments had been, it remained that Elijah was still angry. Searingly angry.

And hurt.

Sam had failed him. Sam had turned his back on his upbringing and his faith. He had spat on all that his father believed.

Nursing his pain, Elijah sat on into the evening, thinking about Sam, and about the woman across the street, the woman who had challenged him on the obscene books she encouraged children to read.

His mission here was becoming clear. He knew what he had to do.

The fire, stymied at the heights for lack of fuel, caught between two brooks that stood sentry over the rest of the forest, nearly died. The last flames vanished, and a smoky pall hung over everything, even filling the valley below.

Across the brooks, still unsettled by the smell of soot and ash, animals tentatively tried to resume their routine. But the deer were restless and slept lightly, awakening frequently to sniff the night air for danger. The birds were completely gone, offering no surety of a timely alarm if they were disturbed. Smaller animals, creeping out of burrows and nests, seemed even more skittish than usual as they followed their various habits of hunting and gathering. Pausing more often than usual, they lifted their heads to test the acrid odor of the air.

The fire slumbered. Hot coals, protected by the thick layer of ash, glowed, awaiting their moment. Only hours before a hungry conflagration, the fire bided its time, showing a patience that few imagined it capable of.

Throughout the night, the forest waited, knowing it was not yet safe. Then, at dawn, a breeze freshened. Blowing across the burned-out area, its strength undimmed by the leaves and needles of living trees and brush, it stirred the ash.

Little wisps of smoke began to rise again. The warmth buried in the protective coat of ash grew hotter. And as the blacked acres heated yet again, the rising air sucked the breeze more strongly into the heart of the sleeping fire.

At first only ash lifted on the breeze. Dead, lifeless, it sprinkled itself harmlessly among the still-green trees across the brook. But the fanning renewed the life in the small coals the ash had covered.

And before the sun had fully risen, sparks were swept up on the eddies of the growing wind.

Most fell harmlessly, burned out before they reached the fresh fuel across the water. But at last one made it, finding a welcoming spot among pine needles so dry they ignited instantly.

The fire spread, needle to needle, multiplying rapidly. Soon there was a large, charred circle ringed in flame. A gust of air lifted those burning needles in a shower of orange lights and deposited them among the needles of parched trees, where they grew hungrily.

A dozen trees ignited with a huge whoosh, the hungry fire drawing more wind to its heart.

And the conflagration once again began its inexorable march, this time toward the pass that led to Whisper Creek.

4

Sam smelled smoke again. It was carried on the clear morning air, again just a whiff, gone so quickly it was hard to be sure he'd smelled it. It unnerved him just the same.

Standing in his driveway, he searched the rooftops of the town and saw nothing untoward. Then he scanned the circle of mountains around the valley. Not a thing.

Nothing except, perhaps, the faintest darkening to the west. As if the sky was not quite true blue. He studied it but couldn't be certain he was seeing anything. Sometimes the sky looked like that before clouds developed, and God knew they could sure use some rain.

He sniffed the air again but detected nothing. His imagination?

Maybe.

"Good morning, Sam!"

He turned and saw his next-door neighbor, Sheila

Muñoz, coming out to get her paper. Sheila was an attractive divorcée who lately seemed to have developed the habit of getting her paper just about the time he left for work in the mornings. And lately, when she came out that door, she was still wearing her nightclothes. Nightclothes that were a little too...suggestive. Not indecent. Just suggestive.

"Morning, Sheila," he called back and slipped quickly into his patrol car. There had been a time in his life when he might have been flattered, but no more. Now he just wanted to escape as quickly as he could.

Gunning his engine, he backed out of his driveway and turned away from Sheila, even though the route to work would be longer.

Coward, he thought almost wryly as he took his alternate route. But he wasn't interested in Sheila and didn't want to give her any idea that he might be. The best way for both of them to save face was to avoid any situation where someone might be embarrassed. Especially in a town this size.

But he kind of felt sorry for her, too. Her divorce was new, and loneliness was a miserable thing. Hector had walked out on her only six months ago, leaving her for another woman. Sam had no doubt that part of what Sheila needed was reassurance that she was still attractive. Well, he wasn't up for that game. She was nice enough, as a neighbor, but there it ended.

"Dinner tonight," Earl Sanders reminded him the

minute he stepped into the office. Apparently he was the first arrival for the day shift.

"I remember."

"Good. I don't want you wiggling out again."

"I won't." What was the point? Earl was going to keep on stalking him like a lion after prey.

The thought caught Sam like a hiccup, and suddenly he laughed. A genuine laugh. A feel-good laugh. God, was he really this morose? Or was it just an ugly habit?

"What's so funny?" Earl demanded.

Sam was still grinning. And for once his face didn't hurt from it. "Me, boss. Just me."

Earl scanned him from head to foot. "I don't see anything funny about you."

"And that's the whole problem, isn't it?" Sam shook his head. "I think I'm getting bored with my own company."

"It's about time. Six o'clock. And bring a date if you want."

"Who, me?"

"Yeah, you." It was Earl's turn to grin. "I figure you could have your pick of about half the single females in the county."

"What's wrong with the other half?"

"Beats me. Maybe not smart enough?"

Sam laughed again, much to his own surprise. "Or maybe just too smart."

"Nah. So, are you going to bring a date, or do you want me to invite some nice lady?"

That sure sounded like an ultimatum, Sam thought, and he didn't like ultimatums. His inclination was to become more stubborn than a Missouri mule when he felt pushed or cornered. But this time, just as his contrariness was rising, he found himself thinking of Mary McKinney. Thinking how comfortable it had been last night to share dinner with her. "Yeah," he heard himself say. "I'll ask someone."

"Great."

As he was walking back out to his car after the morning briefing, he started shaking his head and grinning to himself. Earl was like every other happily married man: he wanted everyone else to be happily married, too. Until last year, when he'd married Meg, Earl had been content to let Sam work out his problems in his own way and time, ready to lend an ear when necessary, but essentially hands-off.

Not anymore. Since his marriage, Earl had been persistently nudging Sam to rejoin the human race.

Well, maybe it was time, Sam thought as he slid behind the wheel. Not to date or anything, but to get over himself. Grieving was one thing, but clinging to it was something else.

And he supposed he'd better ask Mary if she wanted to come with him to the Sanders's house tonight before it got much later. He wasn't so rusty he didn't remember that last-minute invitations could be construed as insulting.

He drove over to her house—it was along his patrol route anyway—and found her in her front garden. Wearing shorts, a halter top and a bandanna over her gorgeous hair, she was kneeling before a bed of marigolds, weeding industriously.

Nice view, Sam thought as he pulled up. Probably giving his father a heart attack, if Elijah was home across the street. It wasn't giving Sam a heart attack, though; it was giving him an equally strong but very different reaction.

He turned off the ignition and sat a moment, indulging himself. Mary had a nice bottom, with little left to the imagination as the shorts stretched tightly over it. Nice legs, too, slender but not skinny.

Just then she straightened and twisted to see who had stopped, giving him a great view of her breasts in their sheath of stretchy red cotton. Yup, Elijah would have a heart attack.

Suddenly feeling guilty, Sam climbed out of his car. Mary smiled and waved, as unself-conscious as a child who had been playing in a sandbox. She clearly had no idea that one of her neighbors would consider her to be indecently dressed. Nor was Sam going to advise her. Elijah had always needed to loosen up a bit.

"Hi," she said. She dropped her trowel and weeding fork and pushed herself to her feet. For an instant Sam could almost see down the neck of her top. *Down, boy.*

Her knees were grungy with dirt, but she didn't

seem aware of it. He smiled to himself. "Morning," he said. "Sorry to bother you but..." It suddenly struck him that he didn't know how to ask.

"But?" She waited with a pleasantly expectant look on her face. "Did you forget something last night?"

"Uh...no. It's... Well, I was wondering. Would you like to go to the Sanders's house with me for dinner tonight?"

Something almost fearful flickered across her face, making him wonder what he'd said. Reviewing his words, he couldn't see anything frightening in them. But they certainly weren't clear enough. "Not a date or anything," he blurted.

He winced inwardly, realizing how that sounded. Man, his social skills had not only atrophied, they'd died. Now she would be offended, and rightly so.

But she surprised him by looking relieved. "Great. Sure, I'd like that. As long as it's not a date."

She looked relieved because it wasn't a date. Sam was taken aback by the disappointment he felt, even though he'd laid the ground rule himself. But no, he must be mistaking a little ego bash for something else. He wasn't capable of getting involved again.

"Good," he said, forcing a smile. "It'll be fun."

"I'm sure it will."

A few moments of awkward silence, as if neither of them knew what to say next. Get back to work, Sam told himself, but that seemed too abrupt right after asking a woman to dinner—even if it wasn't a date. But he wasn't much of a talker, never had been. Although this was even worse than usual.

Mary gave him a sidelong look, as if she were a little uncertain herself. Then she shocked him. ''Your father?''

He didn't want to talk about Elijah. He wanted to pretend the man didn't exist, even if he was right across the street. But Mary's mention had been so tentative. And what if something was wrong? ''What about him?'' he asked roughly.

''He's standing in his window watching us.''

Sam swung around and saw Elijah standing in the picture window across the street. The man didn't acknowledge him with so much as a wave. ''Nosy old coot,'' Sam said, his gut twisting.

''Maybe…maybe he's hoping you'll come talk to him.'' She offered it almost as a question, hesitantly.

''Not a chance in hell.'' Sam turned his back on the old man. ''He probably figures you're in trouble with the law. That's the way his mind runs.'' And he needed to get out of there before the old anger managed to burn through the glacier that encased his heart.

''Well,'' said Mary, an impish smile coming to her mouth, while a strange shadow remained in her eyes, ''I'm sure he thinks I'm a scarlet woman after our conversation about books yesterday.''

Sam gave a bark of laughter. ''Maybe. I'll see you

tonight, Mary. Gotta get back to work.''

He felt her eyes on him as he drove away.

When Sam's car disappeared around the corner, Mary looked again at the house across the street. Elijah Canfield had disappeared from his window.

She didn't want to believe Sam was right about his father. She didn't want to believe any parent was capable of such meanness. But she was also an experienced teacher and she knew better. She'd certainly seen her share of it.

Troubled, she went back to her weeding, trying to ignore a prickling at the back of her neck that seemed to say she was being watched. There was no reason on earth why Elijah Canfield would want to watch her grubbing around in the dirt.

But surely there had to be some way for Sam and Elijah to reconcile?

''Hello.''

The deep voice, so like Sam's, caused Mary to start. Twisting, she found Elijah Canfield standing in her driveway. He was wearing dark slacks and a white shirt with the collar open and the sleeves rolled up.

''Hi,'' she answered, feeling wary.

''I wanted to apologize for the way we got off on the wrong foot yesterday,'' he said, giving her a pleasant smile. He was a handsome man, she thought irrelevantly. Almost as handsome as his son.

Mary sat back on her heels, still holding her weeding fork, and looked up at him. ''We had a significant disagreement of opinion,'' she said, keeping her voice gentle. ''Nothing wrong with that.''

He nodded briefly, an acknowledgment that didn't quite make it to agreement. ''But we're neighbors,'' he said.

''That's right.'' Mary waited, a trick she'd learned with difficult adolescents. Let the silence hang until the other person felt compelled to speak. She certainly wasn't prepared to go out on a limb with this man; she didn't know him. But from what Sam had said, she wasn't inclined to trust him.

''The Lord says we should love our neighbors.''

Mary, who was quite religious herself, wondered if she was going to be treated to a sermon every time she saw this man. ''That's right. But sometimes it's easier to love them from afar.''

Despite the beard, she could see the corners of his mouth tip up slightly. ''I've noticed that.''

Mary smiled, prepared to be as noncommitally friendly as he allowed. ''Is there something I can do for you?''

He didn't answer immediately, and she had the sense that he was struggling with something. After a minute or so, she decided to take the bull by the horns.

''Sam is your son, isn't he?''

Elijah's intense eyes jumped back to her. ''Yes.''

''He's a fine man.''

Again Elijah said nothing, but this time Mary refused to speak, either. If something was troubling him, he needed to tell her or take it back home with him. Their gazes locked and held while time ticked by.

Finally Elijah spoke. "He carries a gun."

"Yes." She wasn't about to say anything regarding that, either. Offering opinions to this man might be dangerous, unless she wanted lectures.

"A man who lives by the sword dies by the sword."

Mary bit her lower lip, wanting to defend the necessity of police officers but realizing that Elijah's real problem was something else. Something she wasn't ready to wade into.

His gaze seemed to bore into her; then he nodded and walked back to his house.

What a strange man, she thought, staring after him. Then a thought struck her: maybe he was genuinely worried about Sam's safety. Maybe his objection was something more than that Sam hadn't become a minister.

And maybe she was being too generous to him. She certainly had a tendency to see the best in everyone other than herself.

In herself she saw only the worst. It was a pain she lived with, one so old it was comfortable.

Shaking her head, she went back to her weeding.

Sam continued to be troubled by the occasional whiffs of smoke he detected and the haziness to the

west. Finally he called dispatch and asked if anyone
had reported a fire.

Nary a whisper about one. But he couldn't escape
the feeling that something was wrong, so he told the
dispatcher that he was going to drive up Reservoir
Road and take a look.

The reservoir had been built to provide water to
Denver and in return had provided a great recreational area for visitors and the residents of Whisper
Creek. The road looped around the entire perimeter
of the reservoir, a man-made lake that looked as if
it had been there forever. Campsites and picnic sites
abounded, and the fishing was pretty good. Branch-
ing off the loop was a rutted dirt road that headed
up to the pass between the two highest peaks visible
from town. From there he could see the valley beyond.

As his car ascended, bumping all the way, the air
grew cooler and thinner, taking on just the suggestion of a chill. Pines shadowed his way, hinting of
ancient mysteries in their depths.

Every time he got out in the woods like this, he
found himself thinking of what it must have been
like a hundred years ago for the first settlers. They'd
come looking for gold but had found silver. When
silver prices crashed, they'd suffered until the next
big boom. Right now they were getting by on jobs
at a molybdenum mine and the surrounding resorts.
It had been a while since times had really boomed.

But the first settlers must have thought that a

bright future lay here. And certainly in the summertime the place was hospitable. Plenty of water, plenty of sun and shade, but cool enough for a person to work hard. Of course, at this altitude there wasn't a whole lot you could grow in the way of crops, but there had always been plenty of deer and elk.

It was easy to imagine setting up camp away from everything and just getting by on the land, maybe trapping beavers for their pelts. He could see why people had come and stayed.

Hell, people still came and stayed. People who wanted to live apart in small houses in the woods. People who were more interested in privacy and freedom than neighbors. People looking for a place where they could be unconventional, or a place where they could walk out their own back doors and ski in the winter. And so many of them came with dreams, just like the first settlers.

His car jolted in a deep rut, shaking him out of his reverie. Better pay attention. The pass was up ahead, but the higher he went, the worse the road grew, because it was so rarely traveled. The only things up here were a couple of microwave repeaters and the kind of woods he always thought of when he read that Robert Frost poem.

The smell of smoke was getting a little more noticeable, too. When his car bottomed out in another rut, he turned it around carefully and parked it to one side on a bed of pine needles. Better to hoof it the rest of the way.

He'd come up another two thousand feet, and he could feel the difference as he hiked up the road. He was well above ten thousand feet now, at a place where even his altitude-adapted lungs labored more than usual.

Most summers, the sky would have been overcast by now, heralding a thunderstorm so regular you could set your watch by it. Not this year. This year the sky stayed perfectly blue from sunrise to sunset, unmarred by so much as even one little puff of cloud.

He was approaching the tree line now, and after climbing another fifty feet he had an unobstructed view of the valley and lake behind him. Another fifty feet upward and he reached the pass.

His puffing lungs forgot to breathe as he saw the smoke filling the valley on the other side of the mountains. Ignoring his fatigue, he trotted forward along the vanishing road until he could look downward.

There was a fire at the north end of the valley. Not too big yet, but a definite threat to the woods down there. A definite threat to Whisper Creek by way of the Edgerton Pass to the north, lower and well-enclosed by trees. Maybe a hundred acres were burning right now, and the valley stretched south of the flames like a smorgasbord.

Sam reached for his radio. With nothing between

him and Whisper Creek, the connection was as clear as a bell.

"We've got a forest fire on the west side of Meacher Peak, about two miles north of Edgerton Pass."

"How much involvement?"

Sam looked again to double-check his earlier impression. "Maybe a hundred acres."

The dispatcher said he would take care of it. Sam stood there for a few minutes longer, looking at one of nature's most ferocious beasts. And for some reason it made him think of his dad.

Although "dad" seemed like too familiar a name for the man who had sired him. In fact, he couldn't remember a time when *dad* or *daddy* had seemed appropriate for Elijah. Sam's tender years had been filled with terrors of the devil, nightmares about burning lakes and the endless screams of the damned. Countless nights, horrific visions of the end of the world had kept him from sleeping after he'd listened to his father preach.

Elijah's brand of religion was all about fear and punishment. For some people that was great and exactly what they needed. For Sam, however, it had driven a wedge between him and his father. To a young boy, Elijah had seemed the embodiment of threat and punitive love. A tall man, a very large man to a small boy, whose face twisted in rage when he spoke of sin, whose voice thundered judgment over every peccadillo. For a sensitive child, it wasn't the right brand of religion.

Sam shook his head and tried to banish thoughts of his father as he drove back down to Whisper Creek. Maybe it was time to consider taking a job elsewhere, because there was no way in a town this size that he wasn't going to run into Elijah around nearly every corner.

He wasn't sure he could deal with that; there was just too much bitterness.

5

The Whisper Creek airport, a small private landing strip, had become a beehive of activity. Fire-fighting planes lined the runway, loading the chemicals they would drop from the air. Smoke jumpers were beginning to arrive in their planes, as well.

Up near Edgerton Pass, a command post had been established. Volunteer firefighters were being gathered there to truck into the valley below and cut firebreaks. Up north, at the far end of the valley, similar crews were gathering to try to prevent the fire from spreading in that direction toward the ski resort towns.

The forest service had taken charge, but Sam was assigned as liaison with the local authorities. There were homes in the valley below, scattered miles apart, homes that would be threatened if the fire couldn't be halted. It would be his job to ensure that any necessary evacuations were made.

At the moment, though, the threat was small and

might be contained. Night was fast approaching, though, and the darkness would hinder their efforts.

The first chemical-bearing planes flew overhead as he stood there, then seemed to vanish into the thickening haze of smoke. Lack of wind hampered visibility by allowing the pall to hang thickly, even as it prevented the fire from spreading too swiftly to contain.

"That won't last," Sam remarked as one of the foresters commented that the wind was with them.

The guy—Sam remembered his name was George Griffin—smiled. "You some kind of pessimist?" George was a short, compact guy in his late forties or so, with steely hair and eyes that perpetually squinted.

"I'm a realist. That sun goes behind that mountain over there, we're going to see some stiffening breezes."

"Yeah." George knew it as well as he did. "We always do. But right now, conditions are on our side. I'll take every break I can get."

Another dumper flew overhead with a loud drone. The first one was already on its way back for another load.

George spoke again. "We can't send the jumpers in until morning. Not enough time before darkfall."

Sam nodded. His mind strayed a moment, wondering what Mary was going to think when he didn't show up to take her to dinner. Maybe he should have dispatch call her. Nah. Right now they were too busy fielding calls about the fire. It wasn't a date, anyway. She would understand.

Just then the breeze kicked up. Not much, just enough to make him feel a chill through his light jacket. George looked at him. The sun was hanging heavy over the western peaks, a baleful red orb blurred by the smoke in the air.

George spoke. "I hope our luck isn't running out."

The trucks full of volunteers pulled out, heading down the narrow, winding road. Their job was to build a firebreak to protect the pass. The guys leaned out, hooting and hollering as they passed. Too high on excitement to realize what they were facing. Too macho to admit it.

The breeze suddenly gusted, carrying away the thickest smoke, leaving the fire visible. It had spread. An angry orange beast devouring the valley's north end.

"Shit," George swore under his breath.

Sam didn't say anything. Even at this safe distance, he was suddenly a kid again, looking into the maw of hell. And even as he watched, hunching against the chilly bite of the wind, he saw another tree go up in a burst of hungry flames. Only it was a tree some distance from the fire. The gust had carried a spark hundreds of yards, starting yet another fire.

"Damn," George said. "Damn."

The beast had leaped its own perimeter, running

free. George picked up his radio and began to bark rapid orders. They couldn't wait for dawn. Not now.

Mary dressed for dinner with rather more care than was her custom in a town where casual dress reigned. She chose a green polished cotton dress and a pair of two-inch heels. Her hair, usually allowed to fall in waves below her shoulders, she decided to put up in a loose knot with a few long curls hanging free.

It was more effort than she wanted to think about, considering that Sam and she had agreed that this wasn't a date. She even went so far as to dab on a little perfume.

At six she peeked out to see if Sam had arrived. Instead she saw her neighbors gathered in their front yards, looking to the west. Curious, she went out to discover what was going on.

"It's a fire," Elvira Jones, who lived in the house on the left, told her. "In the next valley."

Mary turned to see the thick cloud of smoke hovering over the mountains, catching the red of the lowering sun. "How bad is it?"

"Not a threat to us yet," Elvira answered. "But my Bob says they're worried about it coming through Edgerton Pass. He went to volunteer."

Mary immediately turned to her. "You must be worried."

"Nah." Elvira smiled, her crow's-feet deepening. She loved to ski so much that she had a permanently sun- and wind-burned face. "He'll just be helping with a firebreak at the pass. He won't get near the flames."

But Mary remembered fires from the past, remembered how a little wind could create desperate situations. At least there wasn't a breeze right now. Of course, in the next valley that might be different.

"There aren't many people living out that way, are there?"

Elvira shook her head. "Just a few loners. It's too hard to get out of there in the winter."

Mary nodded, trying to remember if any of her students lived out that way. She didn't think so. Elvira was right. There couldn't be more than a half dozen folks out there. As long as they could contain the fire, there wouldn't be much damage to property.

Just damage to the forest. Harkening back to environmental lessons from her college days, she seemed to remember that was actually a good thing, fertilizing the soil, clearing out old and dead growth, making way for renewal. "It's awfully late in the day to be sending people out there."

Elvira shrugged. "They can't just let it burn."

No, Mary supposed they couldn't do that. Glancing at her watch, she saw it was six-fifteen. Sam still wasn't there. Her heart skipped uncomfortably as she wondered if he'd gone to fight the fire, too. After a brief hesitation, she decided to go inside and call.

Sam's number was in the book, but there was no answer. She waited another fifteen minutes, then called Maggie Sanders, the sheriff's wife. She didn't know Maggie well, but she recognized her from the times she'd come to school about her daughter Allie Williams. Allie, in fact, was going to be in Mary's literature class this coming school year.

"Maggie?" she said when the other woman answered. "This is Mary McKinney. I was supposed to come for dinner tonight with Sam, but he hasn't shown up yet, and I can't reach him at home."

"Mary! I'm glad you called. Earl didn't know who Sam had invited, and he was hoping you'd call here. Sam's up at Edgerton Pass, helping the firefighters. A bunch of us are getting some food together to take up there. Do you want to help?"

"Of course I do. But I don't have a car. Mine's in the shop."

"Not a problem. I've got to run by Wiggand's in about thirty minutes. They're making up a bunch of burgers and fries to take up there. I'll pick you up on the way. Say...twenty-five minutes?"

"Sure. I'll be ready."

She changed swiftly into jeans, hiking boots and a T-shirt, then topped off the outfit with a flannel shirt and a light jacket. Even in summer, the nights grew chilly at this altitude.

God, she hoped Sam wasn't anywhere near the fire.

She waited outside for Maggie. It was getting darker now, though the sky above the western mountains was still light and smoky. But now the orange glow of fire was visible to the northwest. Her neighbors had all gone back into their homes, and the street was deserted in the mountain twilight.

A light came on across the street, and a man's shadow moved behind thin curtains. On impulse, Mary crossed over and knocked on Elijah Canfield's door.

Presently he opened it, his white hair looking like a nimbus in the light behind.

"Reverend Canfield," Mary said, "I thought you'd want to know that Sam is up in the mountains fighting the fire." Then, before he could say a word in response, she turned and hurried back across the street. She didn't want to know if he thought she was a busybody, didn't want to hear anything he might have to say about Sam. Any man who could think Sam Canfield had failed in life was a man she didn't want to know.

She was aware that he stood there a while in his open door, but she didn't look his way. He might be staring at her, or he might be staring at the threatening glow over the mountains. He might be stunned, or he might be indifferent. She just didn't want to know.

Maggie Sanders was only a few minutes late. She pulled up near Mary in a silver Suburban and leaned over to open the door. "Hop in."

Mary obeyed, climbing up into the seat and reaching for the belt. "Where's Allie?"

"At a friend's house in town. I didn't want her to be home alone."

Mary felt a shiver of apprehension and glanced at Maggie. "That's right. Your house is close to the pass."

"Yeah." Maggie shook her head and put the car in gear. "I'm trying not to think about that. But there are quite a few houses scattered around out there. And The Little Church in the Woods."

The sun had completely vanished by the time they reached the top of Edgerton Pass. Vehicles were everywhere, pulled off to the side of the road, and a tarp-covered command center was now lighted by gas lanterns.

The smoke from the fire, once again a thick, rising column that reached high into the sky, caught the sunlight, glowing golden and red at the top. Below, in the shadows, it turned silvery-gray, smudgy. Occasionally it would part a bit and reveal the hellish glow of flames.

It was a few miles away, Mary noted with relief as she helped Maggie unload the insulated food containers and pass them out to the men. But even as she felt the relief, she realized how rapidly the situation could change.

"Sorry I didn't call."

The sound of Sam's voice caused her to turn around just as she finished lifting two foam containers from the back of the Suburban. Standing there with the cartons in her hand, she felt relief pour through her, so great that for an instant her knees felt rubbery. He wasn't down in the valley. A little warning bell clanged in her mind, pointing out that she was reacting too strongly, that she didn't know Sam well enough to feel this strongly. But the thought whispered away as he smiled at her.

"Hamburger and fries?" she asked stupidly.

"Sure. Thanks." He took a container and opened it, then took a huge bite of the burger. "Are you mad at me?"

"For what?"

"Standing you up."

It was a good thing it was getting dark, because she could feel her cheeks heat. "It wasn't a date, remember? Besides, I hear there's a fire."

He smiled with his mouth closed, the food bulging in his cheek, and nodded. Other men were approaching, and Mary turned quickly to give them food, as well.

A pickup truck arrived, carrying huge insulated jugs and folding tables. Two mothers who Mary knew from school jumped out, and soon they were all helping to set up the tables near the command tent, on a fairly level bit of pine-needle-covered forest floor. The insulated jugs were full of hot coffee.

Soon another truck arrived bearing cups, water and bags full of chips.

"Instant supper," Sam remarked. "I need to get some of that down to the guys in the trenches."

"I'll drive it down," Maggie offered.

"Like hell you will. I like my butt just the way it is. Earl would have my hide. *I'll* take it."

So Mary found herself helping to load Sam's truck. He'd switched his cruiser for one of the department's Blazers, and they filled the cargo area with food and drink. Moments later Sam headed down into the valley on the narrow, paved road.

Maggie reached out and took Mary's hand. "He'll be okay. George Griffin, that forester guy, told me the crews aren't anywhere near the fire."

Mary squeezed her hand back. "I know. He'll be fine."

Maggie arched a brow. "Are you two an item?"

"No. We're very clear on that. Not even dating."

"Really?" A crooked smile came to Maggie's mouth. "If you say so."

Mary felt a little burst of irritation, then reminded herself it didn't matter whether Maggie believed her or not. Time would tell. Which could, she thought, be the whole problem. Not whether Maggie believed her, but whether she believed it herself. Whether she *wanted* to believe it herself.

Because Sam was an attractive guy. Very attractive. And he seemed both nice and gentle, a rarity in a man. As if he didn't feel a need to prove anything.

Mary sighed and went back to the table to help serve. It didn't matter, she told herself. It would never matter. She wasn't in the market for a relationship, good or bad. And she certainly didn't deserve a good one.

The wind kicked up. It was nearly ten o'clock, and the last of the day's warmth had seeped from the thin air. As cold air sank into the warmer valleys, the breath of the breeze stirred and grew. The fire hungrily sucked it in, feeding the flames with fresh air. The angry red glow brightened.

The planes were still flying overhead, dumping their loads of chemicals on the flames. But even as each load fell and fire winked out beneath the assault, the flames spread elsewhere. Before the wind started, it had looked as if they were winning. In an instant, all that changed.

Like orange lights winking on in the darkness, the flames scattered to trees farther away, jumping long distances. Heading south, heading up the mountainsides. Where there had been only one fire, in minutes there were six or seven of them.

George Griffin was talking anxiously into his radio, calling for more chemicals and water.

The wind, shifting almost wildly, blew smoke their way, blinding them, causing Mary to cough as it burned her throat. Then it blew another way, briefly burying the entire valley in an inky pall. Moments later the pall lifted, blurring the stars and revealing the disaster below.

More fires burned now, individual blots of orange

and red in the darkness. And the conflagration was creeping toward the pass.

Huge tongues of flame leaped upward, more than twice the height of the trees. Even at this distance an occasional loud pop could be heard as a tree exploded in flames. And on the wind they could hear the distant roar, like that of a hungry beast.

A shoulder brushed Mary's, and she looked to her side. Elijah Canfield stood there, staring at the fire. "Where's Sam?" he asked.

"I think he's still down with the crew building the firebreak. He didn't come back up after he took food down."

His eyes, intense even in the dull red glow that was lighting the night, fixed on her. "Doesn't anyone know for sure?"

Mary felt a stirring of impatience, accentuated by her growing anxiety. "That's the last we heard from him. If you don't believe me, there's George Griffin." She pointed. "Why? Are you worried about him?"

Under any other circumstances it would have been an unthinkable question to ask a father, but this father...well, he deserved it.

His gaze seemed to burn into her, but he didn't answer. Instead he strode away toward George.

Maggie spoke from behind her. "Chilly sort of guy."

"That's Sam's father. The Reverend Elijah Canfield."

"Whew." Maggie looked toward him. "Sam never mentions him."

"I'm beginning to understand why."

Maggie faced her. "Trouble between those two, huh?"

"I guess so." She didn't feel free to share what Sam had told her privately, so she opted for vagueness.

"I can't say I'm surprised. Sam is one of the nicest guys you'd ever want to meet, but he's closed off, if you know what I mean. He was that way even before his wife died, except maybe with her."

Mary felt the kick of interest. "Did you know her?"

"Sam's wife? Sure. We weren't best friends or anything, but Earl and Sam have been great friends from the instant Sam moved to town. So Earl would invite me and my late husband over sometimes, and Sam and Beth would be there. She was fun. Outgoing, unlike Sam. Young."

"Young?"

"Not in years. She was close to Sam's age. But...I don't know. She always impressed me as being about eighteen." Maggie shrugged and flashed a grin. "Probably because I had a daughter and she didn't. I was buried in responsibility, and she was still having fun being married and in love. You know what I mean. No criticism, by the way."

"I know." Mary felt the hovering black cloud that never quite left her reach out for her heart. She hadn't told a soul in Whisper Creek that she'd had a son. Not one. She couldn't bear to explain. Or to be reminded.

"Or maybe," Maggie said after a brief pause, "it wasn't that she was young. Maybe it's that I was so emotionally old at the time myself. Going through bad things. Maybe I just envied her vivacity."

Mary nodded. She could understand that. She felt as old as the hills herself in some ways. Too old to laugh easily, too old to take pleasure in much. Too weary. But she didn't want to think about herself. "What was going on?"

"Oh." Meg shrugged. "It's still hard to talk about. But my first marriage...well, we were going through a rough time back then. I was feeling isolated and pretty down."

Mary nodded again. "I can identify with that. Things have a way of...going sour, sometimes."

"They sure do." Maggie sighed. "Then, of course, my husband died, and there was no way to fix anything. Thank God for Earl."

"He's a nice man." Although Mary didn't know him very well. She'd pretty much kept to herself since taking the job in Whisper Creek. Her friendships were all superficial, extensions of her job. She didn't want anyone getting close enough to find out the truth about her. Not only because she felt so guilty, but because she felt so ugly.

"Yes, he is." Maggie smiled. "And so's Sam.

I'm glad he and Earl are friends. Well, maybe you can drag Sam out of his cocoon.''

''Me?'' The thought made Mary blanche. Dragging anyone out of their cocoon meant she would have to come out of hers, and she wasn't about to do that.

She had a sudden, vivid memory of a caterpillar one of her students had brought to her classroom in Denver. Back then, she'd been teaching third grade, awaiting an opening at a nearby high school.

The girl had brought the caterpillar in a mason jar, along with a small, leafy twig. It was a pretty caterpillar, probably why the girl had liked it. Before the morning was over, the caterpillar had started spinning its cocoon.

The excitement in the classroom had been palpable, so instead of asking the girl to let the poor beast go when she got home, Mary had allowed her to keep it in the classroom as a science lesson. They'd all been surprised by how fast the cocoon was created.

Then had come the morning when the butterfly had emerged. Everyone had crowded around the jar, watching excitedly. The creature was weak, its wings folded and stuck together.

At that point, Mary's compassion had overborn the necessity of teaching a science lesson. She'd suggested they let the little butterfly go free. Everyone had agreed.

Outside, they'd waited and watched as slowly the

wings had dried and spread. But one of them was deformed, and that butterfly would never leave the ground. Seeing what was coming, Mary had swiftly herded her students back to the classroom.

An hour later she went out to check. As she had feared, the butterfly had been killed by ants because it couldn't escape. There was little of it left.

And that, Mary thought, was why she needed her cocoon. Her wings were deformed. She knew it. The ants would kill her if she ever emerged.

"Why not you?" Maggie asked, her cheerful voice penetrating the haze of Mary's memory. "You're the right age, you're pretty, you're nice, and Sam seems interested."

"He's not interested," Mary blurted before she could stop herself.

Maggie peered at her, the shadows on her face highlighted by the limited range of the kerosene lanterns. "Not interested? He was bringing you to dinner."

Mary shrugged. "That was...well, it wasn't a date. We agreed on that."

"Oh, my word," Maggie said, and fell silent.

Mary chose not to pursue that comment, even though it sounded disbelieving. What was the point, anyway? What Maggie might think had no bearing on what was actually happening, or on the fact that Mary never would have accepted the dinner invitation if Sam hadn't said it wasn't a date.

"Well," Maggie said presently, then said no more.

Needing solitude, Mary walked away from the food tables toward an area from which she could see the fire better. In the darkness, a red fog seemed to fill the north end of the valley, and here and there tongues of fire burst above it. It was getting closer. Showing no mercy.

But then, the world, or the universe, or whatever you chose to call it, didn't show mercy. Ever. It was a cold, heartless world, where bad things happened no matter how good you were.

"It looks like the fires of hell," Elijah remarked.

Mary started, surprised that he had joined her. She wondered if he was going to stick like a burr to her. And if so, why. "It looks like a forest fire," she said flatly.

His face, only dimly illuminated by the lanterns behind them and the glow from the fire, looked dark, a ruddy black. His shaggy white eyebrows seemed to glow with their own light. They lifted. "You don't believe in hell?"

"Oh, I believe in it, all right. I just don't think we agree on what it is."

"I see."

She averted her face, hoping he would take the hint and leave her alone. He didn't.

She heard what at first sounded like the rush of running water. But then, as the pitch-black treetops began to sway against the slightly lighter sky, and as the kiss of the breeze nipped at her ears, she knew what it was. The wind was coming up strongly.

Not just the earlier occasional gust, this was strong, steady. Exactly what they didn't need.

At first it seemed content to sweep the mountaintop and ignore the valley. Mary tensed as she waited, hoping against hope it wouldn't sweep down the slopes and spread the fire. Beside her, she heard Elijah begin a low-voiced prayer. Almost instinctively, she reached out and took his hand, silently joining him. To her surprise, she felt him squeeze her fingers.

And she wondered yet again why Elijah seemed to be haunting her.

6

Dawn seeped through the smoky haze, bringing a dim gray light to the men who had struggled all night to build a firebreak below Edgerton Pass. Even though the fire was nowhere near reaching them yet, the area still looked as if it had been bombed out. Trees had been cut down, and during the night bulldozers had arrived to shove them away from the cleared area. Now there was nothing to be seen except a wide, barren strip they hoped the fire couldn't cross. There was still more work to be done, more land to be cleared, but the crew that had worked all night was being dismissed as replacements arrived.

Sam was among those leaving. He climbed into his truck, offering rides to some of the other men. The air reeked of wood smoke, enough to make their eyes burn. All of them wore kerchiefs over their mouths.

Climbing up the pass didn't make it any better. It was like driving through a pea-soup fog that stank of burning pitch. It was as if he could have driven off the end of the world at any moment.

The command center at the top of the pass was a hive of activity, but this morning almost all the faces were new. George Griffin was still there, though, handing over the reins to his replacement.

Sam parked, letting the other guys out to go to their own cars. He went over to George and asked, "What's the news?"

"Not good." George sighed. His eyes were red from the smoke, and his face had a gray cast to it. Most of the faces did. Soot was settling everywhere. "We've got four different fires burning now, maybe twenty-five hundred acres each. Hard to tell how bad it is right now, though."

It certainly was. Once again the pall of smoke concealed the fires and most of the valley.

"Go on home," George said. "Get some sleep. We're going to need all the rested help we can get later."

That didn't sound good, Sam thought as he headed back to his truck. Not good at all. He didn't have any experience with forest fires, but he'd read some about them. Fighting them was never easy, and in a place like this, with no road access to the burning area, it was even worse. Everything out there was fuel.

The air stirred a little, and fine ash sprinkled over him. He hardly noticed it; it had been happening all night. Right now he needed his bed and about ten hours of sleep. He figured he could only allow himself six or seven, though. He would have to get back up here as soon as he could.

"Hi." Mary stepped toward him, looking as gray as the rest of them in the dim morning light. Her eyes, too, were red-rimmed and watery looking.

"You're still here?" he asked.

She nodded. "I promised your father I'd make sure you got back here safely."

"My father?" Cripes. Just what he needed to think about right now. Anger stirred in him, a not-quite-sleeping beast. "What the hell does he care?"

"He seems to." She shrugged. "Can I hitch a ride to town? No car."

"Sure. Yeah, sure." He opened the passenger door for her, then slammed it after she'd slid onto the seat. His father. Of all the damn things...

The man hadn't given a single damn about him in fifteen years, at least. Why the hell was he concerned about Sam's health now?

A show, maybe? Perhaps it was uncomfortable for a minister of God to have people know he wasn't even speaking to his son. That could well be. Make it look as if it was all Sam's fault. As far as Elijah was concerned, everything was Sam's fault anyway, and always had been.

But it was way too late for the prodigal son routine. Way too late.

Sam headed the truck down the winding road, taking the corners just a little too fast.

"Sam?" Mary spoke. "Are you okay?"

"Yeah. What kind of crap is he shoveling, anyway?"

"I don't know. Are you sure it's crap?"

He glanced at her, his eyes still burning. Just the smoke, he told himself. "Yeah, I'm sure. He's the man who called me the day after my wife's funeral and told me her death was a punishment for my sins."

"Oh, no!" Mary's tone was full of distress. "Oh, Sam."

He took the next corner practically on two wheels and forced himself to slow down. Maybe he didn't care if he died, but he cared that Mary didn't. "I'm sorry I missed dinner," he said, changing the subject.

"It's okay. Maggie told me you were up here. The fire's more important."

"Thanks for understanding."

"There's nothing to understand."

But he couldn't leave the subject of his father alone. It was like a scab that itched, and he couldn't ignore it. "What did he say to you, anyway?"

"Elijah? Not a whole lot. He doesn't seem like a very talkative man."

"Huh. That's a surprise. Used to be he could never shut up. Always thundering about something and never listening."

"Maybe he's improved with age."

Sam wasn't even going to toy with that idea. Elijah was Elijah. Lions didn't turn into lambs. "That's about as likely as a leopard changing its spots. Besides, what's one of the first things he said to you?"

"Something about the books I use to teach literature."

"Exactly. Give him until the school year starts, then he'll be out to cleanse the school library."

"I hope not."

Sam shook his head and braked for another turn. "Waste of effort. He'll do it. He'll also probably try to close down the X-rated video rental room at Baker's Video Rental. Not that I like those things, but..."

"I always thought it was good they put those tapes out of sight where the kids can't find them."

"Me, too. It shows some responsibility, without interfering with people's choices. And it's all soft-core, anyway."

A little giggle escaped her. "You've checked it out?"

He sent her a sour look. "Only in my official capacity. Somebody complained that they were renting child pornography."

"Were they?"

"Of course not. The woman who complained hadn't even been in the store. She'd heard it from someone, who'd heard it from someone else. You know how that goes. Anyway, the stuff they're renting is pretty much on the level of an R-rated movie, just more of it."

"Well, I'll be the first to admit I don't understand the fascination for those things. But then, I'm a woman."

"I'm a man," he said, stating the obvious. "I don't read girlie magazines, either." Then, unable to resist, he added, "Why settle for pictures if you can have the real thing?"

He heard her gasp; then a deep laugh escaped her. "You are wicked, Sam Canfield. Wicked, wicked."

"So my father always said." But this time he said it without bitterness. Somehow Mary's laughter had taken the sting out of her teasing words—and the sting out of remembering his father. He wished it would last.

As they approached her house, she said, "Why don't you come in for breakfast?"

"I don't want to trouble you."

"It's no trouble. I'm an old hand at fast breakfasts. I can microwave bacon and some sausage biscuits, and make coffee in a jiff. And you need to eat something."

He couldn't argue with that. Nor, he realized, did he want to. Exhausted as he was, he was still too wound up to hit the hay. He figured it might take him an hour or so to wind down from working all night. It always did.

"Thanks, Mary. If you're not too tired."

"I'm as wired as can be. I got my second wind along about 5:00 a.m. And I'm hungry, too."

So he parked in her driveway. For an instant he

wondered if his father was watching from across the street, then told himself he didn't care. It made him uneasy, though, that Mary had intimated his father was showing interest in him. In Sam's experience, Elijah grew interested only when he believed his son was messing up.

The air in town was hazy now, not as bad as up in the pass, but the effects of the fire were reaching here, too. The morning sun, heralding yet another dry day, looked pale through the smoke, and yellowed.

"It smells smokier than a frigid winter night," Mary remarked as she unlocked her door. He knew she was referring to the number of woodstoves that burned around there when it got cold.

But the smoke hadn't penetrated her house, at least not yet, and Sam noticed a delicate scent of lilac on the air. "Is that lilac I smell?" he asked.

"Yes. I love it. It's in the carpet freshener."

Almost in spite of himself, he smiled. "When I was about six, we lived for a while in Michigan. My dad was pastor of a small church up near Saginaw. And we had this huge lilac bush at the corner of the house, just covered with blossoms. I used to like to suck the nectar out of them. And I used to hide under it. Nobody could find me there. I seem to remember spending entire afternoons daydreaming, surrounded by lilacs."

Mary led him into the kitchen, shucking her flannel shirt and hanging it over a chair back. "Did you have to hide often?"

He found himself looking into her green eyes. Sinking into her green eyes. And he saw a gentleness there that made his heart slam. Gentleness wasn't something Sam had experienced very often in life, not even in his marriage. It had an unexpected effect on him, an effect that held him rooted to the spot even as she turned away, apparently accepting his silence as an answer.

"How many sausage biscuits do you think you can eat?" she asked, opening the refrigerator door.

"Uh..." Her question might as well have been spoken in another language. Somehow it didn't connect with his brain.

She smiled over her shoulder. "Why don't you wash up in the bathroom, and I'll make coffee. The caffeine might clear the cobwebs."

He was grateful for the easy escape. Because, for no reason he could figure out, Mary's tidy little kitchen had suddenly seemed as threatening as a dragon's lair. As if something awful might leap out at any moment.

A strange way to react to a gentle smile.

One look in the mirror over the bathroom sink almost caused him to laugh out loud. He looked like a raccoon, so much smoke, sweat and dirt had stained his face. He was surprised any woman would offer him breakfast, looking the way he did.

And now that he noticed, his shirt stank of smoke

and sweat, too. Oh, man. He ought to slink out of here now, before she noticed.

Although how she could have failed to notice, sitting right beside him in the truck cab, he couldn't imagine. Maybe the smoke covered the sweaty smell.

If he'd had a change of clothes, he might have hopped into her shower. Instead he had to strip off his shirt and do what he could with a washcloth and a bar of soap. And when he was done, it was kind of embarrassing to look at the black stains on the cloth. He rinsed it out as best he could, but it was going to take a heavy-duty trip through a washing machine to save it. And it was pretty, too, not just some colorless white cotton of the kind he owned.

That was when he noticed that the whole bathroom was pretty. Lavender and lilac and cream dominated in the shower curtain and rug, along with the soap dish and other stuff he never knew the names of. He bet her whole house was pretty. Feminine.

He and Beth had been kind of basic about such things, preferring instead to spend their money on skiing and a recreational vehicle. Not to mention a boat for fishing on the reservoir.

There was even a tiny old medicine bottle holding a few tiny dried purple flowers.

All of a sudden he was uneasy, feeling as if he'd stumbled into a virgin's bower. Mary McKinney dealt in things he couldn't begin to fathom, things like tiny little flowers and probably satin sachets in her dresser drawers. It was an alien world.

Moving swiftly, he donned his flannel shirt, thinking that he'd wasted the effort of washing himself. Once again he was enveloped in soot and stench.

When he returned to the kitchen, taking care not to peer off to the side at her living room—it was probably dripping with cute feminine things—he found her pouring two mugs of hot coffee. The microwave was humming, its digital display on a countdown. She, too, had scrubbed up a little, washing the ashen color from her face and neck, restoring her rosy color. But as she moved closer to hand him the coffee, he could smell the smoke on her, too.

"I'm afraid I killed your washcloth," he said as he accepted the mug. The cream and sugar were already on the table, in blue willow containers. His mother had done that, too, he remembered with an unwelcome pang. She'd never been content to put the milk on the table in a store container.

"Don't worry about it," she said pleasantly. "It's just a washcloth. Two-ninety-nine at the discount store. I've got bigger worries." Then she laughed.

God, her laugh was incredible. Warm and throaty, seeming to rise from deep within her. Its touch was almost physical.

"Sorry," she said. "I seem to be punchy from lack of sleep."

A helpless smile came to his own mouth, like the harmonic response of a tuning fork. Irresistible.

"Me, too. Tell you what. Nothing either of us says is to be taken into evidence."

She laughed again. The microwave pinged, and she pulled out a clear plastic pouch containing bacon. "This stuff is actually pretty good."

"I know. I depend on the microwave. Without it, I'd either starve to death or go broke from eating out all the time."

She lifted an eyebrow at him, still smiling. "One of those, huh?"

"One of whats?"

"Testosterone-based life-form."

He had an urge to laugh, but instead he played along. "What's that supposed to mean?"

"Oh, you know. Those poor unfortunate creatures who are incapable from birth of cooking or cleaning."

"Ah. You mean I suffer what some folks call testosterone poisoning."

She shrugged, still looking impish. "Same thing, I guess."

"Hmm. Well, I'll have you know my house is pretty clean."

"No underwear on the bathroom floor? No giant dust bunnies under the bed?"

"Well, I can't say for sure what's under the bed...." He trailed off and enjoyed watching her laugh again. Damn, it had been so long since he'd shared anything approaching humor. Who cared if they were punchy from lack of sleep? It felt good.

Using only the microwave and coffeepot, she put quite a meal in front of him: bacon, sausage biscuits, orange juice and coffee, and plenty of it. And once he started eating, he realized he was famished.

She spoke as he bit into his second biscuit. "It must have been hard work, building the firebreak."

He shrugged. "It wouldn't have been quite so hard if I hadn't been spending too much time on my can in a patrol car recently."

One of those enticing smiles flickered across her face. "I could say the same. It's funny, when I moved up here I had all these ideas about cross-country skiing, hiking in the summertime. Instead I always seem to be too busy."

"That's life. There's always something that needs doing." But then he remembered Beth. "My late wife had a different philosophy."

"What was that?"

"That the responsibilities won't go away if you ignore them for a few days. They'll *always* be there. In fact, she used to say that if you let them, responsibilities will expand to take *all* your time."

"How did that work out?"

"Not too bad, usually. Yeah, the bills had to be paid on time whether you felt like it or not, but other things... Well, she used to get up on her day off, and the house would be a mess because we'd been too busy, and the yard would need mowing, or whatever, and she'd say, 'Let's go fishing, Sam. It's a beautiful day.'" He almost smiled, remembering.

"And I'd say, 'But, Beth, I'm supposed to work on the yard,' or whatever it was. Once it was patching the roof because we had a small leak." Mary's green eyes were smiling gently at him, he noticed.

"What did she say?" she asked.

"She'd say, 'Sam, that yard will still need mowing tomorrow.' Or 'Sam, that roof will still be fixable this afternoon.' And off we'd go."

"Sounds like a great philosophy."

"It was." To a point. Sometimes it drove him batty. Things needed doing when they needed doing. Like the roof. They went fishing, had a big early-afternoon thunderstorm, and he'd wound up having to patch the bedroom ceiling as well as the roof. But it would have felt disloyal to say that to Mary, so he kept it to himself.

"Still," Mary said, almost as if she were reading his mind, "I guess you'd need to watch your balance."

"Sure. And I'll be the first to admit that procrastination drives me crazy." He shrugged. "I'm one of those people who just wants to get it *done*. So I guess I've lost my sense of balance the other way lately."

She nodded. "Maybe I have, too. It gets easy to let work and responsibilities substitute for life."

He'd never heard it put that way before, and he turned it over in his mind. "Yeah. Less painful."

"Exactly." She sighed quietly and nibbled on her strip of bacon. Sam was making huge inroads into the mound of food she'd put in front of him. "It makes it easier not to think."

"It sure does." He was tempted to ask her what she didn't want to think about but decided he didn't know her well enough. If she wanted to, she could volunteer. "Used to be I loved to sit out on dark nights and just look up at the stars. I used to feel this, um, connection to something bigger." He was almost embarrassed to say that. It was a part of himself he hadn't exposed to anyone in a long time.

But to his surprise, Mary simply nodded. "I know what you mean. I feel that way sometimes, when I'm walking alone in the woods and the breeze is whispering in the treetops. It's like being in a cathedral." Then her expression turned haunted. "It also gives me too much time to think."

He could identify with that. He gathered they were both running from a bit of depression. Well, hell, most of the world was, one way or the other. He didn't pretend his problems were any worse than anyone else's. He just didn't plan to set himself up for another round.

But as he left Mary's house and headed home, he realized he'd found a kindred spirit in her. And that *really* disturbed him.

7

"**B**rother Elijah," Mrs. Beemis said, smiling too avidly, "you wouldn't happen to be any relation to Sam Canfield, would you?"

He'd only been at the church a few days, but already Elijah had pegged Mrs. Beemis as a gossip and potential troublemaker. She looked like a dear old lady, with gray hair, a surprisingly smooth and rosy face, and blue eyes that peered out from behind the requisite eyeglasses with rhinestones at the outer edges. Everybody's grandmother.

She was also entirely too eager to tell him about her fellow congregants. Properly handled, a minister would find a woman like her useful. But she had to be handled like nitroglycerin. Every church he'd ever pastored had had at least one Mrs. Beemis.

It was Wednesday evening, after prayer service, and about fifty people were milling about in the tiny parish hall, sipping grape juice and soft drinks and eating cookies. Too many of them, thought Elijah, were able-bodied men who ought to be helping with the fire fighting. On the other hand, it *was* his official welcoming party, and many of them may have felt it necessary to be there.

Mrs. Beemis was still waiting for an answer. The longer he delayed, the more likely she was to think he was hiding something. And Elijah had nothing to hide. He hadn't done anything wrong.

"Yes, he's my son, Mrs. Beemis."

"Oh, my, how delightful! He'll be joining our congregation, then?"

It was not a harmless question. Elijah took a second to consider. "We all have to follow our own paths to the Lord."

"Yes, of course we do." Her eyes indicated that her curiosity hadn't been quenched. It was entirely likely that in a half hour she would be phoning everyone she knew to suggest that a preacher who couldn't raise his own son in the faith was one who ought to be watched.

But he would be watched anyway. It was part of his job. Everything he said or did would be examined in minute detail by those with nothing better to do with their time. It was an unhappy fact of his life that he served at the pleasure of his congregation, which meant they pretty much dictated the way their religion was served to them.

And he was getting just a little bit cynical, he realized, feeling as if he were preaching the Gospel according to his current vestry. For a long time he'd overlooked that subtle nuance, but for some reason, over the past few years, he'd been noticing it more and more. Hellfire and damnation preached from the pulpit were great things—unless they struck too close to home.

Maybe it was something about the modern world, but "too close to home" seemed to be happening with greater frequency.

"Well," said Mrs. Beemis, "preachers' kids *do* have a tendency to go a little wild."

For all his problems with Sam, Elijah took exception to that. "He's not wild, Mrs. Beemis. He's just following his own path." Wrong path, but not wild.

"Yes, of course," she said. "He *is* a policeman, after all." With that, she finally drifted away. Apparently she felt she had enough to keep her phone line busy until midnight.

No point in worrying about that now. When he grew fed up with her and her ilk, he would look for another position. It was ever the same: some people weren't happy until they managed to convince themselves they were better than everyone else, even the preacher. So be it.

It had been easier to endure when Belle was still alive, though. He hadn't felt so alone.

Too bad, he told himself. Too bad. Sam had been an embarrassment to him for years. He should have known better than to come to this town.

But he'd come anyway, and that disturbed him. Maybe that was something he needed to pray about.

Or maybe God had drawn him here for some reason. Well, of course he had. Elijah Canfield believed his entire life was guided by God. Even coming to Whisper Creek and seeing his son before he'd seen another soul in town.

That didn't mean he knew what this was about. It felt like wearing a hair shirt. But maybe he was here to call Sam back to the true path.

Yes, that must be it. The boy had wandered too far, and the Lord wanted him back in the fold. It was about time.

Before he had much time to think about how he might accomplish that impossible task, another one of his flock bearded him about what he was going to do about all "them gays in town."

"What gays?" Elijah asked.

"Those two artists." Silence Tippit, one of the vestry members, started the conversation in what Elijah had already come to realize was his usual abrupt way. Silence, a man of about sixty, was short and round, with enough white hair that he reminded Elijah of a polar bear. He was also one of the powers-to-be-reckoned-with.

"There's more than them two artists," said another man, whose name utterly escaped Elijah. The guy was about as nondescript as a man could be. "You got those women living together over on Eighth Street."

Silence shook his head. "Bill, it's just two women

living together. Roommates. There's never been any sign of anything else.''

"Well, that one has short hair and them funny round glasses.''

Elijah felt compelled to say something. "One mustn't judge simply by appearances, Bill. Have they *done* anything?"

Bill scowled. "It's the way they look. And living together. Why don't they have husbands?''

Silence apparently didn't want to argue it any further. "We *do* have a problem with those artists, though," he said, turning to Elijah. "They set a bad example for the youth. When they come to town, they hold hands.''

"Hmm." Elijah didn't like that. In fact his stomach turned over at the mere thought. "Well, I'll certainly preach against sins of that kind. It's an abomination.''

Silence nodded. "Truly, truly an abomination.''

Bill spoke again. "We don't need that kind in town. We need to get rid of them.''

There had been a time when Elijah would have agreed. But the years had taught him how such words could be interpreted and the kind of sin they could lead to. "Bill," he said in his firmest I-am-the-pastor voice, "we mustn't get rid of anyone. Do you understand me?"

"We can't tolerate abomination! That's a sin.''

Elijah nodded. "I'm not asking you to tolerate,

Bill. But remember, we can hate the sin, but we're required to love the sinner.''

Bill scowled. "I ain't loving neither of them."

Silence looked at Elijah, something indefinable in his steady gaze. For an instant Elijah thought his time in Whisper Creek had just come to a close. But Silence surprised him by nodding. "Brother Elijah's right, Bill. We can't allow someone else's sin to lead *us* into sin."

"Exactly," Elijah said, feeling he had just passed a major watershed safely. "We must be good Christians ourselves. I'll preach against abomination, Brother Bill. I may even speak to these young men about their conduct and try to persuade them to live a godly life. I'll certainly tell our youth they mustn't even consider such things, because they're vile. But we must not lift a hand against another."

Bill went away looking unhappy, but Silence clapped Elijah on the shoulder. "We need to live in this town, Brother Elijah," Silence said pointedly. "Some people, like Brother Bill, don't seem to exactly understand that. I'm glad you do."

Elijah felt pretty good. Until he started thinking about Sam again. Until the mental hair shirt started itching like mad.

The fire was getting worse. A pall of smoke now hung over Whisper Creek all the time, dulling the sun, irritating the eyes. Efforts to put it out had mostly become efforts to control it. And for the first time all summer, thunderclouds were beginning to build.

"Rain," said George Griffin. "We need rain, not lightning."

"Picky picky," Sam answered. He'd spent all day working on firebreaks down below and was getting a breather as the next shift of miners coming off work was beginning to show up to help. Five days, and about all they'd managed to do was keep the fires boxed in. Every time they thought they were getting ahead of the game, flames would spring up somewhere else. Sometimes they managed to put them out before they spread too much, sometimes not. It was like fighting that many-headed Hydra he'd learned about when he'd studied mythology in high school. Chop it off here, and another one came at you from somewhere else.

And fire was a big beast, bigger than men, bigger than all their resources.

George turned to him and put a hand on his shoulder. "Sam, go home and get some rest. You've been working harder at this fire than anyone except the smoke jumpers. It'll still be here tomorrow."

Sam was about to argue, but he stopped before the words came out of his mouth. George was right. He was getting a constant cough from the smoke, his eyes never stopped burning, and his body was aching all the time. Toward the end of his shift below, he'd found he was losing his coordination.

"Yeah, I guess I will," he said. "See you tomorrow."

"We'll be here."

The words were grim, and so was Sam's mood as he climbed into his truck and headed home. Bath, bed, about twelve hours of sleep, and he would be ready to pitch in again, he promised himself. It had gone well past the point of being a liaison. They needed every hand they could get to contain the beast.

For some reason, as he was driving through the twilight down the mountain, he found himself thinking of Mary. He hadn't seen her but a minute or two since the morning she made him breakfast. He knew she was still bringing food and drink up the mountain, along with a bunch of other women, but their encounters hadn't been more than a nod and a smile in all that time. He wondered if her car was out of the shop, and if not, how she was getting her groceries. After all, he'd promised her that he would take her to the store.

Okay, so bath, then a call on Mary to see if she needed anything. *Then* bed. He would survive.

His house smelled musty from lack of use. He'd done little enough there over the past week that it smelled unoccupied, except for the faint odor of smoke and ash rising from the hamper where he'd tossed his clothes. Stripping, he threw everything into the washer, including the stuff in the hamper, but he didn't turn it on. Then he stepped into a hot shower, turning his face up to the spray, and forgot all about time as the heat pounded the ache from his muscles and the water cleansed the stench from his pores.

Only when the spray turned chilly did he climb out. After he toweled off, he padded, still naked, to the laundry room and turned on the washer. Cold water wash. He didn't care.

Food was his next priority, but a check of his fridge told him some of that stuff had been sitting there too long. With a sigh, he threw it out and settled for a family-size can of clam chowder.

While it heated, he climbed into some sweatpants and a T-shirt. His mood was sinking, he realized, but he didn't realize how badly until he was sitting at the kitchen table with his bowl of chowder.

Because all of a sudden he was thinking about his late wife. Emptiness filled his gut, a hollowness that wanted to suck him down into its depths. He'd learned how to fight it, how to withstand it, but it never hurt any less.

He missed looking at her across the table. And while he still would have come home to do his own laundry and make his own soup, at least he wouldn't have been sitting alone at this damn table. She would have wanted to hear his stories about fire fighting, and she would have shared the stories of her day, and the silence wouldn't have threatened to eat him alive.

Shit. He was just tired. His defenses were down.

He closed his eyes for a minute, forcing himself to concentrate on the aroma of the clam chowder. The reality of it was something he could focus on to the exclusion of other things.

But then Elijah popped into his head. Damn Elijah.

Anger superseded sorrow. Why the *hell* had that man had to come to town *now?* Even as he asked the question of himself, it sounded stupid. Now, later, whenever—what difference did it make? It wouldn't have been any easier in five weeks or five years, or ten.

He thought he'd built a wall between himself and his father, a wall of disinterest. Or of ice. He'd honestly believed he'd left the pain and anger in the past, where they belonged. He ought to be able to look at Elijah now and feel sorry for him, a man who had lost his wife and driven his son away.

Instead he felt…angry.

Hell.

Finishing the soup in a hurry, he decided to go check on Mary. She was the one thing around here right now that didn't carry bad memories of some kind. One person he could talk to who wasn't associated with his late wife.

With his late *life.*

Mary was up to her eyeballs making sandwiches for the next day. Each day, when they finished their tour on the mountaintop, she and Meg stopped at the grocery to pick up what they would need for the next day. Other women did the same, portioning out the chores and types of food.

Today Mary was making dozens of sandwiches. Her kitchen table looked like an assembly line of white bread, rye bread and whole wheat bread slices. Some were slathered with mayonnaise, others with butter or mustard. Pounds and pounds of cold cuts, contributed by the local market, sat in stacks on one corner of the counter.

They had to be thick sandwiches, because the crews were working so hard, but Mary found herself cringing a little as she heaped a quarter pound of meat on each one. For herself, she would have used only one or two thin slices.

But on went the thick layers of pastrami or ham, bologna or turkey. It was a good thing the market was donating the meat; otherwise someone would have gone broke trying to do this.

But it made her feel good to be doing something useful. Some of the local women were also fighting the fire, but Mary would have been the first to admit she was terrified of fire, pathologically so. She wouldn't even light a charcoal grill.

She had no idea where the fear came from. It was a phobia of some kind, one she'd never had to test. It was the reason, however, that she'd gotten rid of the gas range that had come with the house and installed an electric one. Open flames bothered her.

Even on candles, although she would occasionally light one. When she wasn't alone.

Sighing, she shook her head over the silliness of human nature. How could fears like this grow so powerful, and all from nothing?

Then a thought occurred to her. Suddenly her head snapped up. In her hand were slices of pastrami. She started to turn toward her kitchen door, then realized she was still holding the meat. Putting it down on a slab of rye bread, she wiped her hands on her apron and headed across the street.

Reverend Elijah Canfield answered on her second knock.

"Yes?" he said.

"Can you tell me something, Reverend?"

He smiled and nodded. "Certainly, if I know the answer."

"Maybe you do and maybe you don't. But how come the women in your church aren't helping feed the firefighters?"

For a few seconds he didn't answer.

"You see," Mary plunged on, "there are a half-dozen of us who've volunteered to make food for the firefighters. I'm over there making a couple hundred sandwiches right now. And it suddenly occurred to me that more people ought to be helping. So...don't bother to answer me. But it sure would be nice if somebody would make potato salad or macaroni salad, or even some dessert!"

Finished, she marched back across the street and

into her kitchen, where she went back to work. She didn't care what the man thought of her, but it was really bothering her how few people in town were helping. Oh, a lot of men went to fight the fire, but not nearly as many as could. And right now six women were trying to make enough food for an army.

Apparently the town didn't feel all that threatened at the moment. Well, she ought to know, from her years of teaching, how few people stepped forward to help out unless they had a personal interest. It never failed that one or two mothers in her classrooms would do everything. Or that only fifty parents, in a school with five hundred students, ever showed up for the PTA meetings. The same fifty, every time.

She was putting the top slices on the first batch of sandwiches when her kitchen screen door, which opened onto her driveway, swung open. Startled, she looked up and saw Elijah Canfield.

"You're right," he said simply. "Let me help with those sandwiches."

She was hardly going to tell him to get lost after making a stink about it. So she smiled, waved to the cold cuts and suggested he start at the other end of the counter.

For a few minutes they worked in a silence that was not quite comfortable. Mary didn't usually have a problem with quiet, but it was different somehow with Elijah, as if a million unspoken things were swirling in the air around them, few of them pleasant.

It was Elijah who broke the silence as he started slicing the sandwiches. "You know Sam well?"

Mary hesitated. What did he mean by *well?* "Not really," she said slowly. "He helped me out when someone rear-ended my car. We've talked a few times since." Which struck her as some kind of fib, when she thought about it, because however short a time she had known Sam, she also knew some very personal things about him. Things such as what Elijah had said to Sam after his wife's death. Remembering that, Mary felt a prickle of strong dislike for Elijah. How could someone be so cruel?

"So you're not dating?"

"Heavens, no!" And what business of his was it, anyway? He hadn't talked to his son in fifteen years or more. But Mary bit the words back, waiting to see where this was leading.

But apparently it was leading nowhere. She started to stuff the sliced sandwiches into plastic bags to keep them fresh, then stacked them in a cooler with an ice pack in it. Nothing more was said for a long time, not until all the sandwiches were put away and she was laying out bread for the next round. Firefighters worked up a real appetite.

"It's good of you to do this," Elijah remarked. "You're right. I'll ask the ladies at the church to make some food."

"Ask the men, too. They're not incapable."

Elijah's shaggy white brows lifted, but he didn't say anything.

Mary realized she had been sharp with him. There was really no reason for her to do that, except that she couldn't forget how he had hurt Sam. And that was really none of her business. On the other hand, she didn't feel at all inclined to apologize for her sharpness.

"I take it," Elijah said, "that you think men and women are equally capable."

"In most ways, yes." Nor was she about to apologize for the idea. Men might have a little more physical strength, but that was their only edge in the world at large. "Don't tell me you hold with the notion that women should submit to men."

"The Bible says—"

She interrupted without apology. "It also says that men should love their wives the way that God loves us. Amazing how often that part gets lost in the shuffle."

Elijah stopped spreading mayonnaise and looked at her, his blue eyes as sharp and bright as glacial ice. "You read the Bible?"

Mary slapped a slab of ham on a piece of bread and felt a great deal of sympathy for Sam, who had grown up with this sort of thing. How difficult for a child it must have been. "Of course I read the Bible," she said tartly. "And what's more, I understand it pretty well. One of the benefits of being an English teacher."

''But *how* do you understand it? As a piece of literature or as the word of God?''

''Both, actually. Because it *is* both.''

His icy gaze continued to bore into her for a few more seconds; then he returned to spreading mayonnaise on the bread. Mary realized he was trying not to start a fight. Too bad. Because for some strange reason she was in the mood to have one.

Maybe she was just tired. Or maybe, she thought, she was worried about Sam out there fighting that fire. Sam and all those other men. Every night she prayed that no one would get hurt. And every night she added a little extra prayer for Sam.

She wondered if Elijah bothered to pray for the firefighters, then realized she was being utterly uncharitable. She didn't know Elijah Canfield at all. Other than having a strange opinion about censorship, he might be a perfectly decent man. Well, except for the horrible way he had treated Sam after his wife's death. All the rest of the conflict could be put down to a clash of strong-willed, stubborn men. She'd certainly seen that kind of thing before. But that comment, that Sam was being punished for his sins... That was beyond the pale.

None of those reflections were making her any less crabby, however. Maybe, she argued with herself, it would be best to think of Elijah as a perfect stranger, someone about whom she knew nothing. A new neighbor.

Except that she could still remember the pain in

Sam's gaze when he had talked about his father. Oh, hell.

So she didn't say anything at all. The two of them worked in silence, until the coolers were all full and ready to be taken out to the pass.

Then Elijah broke the silence. "I'll take the food up. You look as if you need some sleep, Sister Mary."

Being addressed that way set Mary's teeth on edge, but she fought to remain pleasant. "Please, just call me Mary."

He tilted his head and smiled, and she could see the hint of Sam's gorgeous smile there. "Sorry. Old habit. You look exhausted, and I'm not. I had a nice nap this afternoon. So I'll take the food up, and you get some sleep."

Part of her wanted to argue with him, and she felt an inward twinge of embarrassment when she realized it was only because she didn't want to relinquish control. Because she *did* need some rest. Not as badly as the men who were actually fighting the fire, but badly enough.

"Thank you," she said.

His smile broadened, reminding her so much of Sam, despite his beard, that she caught her breath. "Sometimes," he said kindly, "it wounds our pride to accept help. But all of us need it from time to time."

"Even you?" The words were out before she

could stop them, and she wanted to clap her hands over her mouth, but it was too late.

Instead of taking offense, he chuckled. "Even me, Mary. And it was one of the hardest lessons I ever learned."

He was, she thought after he'd carried the last cooler out to his car, a far nicer man than she would have imagined. Yes, he made her feel prickly, and she suspected she probably made him feel prickly, too, but at heart he was a decent man.

Of course, Sam had never said his father wasn't decent, or that he wasn't likable. All she knew for certain was that Elijah was rigid. So rigid that he'd created a problem with his son. So rigid that the first thing he'd done when he'd met Mary was bring up the subject of books her students shouldn't be reading.

But how much of that did he perceive as his duty and how much of that was really Elijah? Hard to tell. But her curiosity was piqued, and she decided that she was going to get to know Elijah a little better.

8

Mary had just showered and changed into her pajamas when the doorbell rang. Expecting to find Elijah there, she grabbed a terry-cloth robe and pulled it on over her lavender cotton pajamas. She couldn't imagine what he wanted, unless it was to return the coolers.

But it wasn't Elijah, it was Sam. A freshly showered Sam, wearing clean jeans and a blue polo shirt.

"Hi," he said.

"Hi," she answered, not quite certain what to do. My goodness, how could she have forgotten how handsome he was? Then she saw the burn marks along his forearms and the angry red welt on his cheek. Nervousness and surprise gave way to instant concern.

"What happened to your face?" Without thinking, she reached for his hand and drew him into the house.

"I'm fine," he protested, turning to close the door behind him. "Really, I'm fine."

"You don't look fine. In fact, you look burned."

His finger touched his cheek. "That's not a burn, Mary. Just an abrasion."

"And your arms?"

"Those are cinder burns. No big deal. Just little singes."

She shook her head and drew him into the living room, urging him to sit on the couch. "What have you put on them? Anything?"

"There wasn't anything to put on them. Mary, it's no big deal, really."

She had half turned to go get some aloe from her kitchen when she realized she was treating Sam as if he were one of her students, rather than a grown man who had been taking care of himself for a long time. "Okay," she said brightly. Resisting the urge to sit beside him, she plopped into the easy chair facing him, suddenly aware of her bare feet. "Can I get you something to drink? Coffee? Tea? Water?"

"Don't trouble yourself, Mary. I was just wondering how you were getting on."

Wondering how *she* was getting on? That struck her as being awfully paternalistic, until she realized that she had been mothering him. And all of that, at least on her part, she realized with pinkening cheeks, had to do with how attractive she found Sam. Maybe he found her attractive, too?

Her heart slammed. No. Of course not. Besides,

he wouldn't like her anymore once he knew the truth about her. But she didn't want to think about that now, not with Sam smiling at her across the mere five feet that separated them. Not with his presence filling her house. My word, she could even smell the soap from his shower and recognized the brand. It was a scent she had always liked.

"So how are you, Mary?" he prompted with that kindness that seemed to come so naturally to him.

"Me? I'm fine. But I'm not fighting a fire."

"But you're making tons of sandwiches."

She waved a hand. "That's nothing." She almost mentioned that his father had helped her that evening but bit the words back. She wasn't sure how Sam would react, and she didn't want to destroy the pleasant warmth between them.

"I guess I got you out of bed." He nodded toward her robe and bare feet.

The word bed seemed to suddenly thicken the air. Mary couldn't believe it. She hadn't been this sensitive to a mere word since her early high school days. "Uh...I just showered."

He nodded. Apparently he wasn't feeling as awkward as she was right now. "To tell you the truth, I was hoping to have a little fun."

Fun? *Fun?* Various definitions of the word fun, none of them in Webster's, ran through her head. She was spending too much time with sixteen-year-old boys, she told herself sternly. But nonetheless, her breath locked in her throat.

"You know," Sam said, as if he had no idea in the world how that word had struck her, "I thought we could go over to the Silverton Inn for dancing or something."

"Dancing?" She repeated the word stupidly, unable to believe it. *Dancing?* The man was exhausted from fire fighting, covered with burns and abrasions, and he was talking about going dancing?

"I know," he said. "It's a bad idea. You look as exhausted as I feel. It just popped into my head before I got here."

And now he was backtracking as swiftly and politely as a man could. On his face she caught a glimpse of his sudden discomfort, as if his suggestion had astonished him as much as it had her.

Sympathy gave her a reason to beg off. "Thank you, Sam. But I'm too tired." Not that she wouldn't have loved to go dancing with him. But she didn't want to go, tired or not, unless it was something he really wanted to do. And she suspected he was a long way from wanting to take a woman, any woman, dancing.

"Me, too." He gave a wry smile, and she felt again a shiver of purely sexual pleasure. Good heavens, what a time for her hormones to wake up from their long slumber. "We'll do it another time. A better time."

Which sounded to her as if he were grateful for being let off the hook. Disappointment and relief filled her, and she gave herself an inward mental shake. She was acting nutty. She'd seen this man around town countless times since moving here and had thought only that he was a pleasant-looking man with kind eyes. Now all of a sudden she was feeling as if he were the most attractive male specimen she'd ever seen. Why? Because now she knew that he had been hurt, too? That he had suffered?

That was dangerous, and she knew it. Being a rescuer was often a dangerous and thankless task. It led people to base relationships on shaky foundations, the way she had with Chet, her ex. She'd wanted to rescue him, too, to save him from his unhappy childhood and the broken heart some other woman at college had given him. Instead she'd found herself married to a spineless, selfish whiner who, in the pinch, had turned out to be made of gelatin.

"Anyway," Sam went on, looking more relaxed now, "I got to thinking. Did you get your car back yet?"

"No, they need to order some parts. Maybe three more days."

"Then I should keep my promise to get you to the grocery store."

"No, really." She shook her head and managed a slight smile. "Meg Sanders and I have been going there every day to get food for the firefighters. Trust me, anything I've needed, I've been able to get. You don't have to worry about it."

"Good." Then, as if he realized how that might

sound, he added, "I mean good that you've been getting to the store. Sorry. My brain is fried."

"You really didn't need to come running over here to check up on me, Sam. I'm a big girl."

He looked at her, and finally a long sigh escaped him. "I'm making a hash of this. I think I've forgotten how to talk to people outside my job. Sorry."

"You're tired."

"Yeah, I am. That's still no excuse."

"Sure it is. Which is why I'm not offended that you invited me to go dancing when it was so obvious that that's the last thing on earth you want to do tonight. That you only suggested it because you were feeling bad about not keeping your promise to take me to the store."

He winced. "Ouch."

"Yes. Ouch."

He sighed once more, rubbed his eyes with the heels of his palms, then looked at her again. "Why don't we start over?"

"Start over?"

"Yeah. Like this." Getting up, he crossed the living room and stepped outside, closing the door behind him. The doorbell rang.

Almost in spite of herself, Mary wanted to giggle. She swallowed the sound and went to open the door, struggling to keep a straight face.

"Hi, Mary," Sam said when she opened the door. "I was feeling like a guilty rat for forgetting to take you to the store, so I thought I'd stop by and see if you need anything.''

Mary, amused, looked him up and down. "You don't look like a guilty rat."

"I have a good disguise. Can I come in for a few?"

"Sure." Smiling, she stepped back to let him pass. "Do you want some cheese?"

He looked startled, then laughed. It was such a nice sound, quiet but mirthful. "Just as long as there's no arsenic on it."

"I would never do such a thing," she assured him primly. "But if you're very, very good, I might give you some crackers to go with it."

It was as if a switch flipped. Suddenly the cool air inside her house became thick, heavy with portent. Oh, Lord, she'd forgotten that high school thing about being good versus being nice. But Sam, clearly, had not. His eyes were suddenly narrow and his face soft.

"Oh," he said quietly, "I can be very, very good."

She believed it. Believed it so much that she stopped breathing while her veins ran warm with honey. This had to stop, said some panicked portion of her mind. Now.

He took a step toward her before her alarmed mind could find words to force from her empty lungs. But then he caught himself visibly and shook his head. "Here I go again. Want me to step outside and try all over, or just leave?"

She managed a jerky shake of her head and finally drew a breath.

"Cheese and crackers would be nice if you don't mind," he said, then placed himself firmly on her couch. "Just don't go to any trouble on my account."

Freed, as if silken bonds had suddenly dropped from her limbs, she fled to the kitchen.

Oh, man. Oh, man. How could anyone affect her like that? He'd just been teasing, she told herself. Just joking around the way they all had once upon a time. Filling an awkward moment with an awkward joke. Being a teacher, she ought to know better than to hand out a line like that.

She just hoped he hadn't been able to tell from her expression how strongly she had reacted.

In her refrigerator she had three kinds of cheese: brie, gouda and cheddar. She warmed the brie briefly in her microwave, then prepared a tray with all three and assorted snack crackers.

"Do you want anything to drink?" she called to him. Easier than going back into the living room just yet. She knew the minute she got out there, she was going to feel awkward again.

"Coffee, if you have any. My caffeine tank is reading empty. But don't go to any trouble." That seemed to be his favorite line, as if Sam Canfield felt unworthy of even the barest courtesies.

"No trouble." How much trouble could it be to scoop coffee and pour water into her drip coffee-maker? It wasn't as if she had to go down to the river and pound laundry on the rocks.

She took the tray into the living room and placed it in front of him on the coffee table, using napkins, utensils and coffee as an excuse to dart back into the kitchen.

This was terrible. She hadn't been this uncomfortable around a man since she'd been fifteen or sixteen. A woman of thirty ought to be well past this.

She looked down at herself and was suddenly torn between a sigh and a laugh. Her lavender pajamas, cotton, were relatively new, but her terry-cloth robe was an old favorite, shaggy with pulled threads and bare at the elbows. Sam *had* to have been joking.

Oddly the realization that she looked frumpy made her feel better. The moments past were nothing but a mental aberration on her part. Reassured, she was able to return smiling with the coffee and utensils.

"You make great coffee," Sam remarked with satisfaction. He'd already tucked into the cheese and crackers.

"Thanks. But I think that's a matter of taste, don't you?"

He lifted an eyebrow. "Okay. *I* think you make great coffee."

She felt her cheeks heating. "Sorry, I'm an English teacher. I guess I've picked up a few bad habits.''

''Which is why I should be more careful about how I say things.'' But he was smiling, with the hint of a laugh in his voice. Holding his mug in both hands, he settled back on the couch. Just then, a crack of thunder disturbed the quiet night. ''God, we need the rain,'' he remarked, glancing toward her window. ''But we don't need the lightning.''

''I know.'' A worried frown creased her brow. ''I repeatedly feel amazed by how hard it is to extinguish that fire. I never really noticed before. Forest fires were always something that was background on the news for me, so I never paid much attention.''

''It feels like magic.'' He sipped his coffee and gave another satisfied sigh. ''Black magic. Every time we start to control it in one place, it springs up in another. A little bit of wind, just enough to blow a few embers, and *bam*—there's a new one. I have to admit, I hadn't really thought much about it before, either. Not in any detail.''

Another crack of thunder sounded, loud enough to make Mary jump. She was glad she wasn't holding a coffee cup. ''I hope that's not hitting anything.''

''Me, too.''

Through the window curtains, she saw another flash and started counting.

''Five miles,'' Sam said. Since storms came in from the west, that didn't sound good.

"I wonder what the men out there are doing," she said. "It can't be safe for them to be in the woods during this."

"I don't know. Probably ignoring it. The fire's a bigger threat."

Mary nodded slowly, wondering how many families were listening to those cracks right now and worrying. "What about Joe and Louis?"

"Joe and Louis?"

"Those two painters who live in the valley."

"Oh, they've been evacuated. Everybody over there has been told to get out. Maybe a dozen families."

"Thank goodness. I can't imagine what it must be like to have to leave everything behind and wonder if any of it will be there when you come back."

"Not pleasant. But most of them got enough warning to get the really precious stuff out. That's a blessing."

Thunder boomed again, a hollow, rumbling sound that seemed to bounce off the mountains all around. So loud that Mary's windows rattled. "I don't like this."

"Me, neither. Mind if I get some more coffee?"

"Go ahead."

Feeling stiff and edgy, Mary walked to the window and drew the curtains back. The street was still dry, her lawn still looking nearly lifeless. Her flowers grew bravely, a miracle of constant attention and regular dousing with her dishwater. Lawn watering had been forbidden for the last month, and except for a few hardy weeds, there was little green out there. Nor was anything moving. Not even a breath of air.

The wind would come later. Maybe it was already blowing in the valley across the pass, bringing the kiss of fire to countless other acres of trees. It was a depressing thought.

A movement caught her eye, and she looked across the street. A dark shadow was standing between the white curtains of Elijah Canfield's house. He was looking out, too. Maybe just to see if it was raining, as she was. Then she realized she was fully illuminated by her living-room lamps. And Sam's car was clearly parked out front.

Damn it! Dropping the curtain, she let it fall back into place, swinging around just as Sam returned with his coffee.

"Does your father *always* stare out his windows?"

Sam paused just before he sat, mug in hand. "Occasionally."

"There's nothing occasional about this. I'm beginning to feel like an ant under the microscope."

"Maybe he does it more since my mother died. I'm sorry."

"No reason for *you* to be. You're not responsible." She sighed. "I'm sorry. I guess I'm waspish tonight. Tired. It's just unnerving to feel as if I'm being watched all the time."

"Just now?"

"Yes. But he was probably doing the same thing I was, looking out to see if it was raining at all."

Sam hesitated. "I could go speak to him."

"I wouldn't ask you to do that. He has a right to look out his window, and besides, I'm sure you'd rather not have to talk to him."

"No, I'll go say something to him. He shouldn't make you uneasy. You don't want to feel as if your every move is being watched."

"Well, I'm not sure it is. Besides…" She gave a little laugh. "Lucy Middleton across the way could probably give you a detailed history of my life since I moved here. She seems to know *everything*."

"That's different. She's not a man. And besides, it's probably adding to your unease that he's my father."

It was, though she was reluctant to admit it. But it might not have bothered her at all, except that Elijah had questioned her. "He asked me if we were dating."

Sam's head snapped up. "When did he do that?"

"Tonight."

"What did he do? Just come over here and ask?"

"No, nothing like that." She shrugged, feeling embarrassed over her own part in this. "I kind of…well…I told you I was crabby tonight. I was making sandwiches for the firefighters when I suddenly got teed off at how few people were helping. So I went across the street and suggested that it would be nice if he asked his church to help by making some food. Actually, I didn't exactly suggest it.''

Was she imagining it, or was the corner of Sam's mouth lifting, as if he were trying not to grin?

"Okay," he said. "And that's when he asked?"

"Oh, no. I came back here, and a few minutes later he came over to help me. It was while we finished making the sandwiches that he asked."

"I see." The hint of a smile vanished. "It's none of his damn business. Not anymore."

Mary was suddenly feeling very contrite. She *had* been irritable, and never should have said anything at all. Sam and his father already had enough bad blood between them, and she didn't want to make things worse. "I'm sorry, Sam, I shouldn't have said anything. It was nothing important. Anyway, he's your father. He's probably still curious about your life."

"I doubt that. I seriously doubt that. I'll have a word with him."

"Sam, no. If it bothers me again, *I'll* speak to him. It'll be better that way. After all, we might have to be neighbors for years."

He appeared reluctant, as if he didn't want to let go of the problem. "As far as I know, he's exactly the righteous, puritanical demagogue he seems to be. I don't think you need to fear him."

"I'm not *afraid* of him. Truly, I'm not. It doesn't

have anything to do with that. I'm just irritable. How many times have I said that tonight?''

"I wasn't keeping count.'' That faint grin reappeared, just a hint around the corners of his mouth.

"Well, it gives you some idea how tired I must be. The point is, if I weren't exhausted, I probably wouldn't even notice that he seems to be in my face every time I turn around.''

The grin was no longer hidden. Sam even laughed. And Mary had to laugh, too, at herself. "Like I said…'' She didn't finish the sentence, and he laughed again.

When he spoke, however, his tone was kind, if a bit amused. "You're allowed to be crabby, you're allowed to repeat yourself, and you're allowed to dislike feeling watched. But if you keep feeling bothered, let me know and I'll say something. This is a small town, and folks need to take care not to irritate each other too much.''

He paused, and his gaze grew distant. "He spends a lot of time at the window?''

"It seems like it. But it won't continue. I've never known a minister who didn't have his hands so full he had trouble finding time to sleep.''

"True.'' He was seeing her again. "Well, I'd better skedaddle before I've been here so long he considers you to be a good subject for a sermon on the morals of schoolteachers.''

Aghast, she dropped her jaw. "He wouldn't do that!''

"There was a time when he would have. But I
don't know how he is now. I don't know him at all
anymore."

And that, Mary thought, was one of the saddest
things she'd ever heard a son say about his father.

Outside in the dark, Sam stood near his car and
looked up at the flickering sky. The line of thun-
derheads approaching from the west grew impress-
ively visible with each crackle of lightning, and the
hollow boom of thunder that followed echoed all
around. A bad one. Worse than they usually saw at
this altitude. And at the wrong time of day. Hereabouts, thunderstorms were afternoon occurrences,
not nighttime ones. The weather had been strange
for months now, the winter bringing record snows
in December, almost an entire year's expected snowfall in about four weeks. Since then, there had been
little precipitation of any kind, leading to the current
problems.

Most of the lightning seemed to be leaping from
cloud to cloud, but then he saw a brilliant downward
fork over the pass. Not good.

Worse, the air was still and dry, unsoftened even
by a hint of moisture. He had the feeling that tomorrow was going to be a wretched day.

Then, unwillingly, his gaze strayed to the house
where his father now lived. Elijah was nowhere in
sight, so perhaps he wasn't trying to keep tabs on

his son's relationship with Mary. Not that Sam could imagine any reason he would want to.

But it was still a relief, until he realized that he had thought of himself as having a relationship with Mary. That was as chilling to his heart as the lightning that once again forked downward over the mountains, and as rattling as the thunder that boomed deafeningly.

He forced himself to climb into his car and drive home, but the memory of the minutes he'd just spent with Mary wouldn't leave him alone. He'd been a boor to tease her the way he had, but there had been that electric moment, when…when…

He didn't know how to describe it. It was as if the lightning outside had entered his body. And it had happened so suddenly, so instantly, that in retrospect he could hardly believe it. Yes, he'd noticed before what an attractive woman she was, but he hadn't reacted that way. Not with an urge so strong that it had virtually overwhelmed him, causing him to act in a completely uncharacteristic way. He could be *good? Very good?*

God, he couldn't believe he'd said that. It was a wonder she hadn't slapped him silly. He knew in his heart that she hadn't meant those words the way he had taken them, and he'd seen the flicker of panic in her gaze when he'd responded like some oversexed sixteen-year-old.

He deserved to be horsewhipped.

On the other hand… Well, he *was* a healthy male,

and apparently his needs hadn't died with his wife, although for a long time now he'd been happy to have them gone. Rediscovering them this way, so unexpectedly, didn't exactly thrill him.

He tried to put Mary out of his mind, but she was there as he drifted off to sleep at last, and she followed him into his dreams.

Dreams that were as charged as the raging storm outside.

9

In the morning, the smell of smoke was thicker than ever, and it dimmed the early-morning sun. The night's storm had barely wept, marking its passing only in rare rivulets in the dustiness on Elijah's car. He looked at it with a shake of his head, then looked to the west, where the sky was blackened with smoke. No help.

"You know, Lord," he muttered as he climbed into his car, "a little flooding would be useful right now. Two or three inches of heavy rain, maybe."

The Lord didn't answer. The Lord rarely did these days, and Elijah sometimes wondered if that was because he himself had become more alert to the distinction between his own thoughts and wishes, and those of the God he served.

There had been a time, he freely admitted, where he'd interpreted nearly every inclination as divine revelation. These days, revelations were thin on the ground.

Sometimes he thought he was losing his faith. Other times he reminded himself that everyone had dry periods in their spiritual lives. Hadn't he counseled hundreds through them?

Keep acting as if, he quoted himself. If you keep acting as if the faith is there, it will return in good time.

So he kept acting as if, amidst a terrible drought of the soul.

Reaching the hardware store, he parallel-parked and locked up his car. He needed some washers for his faucets. Apparently his predecessor had let things go a bit, and both the kitchen and bathroom faucets dripped slowly. He wondered what other neglect was going to surface as time passed, then reminded himself that the day's troubles were sufficient unto the day. He would deal with problems as they arose.

Of course, a new problem arose the instant he entered the plumbing aisle of the store. Standing there, surveying some PVC pipe, were two men, one about thirty-five, the other in his late forties or early fifties. Joe and Louis. Good-looking men in shorts and T-shirts. And they had their arms around each other's waists.

The sight angered him, and he recalled the conversation he'd had recently with Silence and Bill. Even so, given where they were, he felt the best thing to do would be to turn away and busy himself somewhere else in the store. This was not the place to approach two strangers and comment on their moral life. The years had taught him at least *some* restraint.

But as he turned, he discovered Mrs. Beemis behind him. Her lips were pursed in disapproval, and as plain as day her face questioned him: Wasn't he going to say something?

Not only was he feeling out of touch with his faith, but at that instant he wondered if the universe had it in for him. Bad enough he should come to the same town where his son lived, but worse that at this moment Mrs. Beemis should appear as if conjured by Satan himself.

He looked back at the men, feeling an uneasy twitch in his stomach. Then, taking Mrs. Beemis firmly by the arm, he ushered her two aisles away, to the tool section where, thank goodness, there wasn't another soul.

"You aren't going to let that pass!" she said disapprovingly.

"Keep your voice down, Mrs. Beemis. This isn't the place nor the time."

"Since when is the place and time a hindrance to imparting moral teachings?"

Good question, he found himself thinking sourly. Once he would have agreed with her. But time had taught him lessons, some bitterly learned. "Time and place make a difference, Mrs. Beemis. If one wishes to be truly heard."

In short, embarrassing those two men in public,

and thus angering them, would deafen them to any message.

"Well," she said, "if you won't deal with it, I will. I wouldn't have believed you could be so spineless."

"Spine has nothing to do with it."

But she wasn't listening, any more than those two men were going to listen to her. She strode away, face twisted, toward the aisle where her intended victims were probably still discussing plumbing fixtures.

Elijah hesitated. He didn't want to embarrass his church by becoming involved in a public scene. Nor did he wish to waste his thunder in a setting where it would be useless. And frankly, he didn't think men of their age were going to be amenable to anyone's opinion of the way they were living. They'd faced a lot of Mrs. Beemises, he was sure. By now a rhino's hide probably had nothing on them.

Short of main force, he didn't see how he could keep the old biddy from doing what she wanted, either. He sighed heavily.

He heard her voice from two aisles over. Strident and critical. Then he heard one of the men say, "Mind your own business."

"It *is* my business!" Mrs. Beemis squawked. "This is a hardware store, not a den of iniquity. Didn't anyone teach you right from wrong?"

"Didn't anyone teach you manners?" was the response.

Clearly the men weren't going to leave the store to avoid a confrontation, and clearly, from the strident sound of her next comment, Mrs. Beemis had no intention of giving ground. Elijah decided he'd better head that way and see if he could prevent things from getting out of hand.

Just as he rounded the corner of the aisle where the two men and the woman were facing off, the younger man said, "Look, you old hag, just get out of our faces."

Concerned faces were now peering around the other end of the aisle, watching.

"Mrs. Beemis," Elijah said in his most authoritative voice, "I think we'd better leave."

"I'm not going anywhere," she said flatly. "If they want to live their lives in unspeakable sin, they should at least have the decency to do it where the rest of us don't have to see it."

The older man snorted. "I was made this way, lady. Just like you were made to be a shrew."

Someone down the aisle gasped, and someone else muttered a sound of annoyance. Judging by the gathering crowd, this confrontation could become serious.

"Mrs. Beemis," Elijah said again, even more sternly, "this is not the time nor the place."

"There's never a wrong time nor place to save souls."

The men shrugged, looked at each other and

turned back to the plumbing display, visibly dismissing the irate woman.

"Don't you turn your backs on me!"

Oh, Lord, Elijah thought. The men ignored her, and Mrs. Beemis put out a hand toward one of them. Instantly Elijah reached out and stopped her.

"Get your hands off me!" she screeched at him.

"Not if you mean to touch anyone else. Do you want to be arrested?"

"What's going on here?"

Sam's voice, as familiar to Elijah as his own, cut across the growing murmurs. Elijah turned and saw his son, in uniform, marching down the aisle toward them. Sam's gaze raked the two men, then Elijah.

"I should have guessed," his son said. Pointing at Elijah, he said, "Out of here. Now."

"I haven't done anything." Although he was sure Sam wouldn't believe that. In the distant past, he *would* have been at the center of this.

"He laid his hand on me," Mrs. Beemis insisted, pointing at Elijah. "He doesn't have the right to touch me."

Elijah turned on her. "Nor do *you* have the right to touch anyone else, madam."

"What the hell is going on?" Sam demanded.

The older man spoke. "This woman came up and started haranguing us about our...behavior. This man got involved."

Sam scowled at his father and Mrs. Beemis, then

jerked his head toward the door. "Outside. Now. Or I'll arrest you both."

Thank the good Lord Mrs. Beemis heeded that warning and marched toward the door. As he followed, Elijah noted that Sam stayed to talk with the two men. Sympathetically, it seemed to him. Sam had always been inclined to sympathize with social outcasts. That hadn't changed.

Mrs. Beemis marched out onto the street, Elijah in her wake...although, were he to be honest about it, he didn't want to be within ten blocks of this woman. He had a sneaking suspicion he wasn't going to last long in Whisper Creek. Either Mrs. Beemis would get him fired or he would get so fed up with her that he would resign. At the moment, the two possibilities appeared equally inevitable.

But the woman wasn't done with him. On the sidewalk, she turned to face him, her finger wagging. "I'm disappointed in you, Brother Elijah. Seriously disappointed. How you could ignore sin happening under your very nose is beyond me."

"Sister...what *is* your first name?"

"Alma." She sniffed, as if he were beneath contempt for not knowing that, never mind that he had a whole congregation of names to learn, and never mind that he was fairly certain no one had mentioned her first name to him.

"Sister Alma, I am not spineless. Neither am I a fool. Creating a scene such as you did won't teach anyone anything except that the members of The

Little Church in the Woods are interfering, intolerant, unloving busybodies.''

''I am not a busybody! It was plain as day what those two were doing, and right in front of me. That makes it my business. As for tolerance, we are not supposed to tolerate sin.''

''But we are also called to love our brothers and sisters, and treat them with the same dignity and respect we want for ourselves. Furthermore, Sister Alma, you might consider rereading your Bible. When you are without sin, when you have plucked the beam from your own eye, then you can cast the first stone, or pluck the mote from your brother's eye.''

''Well, I never!''

''And while you're at it, may I suggest you reread the Beatitudes? You may wish to recall that we are sternly warned against judging others.''

Elijah was now on a roll, and it was his finger pointing at the woman, who was beginning to gape like a fish gasping for air. His voice held the thunderous sound that made him such a popular, memorable preacher. ''Remember, Sister, the admonition when our Lord was asked which was the greatest commandment: 'You shall love the Lord, your God, with all your heart, with all your soul and with all your mind.' This is the greatest and the first commandment. The second is like it: 'You shall love your neighbor as yourself. The whole law and the prophets depend on these two commandments.'''

He was silenced by the sound of slow clapping behind him. Turning, he saw Sam standing there, applauding. Several other people had gathered, but at a look from Sam they hurried on.

"You're still good," Sam said to him.

Elijah didn't know how to respond. For the first time in his life, the sight of his son tongue-tied him.

But Sam didn't wait for a response. "Mrs. Beemis," he said, "the Constitution protects your right of free speech. I can't arrest you for what you said in there. But there's a fine line between exercising your right to express an opinion and disturbing the peace."

"They had their arms around each other!"

"But that's not illegal. They have as much right to shop in that store as you do. So leave them alone. Save your sermonizing for more appropriate venues."

She glared at Sam. "A public place is appropriate."

Sam shook his head. "Not if it leads to trouble. And that was heading toward trouble. Don't incite your neighbors, ma'am. And don't harass them, either."

"I'm obeying a higher law."

"Fine. As long as you're willing to go to jail for breaking human laws, go ahead."

The woman huffed, then turned on her heel and marched away.

Elijah felt a sweeping sense of relief. For a little

while, the Beemis thorn was out of his side. But then he looked again at Sam and felt an uncomfortable pang. For a man who made his living by speaking, he was pathetically speechless right now.

Sam broke the silence. "When did you start preaching tolerance?"

"I always did."

Sam lifted a skeptical eyebrow. "That's not how I remember it."

Once again Elijah was at a loss. He was too aware of his own failings these days to argue that Sam had misunderstood him. Finally he said simply, "I feared for you, boy."

"I'm not a boy." Sam turned and strode away, a good-looking man in his prime. A man any father should be proud of. A son Elijah couldn't seem to forgive.

"We're shorthanded," Sheriff Earl Sanders had said to Sam that morning. "Jeff Bauer is laid up again with asthma from all the smoke, Brad Gomez's wife is in labor, Chas Elgin got a severe burn on his arm last night, fighting the fire, and Irena Figueroa is going to Denver for her grandmother's funeral. Plus Teal is still on vacation, Luci Landro has to go to her son's swim meet, and Phil Potter ate something bad last night and is tied to the porcelain god. That pretty much guts us. Anyway, the pros have pretty much taken over the fire fighting. I need you on patrol."

Sam didn't mind. Over the past days, as firefighters had arrived from all over the country, he'd begun to feel more and more like a fifth wheel. What the hell did he know about fighting a fire, anyway?

On his way in, he stopped by the hospital to see Chas and learned that he was being shipped off to a burn unit for treatment and grafting of the burn on his left forearm.

"It was stupid," Chas said, groggy with morphine. "Stupid. I just wasn't paying close enough attention."

"You were too tired. We get sloppy when we get exhausted."

"Yeah. But we gotta put that fire out."

After that he signed in at a rather quiet, empty roll call, got his assignment and checked over the reports from the night before. It was all the usual stuff: a couple of domestics, a drunk who couldn't find his own house, a DUI, and a half-dozen underage kids who had been found drinking around a campfire near an abandoned mine. He hoped somebody had given them a stern lecture about the danger of building a fire in the woods just now.

His first call had been to the hardware store. Just what he needed to start his day: Mrs. Beemis and his father.

The Beemis woman was a well-known pain-in-the-ass around town. Six months ago she'd raised Cain in a city council meeting by ranting that Bob Hinderhoff ought to resign from the council because

his eight-year-old son had been caught stealing a
package of candy from the drugstore. As if nearly
every kid didn't try that at least once. But Mrs.
Beemis had insisted it was a sign of Bob's moral
weakness and it made him unfit to be a councilman.
She'd raised enough of a ruckus that the police finally had to remove her. That hadn't stopped her.
She'd spent the next week on the front page of the
small local paper, picketing city hall with a couple
of her cronies. The whole town was as used to her
hijinks as they were to the strangeness of the schiz-
ophrenic novelist who had painted every inch of his
house, inside and out, shocking pink, and occasionally paid for half-page ads in the paper claiming that
the government was beaming messages into his
mind.

Such things happened everywhere, but in a small
town everyone was aware of them. And most of the
local people shrugged it off, or found it good for a
laugh.

But finding his father there...well, it hadn't put
him in a good mood. Although he had to admit that
Elijah's little sermon on the street had sounded more
temperate than those he remembered from his youth.
In fact, Sam hadn't found a thing to disagree with,
which nagged at him. Had Elijah lost some of his
self-righteousness? Or had Sam exaggerated what
he'd heard as a youth?

He didn't know what to make of it. And, like most

people, he wasn't comfortable when things fell out of their tidy mental niches.

Then he remembered what his father had said after Beth's funeral. That phone call hadn't displayed either temperance or love. Punishment for his sins. Right.

Sam didn't know what had hurt him worse that night, the revelation of how Elijah viewed Sam's character, the fact that Elijah clearly didn't give a damn for his feelings, or the inevitable sense of guilt that he might somehow have been responsible for Beth's death.

The memory did its work, though, reinstalling the anger and ice in Sam's heart.

By two that afternoon, however, he was ready to turn in his badge and join a monastery of any brand other than his father's. There was something mightily depressing about being called out on domestic disturbances that involved your friends and neighbors, people you actually knew.

The Tenants, Foster and Pat, who lived just four doors down from his own house, got into it over their burned-out yard. Their raised voices drew the attention of a neighbor who called the sheriff. By the time Sam arrived on the scene, they were in the front yard, threatening each other with garden implements and screaming at the top of their lungs.

Sam pulled up and climbed out. Neither of them noticed him, so he slammed his door as hard and loud as he could. That got their attention.

"We don't need you, Sam," Fos said flatly. "We're just arguing."

"I know." Sam was careful to amble slowly in their direction. "It would be kind of nice if you'd put down the rake and the shovel, though." Pat, who was holding the rake like a baseball bat, and Fos, who was holding the spade like a battering ram, seemed to jerk awake.

"Oh, jeez," Fos said, tossing the spade aside. "I was just going to dig up the dead shrubs."

Pat lowered the rake. "Like hell you were. You said you were going to dig up every inch of the sod."

"The damn stuff's dead anyway! I told you not to buy it. Damn it, four thousand dollars on grass! I told you it was too dry."

"How was I supposed to know they were going to tell us we couldn't water? What am I, a mind reader? Besides, you signed the check."

"Only to shut you up!"

They were getting into it again, and Sam deftly inserted himself in the middle. "You know," he said with a smile, "I could sure use a cold drink. Pat, you got any of that great ice tea of yours?"

A minute later they were in the house. Sam made them sit on opposite sides of the kitchen table and mediated as best he could. It took a while, but they calmed down. Pat and Fos, as far as he knew, got along pretty well most of the time. Whatever had set this off wasn't usual for them.

He'd hardly left the Tenants imitating reasonable domestic bliss when he got a call that Ike and Marcia Leip were at each other's throats. He knew Ike and Marcia from the community theater, where he occasionally helped build sets and props. They were both a little freaky, given to extravagant "artistic temperament," but they'd always seemed to get along well.

That afternoon they weren't getting along well at all. In fact, they had devolved into throwing things at each other. Sam was past caring what had started it; he basically gave them a choice: solve it, or somebody was going to jail.

They solved it. In fact, they both seemed pretty embarrassed to have Sam involved, even though Marcia had been the one to call the police.

It was a weird world. Stepping back outside, though, Sam had an idea what was getting to people. The smoke was a constant irritant now, making eyes and throats burn. The sky to the west was a deep gray, fading away to a bluer color overhead, but even so, the day looked hazy and dark. The sun, now in the west, was a dulled, dirty yellow.

Last night's storm apparently hadn't helped at all.

And he found himself thinking of Mary again. He wondered if she'd ever been married, and, if so, had her marriage erupted the way he'd seen today? He and Beth had fought at times, but nothing so loud or violent as what he often saw in his job. He couldn't imagine Mary screaming at anyone, let alone throwing things.

But he didn't know Mary all that well. In fact, he reminded himself, all he really knew about her was that she seemed gentler and quieter than Beth. Not that there had been anything wrong with his late wife. Nothing serious, at any rate. Nobody was perfect, and everyone had to overlook things with their partners. That was just life.

But an almost traitorous thought wormed its way into his brain, asking him if he would have married Beth again if he met her today.

And worse than the question was the answer that came unbidden: He didn't think so.

That hurt, really hurt. His heart squeezed so hard he had to pull his car over to the curb and wait for the pain to pass. Had he really loved her?

Of course he had. Completely. Totally.

But maybe…maybe he just wasn't the same person anymore. That wasn't a flaw in Beth or his feelings for her. That was just an inevitable fact of life. Time had changed him, and Beth hadn't been there to change with him.

But the time they'd had together, well, that had been just about perfect. Maybe not what he would want now that he was older, but certainly what he had wanted then.

And that was okay, wasn't it?

But guilt settled over him like a cloud of doom. It just wasn't right to be thinking this way.

Maybe his father had been right. Maybe he *was* being punished for his sins.

The wind and lightning from the night before had spread the fire. The valley was now dotted with spreading flames. Every firefighter they could find was desperately digging firebreaks and creating back burns, trying to corral the worst of it in the north end of the valley.

In the late afternoon, something went awry. The wind suddenly picked up, and the back burns shifted direction. Instead of the man-made fires being sucked toward the already burning acreage by the fire's own draft, the wind twisted them around. With heart-stopping speed, a wall of fire ignited south of the firebreak, sandwiching in the firefighters. The only choice they had was to get out of there as fast as they could.

And not too far away, a man drove toward his house, unaware that the fire was racing toward him on gusts of dry wind.

10

"Dinner tonight? At the Steak Place?"

Sam's voice coming over the telephone was like a balm to Mary's fatigue. Elijah had been good to his word, and his church members had taken over delivering and serving food to the fire crews, so Mary had stayed at home running a sandwich assembly line. The thing was, it was hot today, and she'd had to keep the windows open or suffocate. Now her house smelled of wood smoke and her lungs felt as if she had bronchitis. That had worn her out more than standing on her feet in the kitchen for so many hours, something that wasn't all that different from her teaching job, although the endless repetitive motions and boredom took their toll, too.

A dinner out sounded like heaven. "Are you sure you're not too tired?" she asked Sam.

"Me? Nah. I got to play cop today. We're short-handed. No fire fighting for me."

She hoped he could continue playing cop, because

she didn't at all like the idea of him being down there in those growing flames. The cable news had picked up the fire as a major story, and she'd spent all day glancing at her TV set to see the frightening pictures of flames reaching sixty to eighty feet into the sky, and the puny, exhausted, blackened firefighters who were too close to them for comfort. Now they were saying a group of firefighters had nearly been trapped between two walls of flame. She didn't want Sam out there. She didn't want *anybody* out there. "What about tomorrow?" she couldn't help asking.

"Same thing. Although, to tell you the truth, I don't know what's worse, fighting forest fires or fighting domestic fires."

She almost laughed, then realized it wasn't funny, even if he was trying to sound light about it. "Oh, Sam."

"It's okay. Nobody bled. So, want me to pick you up around six?"

"That'd be great."

But when she hung up the phone, she found herself wondering why he'd asked her. And wondering why she'd accepted.

Even on their short acquaintance, she had the feeling that Sam was as ambivalent about getting involved as she was. That he had as many, albeit different, reasons for preferring solitude.

But that didn't keep her from putting on a nice

navy-blue linen dress and red pumps, or from using makeup, or from brushing her hair until it shone.

It felt good. It felt good that a man wanted to take her to dinner. And she assured herself that his ambivalence was even more protection for her.

This was an opportunity to have a friend with whom she could share the semblance of normalcy without all the dreaded complications. It would be good for both of them.

Her doubts thus quelled, Mary was waiting for Sam with a smile when he arrived. He apparently liked what he saw, because a smile creased his face as his gaze swept over her.

"You look really nice," he said.

"So do you." And he did, in a white Western shirt, pressed jeans and polished Ropers. Better even than he looked in uniform.

The sun had gone behind the mountains already, leaving the town in a bright twilight that was cooling rapidly. Mary grabbed a sweater and draped it over her shoulders.

Sam was driving his own vehicle tonight, a Grand Cherokee equipped with ski racks on top and a bicycle rack on the back. He opened the door and helped her in, an old-fashioned courtesy that was a rare experience these days. Mary actually appreciated it. Being an independent woman didn't mean she couldn't enjoy the social niceties at times.

Instinctively she glanced over at Elijah's house,

to see if he was watching, but there was no sign of him.

"Is the Steak Place okay with you?" Sam asked as they drove.

"It's great." There weren't a whole lot of choices in a town this size. The fern bar on the corner of Main, the diner, a burger joint and a chain pizza place. And, of course, the two saloons that also sold sandwiches and wings. The fern bar was okay if you were in the mood for a huge salad topped with al-falfa sprouts, but it wasn't the place to get a full meal. And Mary was definitely in the mood for a full meal.

"It'll be nice," Sam remarked, "when Witt Mat-lock gets that new hotel of his done. Hardy Wingate tells me they're going to have a great dining room, and I guess his wife is already on the hunt for a chef who suits her."

"That would be nice. I don't mind going to the Inn for dinner, but the food isn't...well..."

"It's pedestrian," he said, giving her an amused look. "I can turn out a better steak in a frying pan."

She laughed. "So can I. I only go there when I absolutely can't stand the thought of cooking."

"Well, Witt's new hotel should be better. All we have to hope is that it gets enough business so he doesn't have to cut corners."

"Somebody said it's going to look like a huge old Victorian resort."

"Yeah. I've seen the model. Nothing like the

usual Colorado ski-country look. Straight out of the past and the days of the really fancy resort hotels.''

"Maybe it'll be like that hotel in *The Shining*.''

He turned his head and wiggled his eyebrows at her. "Without the evil twins, I hope.''

He was obviously in a good mood tonight, and he was lifting Mary's spirits, as well. As they approached the restaurant on the north side of town, she forgot all about the fire, all about the sandwiches she was going to have to make tomorrow and all about everything else. It was a beautiful evening, if you could breathe the sooty air, and she was in the company of a handsome, charming man. Surely she could be allowed to enjoy herself for a few hours in a fantasy woven from being with an attractive, eligible man.

The restaurant was quiet, serving only one other couple, out-of-towners. The smell of the fire had been kept sternly at bay, and indoors there were only the good aromas of food cooking. It was like another world.

"Ah,'' Sam said, settling back in his chair with obvious contentment. "I feel like I'm on another planet.''

"Me, too. It's nice not to worry about the fire for a while.''

"That's what I was thinking all day today. How nice it was to do ordinary cop work again. Except that I knew the people involved in the domestics.'' He shrugged. "Oh, well. It happens.''

"It must be difficult to deal with, though."

"Today I was lucky. It wasn't so bad."

They ordered coffee, and Sam asked for a seafood appetizer without even looking at the menu. "Do you want any particular appetizer?" he asked Mary. "Or do you want to share mine? There'll be more than enough."

"More than enough for me. I'll just share, thanks." After the waiter left, she added, "You come here often, don't you?"

"It's a dead giveaway when someone has the menu memorized, isn't it?" He smiled. "Sometimes I can't stand any more of my own cooking."

"I know how that is."

"It's not that I can't cook, I just have a limited repertoire that I'm willing to make for myself. Sheer laziness."

"I guess neither of us is a born chef."

He laughed. "It looks that way. Cooking is a necessity for me, not a hobby."

Sam leaned back to allow the waiter to serve the appetizers and coffee. Talking about cooking...man, he was rusty. All his conversation seemed to revolve around work. He was like a fish out of water when it came to making casual small talk with someone, particularly a pretty woman he didn't know all that well.

And he wasn't especially eager to consider why he had asked Mary to dinner. After spending all day counting all the reasons he didn't want to get involved again, on the spur of the moment he'd asked an attractive, single woman out to dinner.

He needed his damn head examined.

Except that he knew what was happening. Something about Mary felt like a cool, refreshing oasis in the midst of a life suddenly full of stress: his father's presence in town, his job, the fire...all of it was weighing on him, and Mary felt like an emotional escape somehow.

So he was sitting there, trying not to talk about the things that were absorbing his attention, namely his father, the fire and his job, which left him with nothing to offer except some inane remarks about cooking.

And Mary seemed to be feeling the same restraint. As if she sensed the boundaries of where he didn't want to go. It was going to make for a pretty silent dinner.

And that made him feel increasingly awkward.

Mary sampled the bacon-wrapped shrimp and pronounced them excellent. Her smile across the table was brighter than the candle that sat between them, seeming to embrace him and warm him. Lord, she was pretty.

"You ever been married?" he heard himself blurt. One of those places he didn't want to venture, so naturally, he'd brought it up himself. He wondered if he could kick himself in the seat, or if that was physically impossible.

Her smile, her beautiful smile, vanished. Apparently the topic was as bad for her as it was for him. "Forget it," he said swiftly. "None of my business."

She hesitated, a profound sorrow shadowing her face. "No, it's okay," she said quietly. "I was married. Seven years."

"What happened?"

"He proved he was the same idiot I married. The going got tough and he got going...far away."

She'd tried to be light about it, but she didn't succeed, and he wouldn't have been deluded, anyway. "I'm sorry."

"I'm better off without him."

She sounded as if she really meant that, but at least he still retained sense enough not to pursue it. There was a disparity between her reaction to the question and the definite way she said she was better off without him. Something else had happened, and while his curiosity was piqued, he knew better than to ask.

Which again left him with little to say. He rapidly sorted through a list of safe topics, discarding them one after another. The weather? Nah. That had been talked to death all over town. The upcoming football season? The current baseball season? Politics? Yeah, right.

But she seemed to feel awkward about not explaining, and before he could think of a way to change the subject, she said, "We, uh, lost our son.

He was only six. And Chet just ran away from it all.''

His heart stopped. He couldn't imagine losing a child; he just knew that it had to be as bad or worse than anything he'd experienced. ''I'm sorry. I'm so sorry, Mary.''

''Me, too.'' She looked away, toward the window that gave them a view of the dying day and the mountains. ''I miss him. I'm always going to miss him. My son.''

He nodded and reached instinctively for her hand, covering it with his, squeezing gently.

He waited, and after a minute or so she visibly shook herself and faced him with a smile. ''But we're here to have fun. So let's eat and laugh.''

After that the appetizer disappeared quickly and was soon followed by their steaks.

''So,'' she said, after taking a few bites of steak and pronouncing it delicious, ''what's the weirdest thing that's ever happened to you?''

He arched a brow and hurried to swallow. ''Weird how?''

''I don't know,'' she said, musing. ''*Twilight Zone* weird?''

He pondered for a moment. ''I guess it was when I was fourteen. Playing out back in the yard. I had one of those pitch-back things, where you throw a baseball into it and it will bounce back to you. So you can play catch by yourself.''

He paused. ''I didn't have a lot of friends that

summer. I think we'd just moved. Anyway, I was playing ball, and I caught a movement out of the corner of my eye, and there was this old lady walking across our lawn, on the far side, near the woods. I looked at her for a minute or two, wondered who she was, what she was doing there. But for some reason I was too...scared, stunned, I don't know what...to say anything. Then she stepped into the trees and just...vanished.''

He took a bite of baked potato, waiting for a response, but she merely sat and listened. So he continued. "Well, for some reason, *that* was when I got curious, so I ran across the lawn to where she'd walked into the trees, but there was no sign of her. No sound. I walked along all the paths...nothing. The woods weren't that thick, and I hadn't been so far away that she could just have vanished in the time it took me to cross the lawn. But...she did. And for the rest of my life, I've wondered if she was really there at all or if I just imagined her." He poked at his salad and looked back at her. "So now you *know* I'm strange, right?"

She smiled. He had a lovely voice. She hadn't meant the conversation to go this way, but it had, and it didn't bother her. "Well, no, not strange. Weird things happen."

"To you, too?"

She nodded. "Let's say the mountains can be very, very disorienting at five in the morning, when the fog is thick and you're camping, and you wake up needing to relieve yourself and not a single other soul is awake for miles around.''

''You were alone?'' he asked.

''No. But my parents were sleeping late. Well, not late…5:00 a.m. isn't late. But…it was just me and the mountainside and the dark fog. And that's when I heard the footsteps, or whatever, something *big* moving in the brush around me. I thought maybe it was a bear, so I ran for the latrine. But it was just…there.'' She suppressed a shiver. ''It wasn't an animal. Don't ask me why I think so. I just know it wasn't. I'm not sure it was human, either. It was…like I could feel it thinking about me, deciding if I was…the right one.''

''The right one for what?''

She shrugged. ''I don't know. I did my business and dashed back to the tent as fast as I could. Didn't sleep another wink that night or the next.''

''Sounds like one of those bad teen slasher flicks,'' he said, smiling. Then he seemed to read something in her face, and his smile dropped. ''I'm sorry. That was insensitive.''

''No,'' she said, shaking her head. ''The really strange thing is that it *does* sound like some cheesy horror movie. Except…I was in it. And I didn't like it.''

He nodded. ''I had the same sort of feeling about that woman I saw. And I've been grateful ever since that I've never had another experience like it.''

''I wish I hadn't,'' she said.

"It happened again?"

She colored faintly. "Never mind. You're going to think I'm off my rocker."

"It's *obvious* you're not off your rocker. Go on, tell me."

She hesitated, toying with her food. When she spoke, she tried to sound lighthearted. "Those footsteps I heard in the brush?"

"Oh, God, don't tell me something attacked you."

Her eyes jumped up, meeting his. "Oh, no! Nothing like that. No, it's just that they…followed me home."

He wasn't sure he understood her correctly. "Followed you home? How? When?"

"It's kind of hard to explain. But after that camping trip, when we came home, I heard the footsteps in the house late at night. Something would wake me, and I could hear them. Sort of. Oh, it's so hard to explain. It wasn't exactly as if I heard them the way I'm hearing you, but I still heard them, if you can get some idea what I mean." She grimaced. "Sometimes language fails."

"I think I know what you mean. Like something on the very edge of hearing."

Her eyebrows lifted. "That's a great description. That's exactly what I mean. Night after night, I'd lie awake listening. I'd hear those footsteps start at the base of the basement stairs. They climbed slowly and walked into the kitchen. Then they'd stop."

"Now that's really creepy."

"I lost count of the nights I lay awake with my heart hammering so hard I could scarcely get enough air in my lungs. Listening. Terrified they'd go farther, that they'd come down the hall to my bedroom. I started needing the hall light on outside my door, not that I ever understood what the light would do. I tried to tell myself it was just some sound the house was making, the heating system or something. But I kept right on hearing it. For years. It didn't stop until I left home."

"That must have been awful! Did you tell anyone?"

"Oh, sure, I told my mom. She asked me to keep quiet about it so my little cousin wouldn't get upset. I thought she didn't believe me, but it turns out I was wrong. She believed me, all right. And years after I left, I heard from her and my cousin that they heard the steps, too, and that they started to go farther back into the house, into the bedroom wing."

"I feel like shivering. But how do you know they were the same steps you heard in the woods?"

"Because…" She hesitated, then blurted it out. "Because I could feel it thinking, 'Is she the one?'"

"The hair on the back of my neck is standing up."

"Mine, too." She gave an uneasy laugh. "I've never told anyone else about that. You must think I was hallucinating."

He shook his head. "You forget, I grew up in a

world populated by demons, devils and angels. In my childhood, the unseen was every bit as real as the seen.''

''Do you still feel that way?''

He thought it over for a moment or two. ''I guess so. My belief structures are less simplistic than they used to be, but if you want to ask me if I believe in angels or the devil, I'd have to say yes. And if I had any doubts, my experience in police work would have convinced me.''

''Why?''

''Because of what I've seen. It's not so bad here in Whisper Creek, but when I was working in Boulder and Denver, I saw stuff that could chill your soul. Things that couldn't be called anything except evil. People so far removed from basic conscience that it was as if they didn't *have* a soul. But I saw other things, too. Miraculous things. Things that make me believe angels watch over us sometimes.''

''Not chance?''

His steady gaze met hers. ''What do you think?''

''I'm a religious person. I go through most of my life feeling that everything around me is a miracle. Other times...'' Her face darkened, but she made a visible effort to lighten her mood. ''Sometimes I feel as if we're all lost and abandoned. Victims of random chance.''

He nodded and touched her hand again. This time, while it was also comforting, the touch was electric. He could almost hear the snap in the air. He jerked his fingers back. "We all feel that way sometimes. It's the old question: why do bad things happen to good people?"

"Why do they?"

He shook his head. "I don't know. I guess we're supposed to learn lessons from it. Deepen our compassion and sympathy and love for our fellow man. That's all I can think of."

She nodded slowly and drew a long breath. "Maybe so. I have to believe there's something positive in it all."

"Otherwise we'd give up completely."

They shared a long look of understanding, then resumed eating.

"So," Sam asked, "have you had any other spooky experiences?"

"No, thank goodness. That was it, and that was quite enough for one lifetime."

"So what do you think these experiences are?"

"I haven't the faintest idea. I'd say brain glitches, except I find it hard to believe that leaving home would have made me stop hearing those steps if they were caused by something in my brain."

"Or that your family would have heard them if it was just in your brain."

"Power of suggestion," she suggested.

"But you don't really believe that. And frankly, neither do I." He pushed his plate to one side and nodded for the waiter to refill their coffee cups. "The thing is, the whole idea of ghosts doesn't fit with my religious beliefs. The idea that spirits could get trapped here on earth just doesn't sit well with me."

"But demons do?"

He laughed. "I never said I was consistent. Maybe there was a demon after you. But a ghost? That means something isn't working right in the way things are set up."

She nodded and pushed her own plate aside. "I see what you mean. I sometimes thought that maybe what I was hearing was some kind of psychic impression left behind in the house. Except that doesn't explain what I heard in the woods."

"Hmm." He thought about that, drumming his fingers absently on the table. "Well, my father would tell you that a demon was after you."

She shivered visibly. "The thought crossed my mind more than once when it was happening. Do you think that?"

He shook his head. "I have to admit I don't. I'm more inclined to believe it might have been some sort of poltergeist phenomenon."

"What's that?"

"Well, the name means noisy ghost. But what the experts think is that kids in adolescence give off some kind of strong psychic energy that can cause noises, or even cause objects to move. So maybe nothing followed you home. Maybe what happened in the woods somehow triggered your unconscious to imitate the experience."

"But why did it continue after I left?"

"How old was your cousin?"

All of a sudden she smiled faintly. "Twelve. She had just turned twelve. I like your explanation."

He shrugged. "I don't know if it makes any more sense than demons. Except that if you accept the existence of demons for the sake of argument, I'd have a hard time trying to figure out a reason why any demon would do exactly the same things night after night like that."

"Good point." She looked as if some kind of weight had lifted from her shoulders.

"Of course," he added wryly, "none of this explains my disappearing woman."

"I guess not." But she was still looking relieved.

"I got called in on a poltergeist case once, in Boulder."

Her eyes widened. "For real?"

"For real. How else do you think I know what it's called and what it's supposed to be?" His mouth quirked as he spoke, and she laughed. He loved the sound of her laugh, a gentle ripple of sound.

"So tell," she asked.

The waiter interrupted just then to take their plates and ask if they wanted dessert. Sam looked questioningly at Mary.

She shook her head. "I think I'm too full."

"I'm not. Share a piece of turtle cheesecake with me?"

"Maybe a spoonful."

He grinned. "That's enough to justify it."

The waiter departed, leaving them once again alone with the flickering candle between them. He could tell the candle bothered her, but she seemed to have shoved that aside. It was, Sam thought, almost like sharing ghost stories over a campfire.

"The poltergeist," she reminded him. "What happened?"

"First, let me tell you that I never actually saw or heard anything. In fact, at the time, I felt kind of stupid even being there. I was almost positive it was some kind of scam."

She nodded encouragingly. The cheesecake materialized in front of them with two spoons. Mary picked one up at Sam's insistence and tasted the dessert. It was, as everything else had been, perfect.

"So what was going on?" she prompted.

"I don't know. What I do know is the department got a hysterical call from a woman who insisted somebody or something was in her house, that it was vandalizing the place. I was the lucky one who got dispatched.

"When I got there, everything was quiet. Well, except for the woman and her two daughters. They were pretty hysterical, and the father was half-stunned and half-ready to kill someone. Apparently odd things had been happening for some time, and it had finally gotten out of hand."

"What kind of odd things?"

"Noises, mostly at night. The kids and the mom

described it as scratching and knocking. The dad said he never heard it. Then things got stranger. Fires started in wastebaskets. At first the parents thought it was one of the girls doing it. The dad got pretty frosted, I guess, and he and the mom started watching the girls like hawks. Then it escalated into vandalism. Tearing off the wallpaper, scribbling on the walls and mirrors in something like lipstick. Things being smashed when nobody was in the room.''

''Boy! What did you do?''

''All I could do. I talked to the girls, tried to frighten them a little about what would happen if they or one of their friends got caught doing any of that stuff and wrote up a report. What else could I do? There was no evidence at all of any involvement outside the family. At that point it was a matter for somebody besides the police, unless one of them was going to point a finger. And nobody was pointing fingers. By that time the parents were convinced the daughters weren't involved.''

''Poor people. So they never got any help?''

''I didn't say that. A few months later I heard they were working with a parapsychologist. It was certainly more up his alley than it was mine.''

''I've heard about things like that, but I never knew anyone who was personally involved.'' She laughed and took another spoonful of cheesecake. ''Well, except for me, I guess. You know what I mean.''

"I wasn't exactly involved, though. Nothing much a cop can do about something like that. What am I going to do? Arrest a poltergeist? Arrest a kid who doesn't have the foggiest idea she's doing anything? Not likely."

"It must have felt awful to be unable to help."

He was surprised by her understanding. "It was," he admitted. "They were as upset and scared as anybody who's had a home invasion, and I couldn't do a thing to ease their minds."

A few minutes later, when they stepped outside, the stench of smoke hit them in the faces, almost like a slap. Sam's eyes started burning immediately.

"Back to reality," he said. It wasn't a happy thought.

11

The smoke in the air hid the stars in the sky as Sam and Mary crossed the gravel parking lot to his car. Just as he was about to help Mary in, a car came roaring down the highway and sprayed gravel as it turned into the parking lot. It stopped with a jolt right next to Sam.

The man inside jumped out. It was Louis DelRay. "Sam, Sam, thank God I saw you. It's Joe. He went back to the house this afternoon. And he hasn't come back!"

"What the hell was he doing? And how the heck did he get through the pass? They're not letting anyone through there except firefighters."

Louis shook his head. "Joe took the back way in."

The back way in. Sam knew it, sort of. He'd traveled it maybe once in the few years he'd lived here. It was little more than a leftover wagon rut from the last century. Passable by a high-sprung four-wheel drive and little else. These days it was seldom used except by ambitious hikers.

"Why did he go back?"

Louis sighed. "He realized he'd forgotten to pack the pictures of his mother. She's dead, you know. I'd have stopped him or gone with him or something, but I didn't know what he'd done until I found his note. He said he'd be back no later than six." He shifted his weight impatiently, his face a mirror of worry and fear. "I've got to get in there. I've got to get him out. If you come with me, maybe they'll let me through the pass."

Sam shook his head firmly. "No. Trust me, they won't. Not under any circumstances. I'll radio and see if I can get one of the fire teams to look for him."

"I can't wait! He could already be in trouble. And this car won't make it in the back way."

Sam reached out and gripped his arm. "Listen to me, Louis. The firefighters can get to him faster. If you go back there, all you'll do is make it necessary for the teams to search for someone else. You'll put someone else at risk. Do you understand?"

Slowly, reluctantly, Louis nodded. It seemed to Mary that his eyes grew wet.

"I'll get help, Louis. I promise. You see Mary home for me. We'll find Joe."

Mary wanted to stop him, wanted to tell him not to do anything crazy. But she bit back the words and climbed into Louis's car with him. It occurred

to her that she ought to be annoyed about being
dumped on a total stranger like this, but the thought
seemed so selfish and childish that she dismissed it
immediately. Some things took priority, and she
knew Sam wouldn't have turned her over to Louis
if he didn't have to.

Louis jammed his car into gear as soon as they
were both belted in. "Sorry," he said, "but I'm going up the pass just as soon as I drop you off.
Where's your house?"

"On Maple."

He braked at the edge of the parking lot before
getting on the highway and watched Sam speed off.
Sam's vehicle was no longer a private car. He'd
slapped a whirling blue light on top of it.

"God," Louis said, closing his eyes for a moment. "I'm glad I ran into him. He's the only guy
in town I trust to give a shit what happens to Joe."

Mary forgot her own fears for Sam and looked at
him. "Why? Joe's a human being."

"Yeah." Louis gave a bitter laugh and pulled out
on the highway heading toward town. "By the way,
my name's Louis DelRay."

"Yes, I know. And your partner is Joe Canton."

"Right." He glanced at her, his eyes dark and
brooding. "See? We've never talked, but you know
who we are. That's what I mean. The whole town
knows the two queer artists, and most of 'em would
be glad if we lived on another planet."

Mary didn't know what to say. It was true that

she'd heard of them, even had them pointed out to her once or twice. She'd always avoided any derogatory talk about them, but she wasn't a fool. She knew what Louis meant. "I'm sorry."

"Yeah, so am I. But hey, that's the way they slice the loaf. I got the heel."

His wheels screeched a little as he went round a curve. Mary instinctively reached for something to hang on to.

"Sorry," he said, and slowed down. "I just want to get back up there."

"I understand. It's okay."

"No, it's not okay to scare you. Who are you, anyway?"

"Mary McKinney. I teach English at the high school."

He nodded. "Nice to meet you. Wish the circumstances were better."

"Me, too."

"We keep pretty much to ourselves, Joe and me. I suppose we could move to some big city where there're others like us, but... Hey, what can I tell you. We both crave the solitude and the mountains."

"You're artists, aren't you?"

"Yeah. I sculpt, Joe paints."

"Were you able to get all your work out of there?"

He nodded. "The first things we packed. I had to leave some marble behind—too big to carry out—

but if it burns it'll probably be okay. I mean, it's marble. I suppose the heat could crack it, but I can work around that."

"Do you only work in marble?"

"Depends on what I'm doing. I like granite, too. And sometimes agate. Limestone is good for some things."

"What kind of things do you sculpt?"

"Depends on whether I'm working to please myself or to make money."

"I can understand that. We all need to live."

"Yeah. And isn't it amazing how hard we make it on each other sometimes?"

"Yes," she agreed quietly. "It is."

They were in town, nearing her house. He turned onto Maple with a squeal of tires.

"Four doors down on the right," she told him. "Thanks for the ride."

"My pleasure." He stopped with a sharp jerk, and Mary reached for the door handle, well aware that he just wanted to get up to the pass.

But she paused and looked at him. "Louis...let the pros handle it. They're more likely to get Joe out than you are."

He looked straight at her. "If we don't get Joe out, I don't give a damn what happens to me."

"I do," she said firmly. "And I'm sure there are others who would, too. Besides, it's like Sam said. If you go out there, you might only be endangering others."

The smile he gave her was lopsided, humorless. "You really are a teacher."

Flushing, Mary climbed out of the car and stood on the curb, watching him tear away. After a moment she noticed that Elijah was standing across the street in his yard.

"Are you okay?" he asked her.

"Why wouldn't I be?"

"Interesting company you keep."

Her temper flared. "What do you mean by that?"

"Just that I think a schoolteacher should be more careful about the types she hangs out with."

"Where do you get off telling me who I should be seen with?"

"I'm only concerned about what's best for you."

Her mouth opened with a sharp retort, then closed as she realized that his tone hadn't been at all critical. The man really *was* concerned.

"I'll be fine. Of course, there wouldn't be any problem at all if people didn't have strange prejudices."

"Perhaps," he said noncommittally.

"Anyway," she added kindly, before turning to go inside, "you might be interested to know that your son is on the way to rescue one of those *types* from the fire."

She didn't mean it the way it sounded. She'd genuinely felt he might want to know that Sam could be going into danger. He was Sam's father, after all, and whatever the bad blood between them, she just couldn't believe that there was no genuine love left there. But as soon as she spoke, she realized how spiteful the words had sounded.

"I'm sorry," she hastened to say. "I didn't intend to be mean."

He waved the apology aside and started across the street toward her. "I deserve it, regardless. What do you mean? What happened?"

When he reached her, she saw genuine worry on his face. Maybe she would have been kinder to leave him in ignorance. Maybe she was every bit as mean as her words had sounded.

"Joe Canton went back to his house in the valley," she explained, keeping her tone gentle. "His partner said he'd promised to be back by six."

"But he's not. And Sam went after him." Elijah's face darkened.

"I don't know if Sam will go personally or if one of the fire teams will be sent."

But she knew. In her heart of hearts, she knew. Sam wasn't the kind of man to send someone else where he wouldn't go himself. How she knew that she couldn't say. She was just sure of it.

And so was Elijah, to judge by the look in his eyes.

"Come in," she said in a rush of sympathy. "Come inside and have some tea with me."

To her amazement, he followed, taking a seat in her living room.

"I'll just go make the tea," she said. "Back in a moment."

He didn't respond but looked far away, as if his mind were roving over possibilities she'd been trying to avoid thinking about.

Elijah could be such an irritating man, she thought as she boiled water and dropped some tea bags into the pot. He had a way of saying things that sounded judgmental, as if he were declaiming truths from on high. Maybe that was just a bad habit developed over a lifetime of being a minister. Maybe he didn't mean to sound that way. He certainly had handled some of her bristling and criticism in a humble manner, when he might just as well have erupted at her.

And boy, did he make her bristle. But maybe that was his unfortunate manner rather than his intent. Having dealt with him only a few times, she could readily understand how he might have clashed with Sam, and how painful that clashing would have been for a child. But maybe Elijah was a better man than his abrasive personality would lead one to believe. And maybe he cared more for Sam than he knew how to admit, and more than Sam wanted to believe.

Watch it, she told herself sternly. Don't make judgments too quickly. It could hurt Sam. It could hurt Elijah. It could hurt her.

Looking for the best in people was one of her lifelong traits, though, one she sometimes had to rein in. Life had taught her that there were truly bad people around. But she still didn't seem able to entirely quell her tendency to make excuses for other people.

Carrying the pot, cream, sugar and two mugs on a tray into the living room, she placed them on the coffee table in front of Elijah. "I hope you like Earl Grey."

He half smiled. "My favorite."

She poured cups for them both, taking hers black, and watched as he loaded sugar into his cup. So much sugar that she was certain it couldn't all dissolve.

He spoke. "You like my son, don't you?"

Mary hesitated, uncertain how to take that. "He's a fine man, yes, if that's what you mean."

His blue eyes lifted from his cup to hers. "I meant something more than that."

She shook her head. "I told you, we're not dating. We're just…friends. Casual friends."

He leaned back against the couch, cradling his mug in both hands. "It gets so chilly at night here, doesn't it?"

"Yes. The thin air."

"So I understand. And the older I get, the more the cold bothers me. I probably should have looked for a church farther south."

"Why didn't you?"

"I don't know."

But Mary was of the opinion it was no oversight or mistake that had brought him to Whisper Creek.

Whether he was conscious of it or not, he had come to be near his son.

And wasn't that leaping to conclusions? she asked herself. She'd better watch it. He might have come here for no other reason than that he liked the hiring committee and hadn't realized that the evening chill would bother him.

It was her night, it seemed, to be caught in awkward silences. First with Sam, now with his father. Elijah didn't have much to say, which was rather odd in a man who had up until now offered his opinions about a lot of things without even being asked. And she didn't know what to say to him. Sam was the topic that kept coming to her mind, but she didn't want Elijah to get the wrong idea, and she wanted even less to tread into the quicksand of their relationship.

"I just hope he's okay," she finally settled for saying.

"That always was Sam," he answered. "Rescuing fools from their own foolishness."

For a moment she thought he was commenting on Joe and Louis's lifestyle—was that the right word nowadays? no, orientation—but the look on his face didn't bear out the thought. As if sensing that he might be misunderstood, he continued.

"Going back into a fire zone like that. It was foolish. But Sam was never one to let fools suffer for their mistakes."

"I'll bet he learned that from you," she said.

"You don't see me driving into that valley, do you?"

"No," Mary said. "But you've spent your life driving into people's spiritual valleys. Trying to rescue people from the devil, or themselves, or whatever."

Elijah nodded slowly. "I guess that might be right. But Sam takes too many risks. There's a difference between looking out for your neighbor and driving into a forest fire."

"'Greater love hath no man than to lay down his life for a friend.' Isn't that in the Bible somewhere?"

He seemed taken aback, surprised. "You *do* know your Bible." He had said that the first time they met, but it still seemed to surprise him.

"I love that verse," she said. "But isn't that what Sam's doing?"

Elijah paused for a long moment. "I just want him to come home."

Sam's Jeep bounced along the trail, another Jeep following him with four firefighters. He'd harangued them at the checkpoint until they'd broken down. "You're not going in there without us," a squat, soot-covered fireman had said. "That's the first rule of fire fighting: never go in alone."

Louis had pulled up just as they were about to leave, demanding to come along. Sam had threatened him with arrest if he didn't head back to town.

He had agreed only when Sam reached for his cuffs. Now Sam was jolting around in the seat, fighting to control the wheel, a rebreather unit thunking in the seat beside him. He rounded a corner in the forest and slowed to a stop. A wall of flame had spread across the road.

"No way," one firefighter said, shaking his head as he climbed out of his Jeep. "No way we go in there."

"Don't you have those fire-retardant suits?" Sam asked. "His house is only another couple hundred yards, I think. We can't just leave him to die...." Sam paused. In the heat of the moment, he hadn't even asked the man's name. He extended a hand. "I'm Sam."

"Paul," the man said, taking his hand quickly. "And you *think* it's only another couple hundred yards. Even if you're right, that's too far. Or it's not far enough." Paul looked at the fire. "The house may already be gone, and your friend with it. And as for suits, those flames can reach two thousand degrees. They'll melt the suit right on a man. We can't get in. Period."

"I'm not leaving a man to die," Sam said. "There has to be a way."

Another of the firefighters stepped forward. Younger, blond hair turned gray by ash and smoke. "Paul, they're dumping mud on the far side of the ridge. Maybe if one of the planes has something left in its load..."

Paul turned and started to argue, then stopped. Instead he simply nodded and spoke into the microphone clipped to his vest. "East range chief, mobile two, over. Yeah, we have an urgent rescue and we need some mud." He looked at his map and barked out coordinates. "Yep, where the backfires turned. There's an old mining road. I'll flash our strobe to let him know where we are."

The voice on the radio crackled in objection. Paul let out a sigh. "I know they're busy. But we've got a man trapped, and he may be dying while we're arguing." The voice crackled again, and Paul shook his head. "If that's the best you can do, I guess it'll have to work. We're marking now. Mobile two out."

"So?" Sam asked.

Paul ignored him for the moment, turning instead to his crew. "John, get the strobe up on the roof of the Jeep and stay clued in to the radio. Greg, Larry, suit up. We have maybe two minutes."

The men scrambled into action as Paul turned to Sam. "They're diverting a plane that was on its way back. It's gonna dump some mud on the road there, and we're going in right behind it. If he finds us. If he drops on target. If the mud knocks the fire down. It's going to get messy, so get in your Jeep and stay there."

Sam shook his head, reaching into the Jeep for his rebreather. "I'm going with you."

"The hell you are," Paul said. "Look, this isn't

about courage. It's about training and experience. You'll just be a liability for my men.''

"And you don't know where the house is,'' Sam said, shrugging on the tank and pulling the mask over his face. "What's more, we're wasting time talking. And Joe Canton can't spare the time.''

"Fine,'' Paul said, donning his own tank and mask. "But you stay with my men. If I say pull out, we pull out. No matter what.''

"Deal,'' Sam said.

They hunkered down behind his Jeep while one of the firemen stood on the roof of their vehicle, aiming a strobe light up through the forest. Soon the roar of flame was joined by another roar, a deep-throated rumble from the sky above. Sam couldn't see the plane. He hoped the pilot could see the flashing light. If not...

The rumble grew, then passed directly overhead. "Duck and cover!'' Paul yelled, pulling Sam's head down.

A rain of thick, gooey fluid fell around them, instantly staining everything a bright red. Too thick to evaporate in the heat as it fell, it hit his back with a wet, stinging thud. In an instant the temperature around them dropped forty degrees. Sam looked up, wiping a few droplets of mud from his mask. The road ahead was clear, but only barely, the flames beaten back only a few yards on each side.

"Go-go-go!'' Paul yelled, already up and moving.

Sam jumped up and jogged alongside the others,

the tank shifting and bouncing on his back. He tried to tighten the straps as he moved. A quick glance to either side told him they didn't have much time. The mud had damped the flames, but it would dry in minutes, and the fire would return in full force.

"Just ahead on the right!" he called, pointing over Paul's shoulder.

"It better be," Paul said, looking around. "If it's not around this corner, we're pulling out."

Sam understood the cold moral calculus, even if his heart rebelled against it. Joe Canton was a man worth saving. But so were Paul and his men. Getting them killed wouldn't save Joe's life. If he was still alive.

They rounded the corner and Sam pointed again. "There's the house!"

Paul nodded. Flames were already crackling across the tiny, spare yard, clawing at the base of the walls. Windows had shattered. "Come on!" he yelled, waving an arm forward.

By the time they reached the house, Paul already had the fire ax raised. He swung it at the door, next to the knob, a hard blow. The frame splintered, and the door sagged inward.

Sam followed the men in. There was no one in the front room. He started toward the hallway off to the left, but Paul grabbed his arm. "We go in twos. Greg and Larry, you go right. Sam, you're with me." He looked at his men. "Count to thirty and get out, no matter what."

Sam heard the groaning yawn of overheated timbers stretching. The fire had reached the back walls. Remembering what little training he'd been given on the job, he touched each doorknob before opening it. A hot doorknob would mean an active fire in the room beyond. He opened the first door. It was the two men's bedroom, and empty. Paul stood in the doorway while Sam ran in to check the attached bathroom. Also empty.

"Ten, eleven, twelve," Paul called out aloud, pointing down the hallway.

Sam hurried back out, and they tested the next doorknob. It was warm. Maybe there was time. He opened the door and felt a rush of heat. On the far side of the room, the curtains had already ignited. A pair of metal file cabinets stood along one wall.

Curled on the floor, eyes clenched shut, papers clutched in his hand, was Joe Canton.

"Joe!" Sam called. But his voice was lost in the roar of the fire. A chair under the window was already smoldering. The room would be alight in moments. Sam crossed the room quickly and grabbed Joe's shoulder. The man looked up, terror filling his eyes. "Come on, Joe! You're okay. Let's go!"

A pall of smoke hung in the room. Joe tried to stand, but in doing so he sucked in the smoke and bent over, coughing and retching. Sam grabbed the man and slung him over his shoulder, turning to the door. The carpet had now caught, and flames licked their way across the room. He looked at Paul, who waved his arm desperately as if to say *Get out now!*

Sam crossed the room as quickly as he could, ignoring the heat on his legs. Paul had moved out ahead of him, and when Sam stepped into the hallway it was empty. He cursed and headed back toward the front of the house. As he passed the next door, Paul emerged from the master bedroom holding a wet towel. He clapped it over Sam's legs. Only then did Sam realize his trousers had been on fire.

"Go-go-go!!" Paul called. Outside, Paul counted "twenty-six, twenty-seven," looking at the door. His men tumbled through exactly at thirty.

In the darkness and smoke inside the house, there had been no way to tell the others that Joe had been found. Now they offered quick, grim nods of relief as they set out to the road and back toward safety. The mud was almost dry, and the fire was already pressing back onto the sides of the narrow road.

Sam labored under the unfamiliar tank and the weight of Joe Canton, stumbling in a slow jog. He knew the others were chafing at his pace. He also knew they wouldn't run on ahead and leave him. As they passed through the drying mud, the flames on either side seemed to scream in rage. Sam felt the skin on his face dry and tighten around the edge of his mask. There was no stopping here. Even to pause would let the fire feed on them.

Finally they passed through the worst of it, shambling along, guided only by the feel of the road beneath their feet. They were only a few feet from Sam's Jeep when they saw it through the smoke. Sam tumbled Joe into the back seat and climbed behind the wheel.

"Wind shift!" Paul called out.

Sam turned. The wall of flame had reached across the road again and begun creeping toward them. Paul and his men were already piling into the other vehicle, where John had begun radioing in the good news the minute he'd seen them coming through the smoke. Sam turned the key in the ignition, slammed the truck in gear, twisted in his seat so he could see out the back window and stomped on the gas. The Jeep shot backward, and Sam yanked the wheel to move around Paul's vehicle. Then Paul was also moving, and they backed down the road, bouncing wildly, until they found a small clearing in which to turn around.

"Damn fool," Paul said, leaning in to talk to Sam through the window when they stopped at the checkpoint. "We could've died in there."

Sam nodded. "But we didn't."

"Get him to the hospital," Paul said, reaching for his microphone. "East range chief, mobile two over. We got him out, Doug. Thanks for the flyby."

"Tell him thanks from me, too," Sam said, backing away.

But Paul had already signed off. "Just get that jackass to the hospital and make it worth our while."

* * *

Louis was waiting at the entrance to the E.R. "I think he's okay," Sam said as attendants bundled Joe onto a stretcher and wheeled him in. "Maybe smoke inhalation."

Louis seemed about to hug him, but instead he simply held out a hand. "Thank you for saving him."

"When he wakes up," Sam said, "chew his ass for being an idiot. He almost got four men killed."

"Gladly," Louis said, nodding. "But he's my idiot. And I love him."

"He's lucky to have you," Sam said. He looked down at his charred trousers, then up at Louis. "Hell, after today, he's lucky all around."

12

Sam's lower legs were stinging, but he didn't want to look. As long as they hurt, the burns couldn't be too serious. In fact, he could remember worse pain from bumping his hand into the side of his oven.

He had to pass near Mary's house on his way home from the hospital. Realizing she was probably on tenterhooks about what had happened, he turned down her street and parked in front of her house. The lights were on, so she was still up. He spared a glance for his blackened jeans, then decided he could pass the damage off as ash so she wouldn't worry about it. Hell, he was dirty and sooty from head to foot. But he was still walking, and that ought to be reassurance enough.

He looked even worse than he thought, though. He could tell that from the expression on Mary's face when she opened the door. She was still wearing that pretty dress she'd worn to dinner, but he had a sneaking suspicion he no longer resembled the man who had picked her up.

"My God, Sam," she said in a throaty whisper. "My God." Reaching out, she grabbed his hand and pulled him into the house. "Is there anywhere you're *not* burned? Why aren't you in the hospital?"

"I'm not burned," he lied. "It's soot."

And that was when he saw his father. The man had been sitting on the couch, but now he got to his feet, drawing Sam's attention to him.

Whatever Elijah was thinking, it was, as usual, expressed in stern lines. His was a face Sam had rarely been able to read. "Your legs," Elijah said.

Mary looked down and gasped. "Your pants are burned!"

"Just singed." What he wanted to do was ask what in the hell his father was doing in Mary's house. In some deep, inescapable way, he felt betrayed. She was associating with the enemy.

But the enemy spoke. "We were worried about you," Elijah said. "Risking your neck like that..."

"No risk," Sam said shortly. "I was with an experienced crew." It was a lie, but he wasn't going to have Mary needlessly upset. Even if she was consorting with Elijah. "I'm *fine*. And if anybody's interested, we got Joe out. He's in the hospital for smoke inhalation, but otherwise he's fine."

"Thank God," Mary said prayerfully.

Elijah's gratitude was conspicuously absent. Sam felt a surge of the old rage but bit it back out of deference to Mary. Damned judgmental old fool, he thought angrily. Elijah's spots were never going to change.

"Well," said Sam flatly, feeling his heart turn to stone as he looked at the two of them, so cozy in Mary's living room, "I'll be on my way."

"Sam, no." Mary reached out, taking his hand again. "You're exhausted. You need to unwind. Why don't you take a shower here? It'll help get rid of the tension."

He gave her a humorless smile. "No change of clothes."

"I'll get something from my place," Elijah said, heading for the door. "We're still pretty much the same size."

"Thanks," Mary said. Sam said nothing, just felt the deep burning that never quite seemed to go away when anything to do with Elijah was involved.

"Come on," Mary said, tugging his hand after Elijah left. "You'll feel better. I'll make you a snack. Something to drink…"

He was weak. He didn't want to go home to his empty house. Not yet. And Mary's soothing, concerned tone worked on him like a spell. Had he been strong, he would have marched out. But he was feeling weak, feeling in need of a little TLC.

He told himself it was the adrenaline wearing off. Somewhere inside, though, he realized he didn't want to relinquish Mary to his father.

"Okay," he finally said. "Can I have a garbage

bag for these clothes? They're shot, and I don't want them messing up your house.''

"Of course.''

She gave him one of those big green lawn bags and he took it into the bathroom with him. Judging by the stinging of his legs, he didn't think he was up to hot water. Cold shower. Just what he needed.

And the water was *cold*. At this altitude the ground rarely warmed up enough to take the chill off the water pipes. It felt like a bath in ice, and he shivered as he soaped and then soaped again, trying to wash away the mud and the soot. His legs were red, but there were no blisters, and though the water made him shiver, it felt good on his scorched skin. Really good. With the pain easing, he felt himself relaxing a bit.

When he climbed out to towel off, he discovered that clothes lay in a neat pile on the toilet seat. Resistance rose in him, but he told himself not to be an ass. It was only as he was patting his legs dry— gently, so as not to abrade the tender skin—that he realized all the hair had been singed off them.

Somehow that brought home the danger he had been in even more than the charring of his jeans. For a moment he closed his eyes and said a prayer of thanksgiving, a prayer that Joe was safe, a prayer that they were all safe.

Then, eating his humble pie, as it were, he pulled on his father's clothes: boxer shorts, a polo shirt and, thank goodness, a pair of khaki shorts. Nothing to rub on his tender skin.

When he returned to the living room, garbage bag of ruined clothes in hand, Mary took one look at him and exclaimed, "You're burned!"

"Just a little red. Nothing major."

"Sam, I can see where flames licked you!"

Elijah spoke. "So can I, son."

He hated it when his father called him son. The word had come to mean a lot of things through his childhood, few of them good. It made him feel about three feet tall again. He had to bite back a demand that Elijah call him by name. He didn't want to get into this in front of Mary.

But Mary had other things on her mind than who called whom what, apparently. She turned on all the living-room lights and knelt on the floor to look at his legs. "Sam, these are first-degree burns!"

"They'll be fine. I get worse burns cooking."

"But not over so large an area."

"I'll be fine," he said again, his tone brooking no argument.

Mary shut up, but she didn't listen. She rose and disappeared down the hallway, returning in half a minute with a big bottle of green gel. "Aloe," she said firmly. "If you won't put it on, I will."

"Swallow your pride, Sam," Elijah said. "Do it."

"You're one to talk about pride."

Mary's eyes snapped. "The apple doesn't fall far

from the tree. Now put this gel on or both of you are going to hear me say some words schoolteachers aren't supposed to use.''

She took the garbage bag from Sam and handed it to Elijah. ''Put this in the trash can for me, please? It's out the kitchen door.'' She pointed.

Elijah went meekly enough, but his gaze met Sam's for just an instant, and Sam thought he saw something like amused understanding there. It made him so uncomfortable that he looked quickly away.

Mary shoved the gel into his hand. ''You or me, Sam. Your pick.''

He sat obediently and opened the bottle. The thought of the sticky gel all over his lower legs didn't thrill him, but neither did the stinging, which was beginning to get rather nasty and persistent. ''Okay, okay.''

He really wouldn't have minded Mary doing it, he realized. Feeling her small hands sliding over his skin so gently... No, he wouldn't have minded at all being babied that way. But Elijah was here. Damn the man's eyes.

He corralled his thoughts, which were straying down some rather enticing lanes, and focused on squeezing the gel onto his legs. It felt almost as cool as the water on his skin, and after a moment he didn't mind that he was making himself sticky all over.

Elijah returned and resumed his seat on the couch. Sam was careful to take the wooden rocking chair at the other end of the room. Mary disappeared for a few seconds and returned with a damp paper towel for him to wipe his hands on.

"You must need something to drink," she suggested as she took the towel and bottle of gel from him.

"Water, please. I could probably drink a gallon right now."

Mary disappeared again, and Elijah spoke. "Your cheeks look burned, too."

"No worse than a sunburn," Sam said, touching himself lightly with his fingertips. Imagine that. They were being civil to each other. He wondered how long that would last.

"You took a terrible risk."

Here it comes, thought Sam, stiffening. The lecture. When Elijah was around, there was always a lecture.

"The man would have died if we hadn't gone in for him." He felt Mary enter the room behind him, but he didn't turn around to look.

"And you might have died trying to save him," Elijah snapped. "You could have let the firemen look. At least they knew what they were doing."

"They didn't know how to find the cabin. I did."

"You could have given them directions." Elijah got to his feet, flinging out an arm. "That's my Sam. Always the hero. Always sticking your neck out even when it's not appreciated."

Sam got to his own feet. "It's appreciated."

"You think this town is going to make you a hero because you saved one of *them?*"

Sam heard Mary's gasp behind them. Reining in his own temper with difficulty, he said, "So loving and tolerant, Dad. What happened to the man I heard lecturing Mrs. Beemis earlier about tolerance and the commandment to love? You always were a narrow-minded bigot."

"I'm no bigot. But maybe you ought to stop rushing in where angels fear to tread. You could have been killed. And for what?"

With that Elijah stormed out of the house, the door slamming behind him.

Silence reigned for a few minutes; then he heard Mary draw a breath. "Wow," she said.

"Yeah." Sam's tone was bitter. "Everything I've ever done was wrong. No surprise there."

Mary came to him, glass of ice water in hand. It seemed to him her eyes slid away uneasily. Well, of course. Who would want to take on a man with a father like that?

And why the hell did that question even cross his mind?

He took the glass and drained the water in one long gulp. "Thanks."

"I'll get you more."

He let her do it, instead of offering to refill the glass himself. He needed a minute to calm down, and so, probably, did she.

He should have known his dad wouldn't applaud

his action but would see it as foolhardy. Hell, yeah, it was foolhardy. He knew it himself and didn't need the old man to tell him. But a man's life had been at stake, and there had been no way he was going to sit around twiddling his thumbs when he could do something about it. No way. But Elijah, as usual, had managed to turn it into an act of folly.

Mary returned with another glass of ice water. He accepted it with thanks and sat again in the rocking chair, taking care that his gooey legs didn't touch anything.

"I'm sorry," he said. "Sorry you had to see that."

She waved a hand. "It's all right."

"I guess if I'd helped rescue a good Christian, he'd feel better."

Her gaze grew thoughtful. "Are you sure of that, Sam?"

"What does that mean?"

"Only that...I think he was upset because you could have been seriously hurt, not because of who you saved. I mean...I shudder when I look at your legs. Can't you see it? It's almost like the flames branded you."

"It's a minor burn."

"Right. But I can see how close it came to doing real damage. Your pants were on fire, weren't they?"

He shrugged. "Maybe for a few seconds. I think

it was the starch I put in them. The denim was still holding together.''

She shook her head and sat on the sofa. ''You can minimize it however you want, Sam, but you came awfully close to being killed. And I don't think it's the person you saved that really has your dad upset.''

''What are you? Pollyanna?'' He leaned forward, gripping the glass in both hands. ''Look, Mary, I know you're a nice person. But some people aren't as nice as you. In my dad's church, you have to be a saint—or at least look like a saint—to be accepted. No sinners need apply. And people like Joe and Louis are at the top of the list of sinners.''

She sighed. ''Maybe so,'' she said quietly.

''Not maybe. I grew up with him and his churches. I know what I'm talking about. If I'd saved a church warden, he'd be singing my praises.''

Mary didn't look as if she were ready to think so poorly of anyone, but she didn't argue with him. Instead she tucked her feet up beneath her on the couch and folded her hands together.

''How are the burns feeling?''

''I hardly notice them,'' he lied.

''Promise me if they look any worse in the morning you'll go see a doctor?''

''Sure.'' It was easy to promise. He planned to be fit as a fiddle by then.

''It must have been frightening out there.''

"I didn't have much time to think about it." He sighed and let himself lean back and relax. "I suppose it was, but I was so focused on getting to Joe, I didn't think about it."

"Adrenaline?" she suggested.

"Probably."

"What happened?"

"The fire cut the road a few hundred yards from their cabin." He sketched briefly, without any frightening details, how the plane had carved a path for them, and how he'd found Joe. His voice trailed off as he remembered. "The room he was in was already starting to burn. I think he'd given up."

"Oh, no."

"At least we got him out." He shrugged as if it were nothing.

"With your pants on fire."

"Apparently so."

Mary bit her lip and closed her eyes for a few moments. He wondered what she was thinking but didn't ask. He figured he probably didn't want to know. Her thoughts were probably running like his dad's. After all, the two of them had been hanging out together.

That stung. That really stung. It was as if his dad was taking something else from him.

"I'm glad you're all right." Her green eyes were wide, honest, as she looked at him. "I was so worried. More worried than I even realized."

"All's well that ends well."

"I suppose so." She drew a shaky breath and smiled. "I'm glad you're okay. I'm glad Joe is okay, too. I felt so bad for Louis."

"Me, too. A thought that probably would never cross my father's brain."

"Don't be so hard on him, Sam. I think maybe he's changed a bit."

He snorted. "I'll believe it when I see it."

"Then maybe you should give him a chance."

"Maybe he should give *me* one." He was getting irritated again, and his legs were hurting like the devil. He wondered if the burns were worse than he thought, but when he glanced down at them, they looked just the same. Like a scald.

"I can't imagine anything worse than burning to death." Mary averted her face quickly, concealing her expression. "I'm so glad it came out all right."

"Me, too."

It was time to go. He was very tired and suddenly wanted nothing so much as he wanted his own house, his own sanctuary, his own bed. "I've gotta go."

She rose with him, looking at him as if there was something she wanted to say. He waited, but nothing was forthcoming, so he headed for the door. She trailed after him, and he turned around to say goodnight.

All of a sudden he was aware of her in a wholly new way. Aware of the way soft tendrils of her red hair brushed her cheek. Aware of the misty green of her eyes, a color almost like what he imagined Ireland must look like on a foggy morning.

Her scent. It suddenly filled his nostrils, a mixture of faint lilac with a hint of woman's musk. Her breasts filled the bodice of her dress, gentle mounds promising hidden delights. Her tiny waist...

His brain shut down the inventory as his body took over. Without even planning the move, he reached for her, surrounded her with his arms, and drew her close until their bodies were pressed together.

For an instant she looked startled; then her face softened and her eyelids fluttered, and she seemed to melt into him.

Her lips were sweet, tasting faintly of tea, soft against his, inviting. Everything about her was soft, a softness he wanted to sink right into, a softness he wanted to wallow in. Her mouth opened easily, eagerly, to him, inviting him into warm, moist places that made him think of other warm, moist places.

The burning of his legs was forgotten. The throbbing in his groin, as deep an ache as he had ever known, overrode everything else. He wanted this woman. He wanted to lay her down and open her like an anticipated gift, with care and tenderness and impatience all combined. He wanted to learn her secrets, every one of them, and fit himself into her world in the most intimate way he knew how.

He wanted to love her with his whole body, and feel her shudder with joy and release beneath him.

He wanted her.

And she seemed willing.

But just like that, the wounded part of him slammed on the brakes. No!

The word was as loud as a thunderclap. For an instant he thought he might have said it out loud. But it effectively doused his desire and snapped him back to his right mind. What the hell was he doing?

He dragged his mouth from hers and stared down into her flushed, soft face. Ripe for the plucking. But he didn't dare pluck.

Searching for whatever remaining grace he could find, he said huskily, ''Good night, Mary.''

And skedaddled out her door as fast as he could go.

Mary stood where he had left her, stunned. She felt as if a whirlwind had just ripped through her life and left everything in shambles.

She was shaking, filled with a longing stronger than anything she had ever felt before. That one kiss could do this to her was terrifying.

She stumbled over to the couch and sat. The shakiness made her feel weak, as if she'd just run ten miles. Or as if something terrible had just happened. Maybe something terrible *had* just happened.

Because she didn't want to do this again. She couldn't bear taking these risks again. And worse, she knew it would only be doomed anyway. Once he learned the truth about her, he would dump her like yesterday's paper.

She might try to tell herself that Chet had been weak, a useless excuse for a man. And in a lot of ways he had been. But she knew why he had left her. He had left her because she was responsible for the death of their child.

That was something nobody could forgive. Nobody.

Not even Sam, with his good heart and generous nature.

Most especially not Sam.

13

The valley burned. More of it was on fire now than not. Huge black scars marked the flames' passing, and the untouched green was diminishing hour by hour. The firefighters were exhausted. Supplies were arriving from all over the country, as were more firefighters, but everyone pretty much figured they were going to lose the battle in the valley.

They needed rain desperately. Heavy, drenching rains for several days, something that was all but unheard of at this time of year. Even a return to the regular afternoon thunderstorms would be an improvement. But the sky remained beautifully, stubbornly clear.

Nearly a week had passed since Sam had rescued Joe. During that week, victory against the fire had come close, then slipped away again. And now the flames were heading toward Edgerton Pass, toward the firebreak that had been built in the earliest days of the fire. Would it hold? No one was betting on anything anymore.

"They're sacrificing the valley," Earl told Sam when he came to work. "I talked to them just a few minutes ago. They're going to try to contain it there."

Sam nodded and took a seat facing the sheriff. "I figured that was the tack they'd have to take."

"Not many choices left. How are your burns?"

"They're fine." Ugly, but fine. Apparently they'd been just a wee bit worse than he had thought, because now they had a brownish look to them. But it didn't matter. He was getting around with no permanent damage.

Earl leaned back in his chair. As usual, it creaked and protested.

"Ever hear of oil?" Sam asked, his sense of humor not at its best so early in the morning.

"Yeah, but the chair hasn't." Standard response to the old joke. He sighed and looked at the contour map of the county. "We're in trouble."

"Could be." Sam didn't need it all explained to him.

"Fire danger's so high on our side of the mountains, all it'll take is a spark."

Sam nodded.

"It's time," Earl said, his voice heavy with reluctance. "We need to start telling people to get ready to leave in a hurry."

"I agree. Tell 'em to pack the stuff they can't replace so they can grab it and run."

Earl nodded and rubbed his eyes. "I've been worrying about it all night. I don't want to panic anybody, but..."

"I don't think they'll panic. These folks have figured out the risks by now. Especially the ones outside of town. Even if the fire doesn't leap over, one could start here from a cigarette butt or a spark from a chain saw. And from the looks of it, stopping it wouldn't be easy."

"Or maybe even possible. They need to clear brush and dried wood for at least eighty feet around their houses. How many do you think will do it?"

Sam didn't know. An awful lot of houses were built right under towering evergreens. Thick layers of dead pine needles that could flash into conflagration in an instant, covered the ground. How was any homeowner going to manage to clean all that up, as well as clear away brush and deadwood for eighty feet around his house? And what was he supposed to do with it if he gathered it all up? He couldn't burn it.

"Let's just make that an advisory," Sam said. "Let them that want to, do it. But with no way to predict if there'll be a fire, or if any particular home will be threatened by it..." He left the thought incomplete. "I guess we all need to pray."

"Yeah." Earl sighed and rubbed his temple with his fingertips. "I guess this must be what it's like to wait for a hurricane. Go? Don't go? Will it hit here? Will it miss? Hell. Get together with the fire chief and figure out what we should tell people. Then we'll have our guys distribute fliers on their patrols.''

The fire department had its main office on the other side of the building. Sam strolled over there with a cup of coffee and found Matt Dunegan bent over a bunch of maps not so very different from the one Earl had tacked to his wall.

Matt was in his late thirties, a compact guy with plenty of muscles stretching his uniform. The minute he set eyes on Sam, he said, ''Where's Earl?''

''He sent me over to see what you want us to tell people about the fire danger and possible evacuation. He's meeting with the county commissioners in fifteen minutes about the budget.''

''Yeah, I'm up for that next week. But right now we got bigger fish to fry.''

''Not as far as the commission is concerned.''

Matt made an impatient sound. ''If we get a fire going here, that tune'll change.''

''Well, of course. So let's do what we gotta do.''

Matt pulled one of the maps over so that it was right in front of them. ''First, evacuation routes. No surprises there. There's only three ways out of here right now, and two of them are to the north. I need you guys to plan on closing whichever routes we need to use to two-way traffic, so we can have all lanes headed out of here.''

"That's easy enough to do." Pulling his notepad out of his hip pocket, Sam made a note of that. "I'll make sure the neighboring counties will cooperate."

"Good. Now, it seems to me it would be wise to advise people to clear all combustibles from around their houses. Especially the folks living out of town in wooded areas."

"Eighty feet, right?"

"That's the ideal. I'm not counting on it. But if they want to try to protect their homes, that would be the thing to do. Or as much of it as they can. We're living in a tinderbox, Sam."

Twenty minutes later, they'd assembled a list of dos and don'ts and warnings to be handed out to everyone in the county. Sam threw it together on one of the station computers and headed out for the printers to have it photocopied. Two hours later, he was back at the office with five thousand fliers.

Earl returned from the commission meeting just after lunch hour. His face told the story. "Naturally they don't want to increase our budget, not even to cover cost of living raises."

"Naturally." It was an annual rite.

"I'll take another stab at it next week. As usual. What have you got for me?"

Earl reviewed the flier, nodding his approval. "Thanks, Sam. Let's have the day shift put in a little overtime tonight. I want to get these personally into the hands of as many people as possible."

So it was that two-thirds of the deputies were out

around dinnertime that evening, knocking on doors and handing out the fliers. And somehow it came about that the end of Sam's route brought him into the neighborhood where his father and Mary lived.

He hadn't seen either of them in the past week. Mary had evidently gotten her car back, because it was parked in her driveway. Seeing it sitting there suddenly made him conscious of how badly he'd behaved.

What the hell was he doing? He'd asked the woman out to dinner, then he'd kissed her...and then he'd avoided her like the plague. At the very least he owed her a giant apology for acting like a slug.

In fact, he thought, as he parked his car and worked his way down the street on foot, he had no excuse for burying his head in the sand this past week. Worse, he couldn't understand why he'd done it. It was almost as if he'd gone into denial about what had happened, as if he'd forgotten it.

Except that he'd never forgotten it; he just hadn't been able to *think* about it. Not at all.

Now it was staring him in the face, and he was feeling like a major jackass. Time to face up to it and apologize.

He left his dad's house for next to last and Mary's house for last. It wasn't cowardice but a clear-eyed view of what was likely to happen. With one or the other of them, if not both, he was apt to get involved in some kind of protracted encounter.

It was nearly dark when he walked up to his dad's house and knocked on the door. The last few fliers were in his hand.

The door opened, and Elijah stood there, looking tired. "Is this an official visit?"

Sam handed him a flier. "We're handing out instructions for what to do if we have a fire outbreak nearby."

Elijah nodded and took the sheet of paper. He scanned it. "Looks good. Come in, son."

Sam was about to refuse, claiming business, but the way Elijah stood back and held the door wide seemed to offer him no excuse. As soon as he stepped inside, though, he knew he'd made a big mistake.

Both the easy chair and the rocker in the living room were mementos from his childhood. The easy chair in which his father had always sat was looking a lot more worn and battered these days, but the rocking chair didn't seem to have changed at all. It was still furnished with the pillows his mother had painstakingly embroidered by hand, claiming that busy hands made for a peaceful heart.

Sam felt his throat tighten with a sense of loss. He missed his mother. He'd been missing her since the day Elijah cut him off. Oh, Belle had called him on the phone regularly, keeping in touch, but he'd never set eyes on her again. And that was Elijah's fault.

His eyes felt hot as he looked at his father.

"I miss her, too," Elijah said, as if he'd read Sam's face. He nodded to the rocker. "Every time I look at it I miss her."

Sam didn't answer, because he knew if he did he was going to say something about how his father had cut him off from his mother. And he didn't want to get into that now. He was, he told himself, past it. But like any man dealing with a poisonous snake, he wasn't fool enough to give the snake another opportunity to bite him.

Elijah seemed to be waiting for Sam to say something, but when he didn't, he offered, "Would you like to join me in a soft drink?"

Sam suddenly remembered Elijah's passion for anything carbonated. The man would even drink club soda straight on occasion. And tea. Iced tea with heaps of sugar in it, so much that Elijah had to stir the glass every time he went to take a sip, and it would still settle a half-inch thick at the bottom. "Uh, no thanks. I have to finish handing out the fliers."

Elijah nodded slowly. "I understand."

Sam had the feeling that he'd said the wrong thing; but Elijah had always given him that feeling, and he was past worrying about it. Or so he told himself.

He hesitated a moment longer, feeling as if he ought to try salvaging something from this ruptured relationship, yet also feeling that there was nothing left to salvage. The old man hadn't changed. Look how he'd reacted last week after Sam had saved Joe. More concerned about the type of person Sam had saved than about anything else. Elijah hadn't changed one little bit.

Shaking his head, he headed for the door. Some things could never be salvaged.

"Sam."

Elijah's voice stopped him, but he didn't turn to look at his father.

"Sam." Elijah repeated his name, sounding oddly helpless. "I didn't mean what I said. I was...upset."

"Sure." Sam turned. "You've always been upset with me from the time I can remember. I was never good enough for you. Never. And now you're going to expect me to count the value of a human life by whether you think the sin they've committed is beyond redemption? I don't think so."

He heard his father call his name again, but he was already out the door, striding across the street to Mary's house. He expected no better from her, since she seemed to be on his father's side, for some unknown reason. God, he would never understand a woman's mind. All of a sudden he didn't feel so bad about not having called her in a week. Complications like this he didn't need.

He rapped sharply on Mary's door, an official sounding thud. She answered a few moments later and looked at him expressionlessly. "Yes?"

He handed her a flier. "Recommendations in case we have a fire in the vicinity."

"Thank you." She accepted the flier, started to close the door, then hesitated. "I'm glad to see your legs are okay."

"They're fine." Turn and leave, he told himself. But now he couldn't even use the excuse of work. He was done for the day. And for some strange reason his feet felt rooted to the spot.

"Are you always so unforgiving?" she asked.

That about did it. Something in him seemed to crack wide-open. "What the hell are you talking about? My relationship with Elijah is none of your damn business."

"No, I suppose it isn't," she said frostily. "But I wasn't talking about that. I was talking about you and me. You're still angry that I defended him, aren't you?"

Well, he was. And the realization didn't sit too comfortably on his shoulders. "You answered the door like you didn't know me."

"How else was I supposed to act? You take me out to dinner, kiss me like there's no tomorrow, then walk away and don't ever call again. I'm not a disposable tissue, you know."

Now he was feeling about two feet tall, and he didn't like it. But there was no question that this time he deserved it. "I'm sorry."

"Really? Well, I suppose I can be about as forgiving as you are." She started to close the door.

"Mary, please."

She paused. After a moment she looked at him and sighed. "Oh, hell, come on in."

Mary didn't swear. He'd already figured that out, and it had him minding his own language, at least when she was around. If she was swearing, she was *really* unhappy with him.

He stepped inside and closed the door behind him.

"Have a seat," she said, nodding toward the sofa. She didn't offer him any refreshment, and she took the rocker, well away from him. And then she didn't say a word. She wasn't going to make this easy on him.

He supposed he didn't deserve for her to. "I'm sorry," he said again. "Can I plead confusion?"

"Sure, why not."

Unyielding. He got a glimpse then of the steel in Mary's spine. He had to admit he admired it, even when he was in trouble because of it. The thing was, he didn't know how to begin.

With his father, he supposed. It was the one point of certainty in the midst of something that felt like insanity.

"Okay," he said. "My father got my dander up."

"No kidding."

"I'm sure you can see why."

After a moment, she nodded. "Yes, I can. But I still think you misunderstood the direction of his real concern. And I am *not* a Pollyanna."

He had to admit that hadn't been a nice thing to say. "I'm sorry," he said again.

"You ought to be. Calling names is a juvenile way to argue."

"Yes, ma'am," he said meekly. "I admit I was mad. And I said some things I probably shouldn't have said. And I acted like a two-year-old, not calling all week. I was..."

What was he, exactly? He wasn't sure he could answer that question. Pissed at his dad, certainly, but there was nothing new in that. Pissed at Mary? Maybe a little, because she had tried to defend his father. Pissed at himself? Most certainly. He never should have kissed her.

Because kissing her had filled his dreams for a week now, and along with the waves of desire that nearly overwhelmed him every time he thought of how she had felt in his arms, a wave of panic would also nearly drown him. Care like that again? Only if he had a lobotomy.

So what was he doing trying to make peace with her?

"Well," she said briskly, as if the conversation was over, "I forgive you. Don't let me keep you from your appointed rounds."

He knew with gut-deep certainty that he couldn't leave things like this. No way. He would be miserable for days. Weeks. Maybe even months. Longer than that he refused to allow. He had to set things right with her, though he was damned if he knew why.

"I'm done with my rounds. I saved you for last."

It was a big admission, but he couldn't tell how she received it. Her usually expressive face was revealing nothing right now.

"Am I supposed to feel flattered?"

Ouch. This wasn't going well at all. Not that he could blame her. If he hadn't lost his mind and kissed her, he wouldn't be in this pickle right now.

But Sam was a nice person. A good person. And he didn't at all like feeling that he had wounded Mary. She didn't deserve it.

"I'm sorry," he said again, feeling like a broken record. "I didn't mean it that way. I meant that I wanted us to have a chance to talk. So I could apologize. I behaved badly."

She looked down at her folded hands for a moment. Finally she said, "Maybe I behaved badly, too. I mean, I shouldn't get involved between you and your father. You know him better than I. It's just that I saw how worried he was until you showed up, and he wouldn't be the first man I've known to express his worry by getting angry and acting like a jerk. I teach classrooms full of that type."

She was right, of course. He was guilty of a bit of that himself, and he'd known plenty of other people who were, too. But Elijah?

He supposed he ought to think about that. Except that thinking about Elijah always made him so angry he couldn't think straight. Now how did you noodle over a problem like that?

"I guess," he said slowly, "it would be fair to

say I'm not entirely rational where my father is concerned."

She gave a half smile. "I guess I should say that I can see why not. What he said to you when your wife died was awful."

"It was," Sam agreed without elaboration. What was there to say about it? Elijah's words had rung like a death knell in his heart.

"Of all people, a minister ought to know better than to say something like that," Mary said quietly. "I'm sorry, Sam. I can understand why you don't think his anger was driven by worry. I should have recalled that before I defended him."

Sam shrugged. "You're a kind person, Mary. You want to see the best in everyone."

"Maybe it's just a bad habit."

"Don't start thinking that way. You keep right on thinking the best. Most of the time you'll be right."

Then he felt an uncomfortable prickle of conscience. He was making it sound as if his father had no redeeming qualities at all, and that wasn't true.

"My father..." He paused. "My father's not a bad man. Not at heart. I know that, even though we have some serious differences. He was raised in a spare-the-rod-spoil-the-child house, and he pretty much carried that over to raising me."

"He seems like an angry man."

"He is. The way he was treated as a kid...well, today we'd call it child abuse and take the kid away. He did better than his own father, but he stayed pretty angry. Angry at injustice. Angry at sin. Angry at pretty much everything."

"Including you."

"I'm sure I deserved some of it. I was no angel." He rose from the couch and walked over to the window, pulling the curtain aside and staring across the street. The lights were on at his father's house, but no one was visible in the windows.

Mary spoke. "You can't blame yourself for your father's problems, Sam."

"I don't. But...I think the real problem was that because I deserved his anger so many times, I thought I deserved it *all* the time."

"And so you felt as if *you* had no redeeming qualities?"

"Maybe. I know I felt I couldn't do anything right. Sometimes I even gave up trying."

"That's understandable."

He heard the rocker creak, then saw her reflection in the window glass as she came to stand behind him. "I'm sorry, Sam. No child should have to deal with that."

"It wasn't all bad, you know. He was proud of me sometimes, like when I preached my first sermon when I was thirteen."

"You preached at thirteen?" She sounded amazed.

"It's not unheard of. Although now I wonder what I could possibly have had to say at that age that anyone else needed to hear."

"Sometimes we just need to listen to children. To know what's in their hearts and minds. It's a good thing."

"Yeah. Except he supervised the writing."

"Oh."

He saw her head bow a moment. Then she raised it again. "What would *you* have said if you'd written it?"

"After all these years, how would I know? I chose the text, though. It's funny, because I heard my father refer to it last week when he was lecturing someone. 'Let him who is without sin cast the first stone.'"

"That's a revealing choice."

"I guess. I was raised to believe that anything I did wrong was my fault, and anything I did right was because of God. So inherently I was bad and could only be good when God stepped in."

He saw Mary shake her head. "I hope you've gotten past that."

"I don't know." He dropped the curtain and faced her. She looked at him, sorrow in her gaze. Then, with a sigh, she returned to the rocking chair. "You know, Sam, nobody's all good or bad."

"I know that now. I think."

"I hope you do." Her face grew shadowed. "I've thought a lot about it. Probably because I deal with young people at the most difficult stage of life. But it seems to me that when God created us, he didn't make us little gods. He made us human. He created a flaw in us—and if he put it there, maybe it's not a flaw at all.''

"How do you mean?"

"We try, we stumble, we fall. We're not perfect. As I tell my students, the only time we fail is when we don't get up, dust ourselves off and try again. And sometimes I think that if we were all perfect, God would fall asleep at the wheel out of boredom. As a priest friend of mine once said, 'God loves a good story.'''

"I like that." He returned to his seat on the couch and crossed his legs, left ankle on his right knee. His gun belt was digging into his side, so he shifted a little and tried to ignore it.

"I like it, too," Mary agreed. "It doesn't always help, though. Things still…hurt. Sometimes almost too much to get out of bed in the morning. But if you think of watching a movie, how interesting would it be if everything in the story went perfectly? How many movies about perfect people who never have problems would we watch?''

"Very few." He smiled crookedly.

"And not only would God fall asleep, so would we. Or we'd die of boredom."

"That's an interesting way to look at life."

"Sounds good, doesn't it? Much harder to actually keep that perspective when things go sour, though."

He laughed because it was so true. "Amen to that. But it would always make sense in retrospect." He liked the way she thought about things. Either she was indeed the Pollyanna he had called her last week, or she had learned from experience. And something about the way she looked suggested to him that she had learned from bitter experience.

It was on the tip of his tongue to ask about her past—her marriage, in particular—but he swallowed the words. This accord between them was too new for him to risk upsetting it by prying. So he let the thought drift away on the gentle tide of comfort he was beginning to feel in her presence and promised himself that he would learn more about Mary later.

She seemed more relaxed now, too. As if their talk had eased some concern of hers. Maybe all she had needed was to be reassured he wasn't the total cad he had appeared to be.

So why was he reacting like a cad? His body was so aware of her again, so hungry for her touch. It had blown up out of nowhere, it seemed, needing only a moment of comfort to erupt like a smoldering volcano. Just like last time. But he wasn't going to react the same way. He wasn't going to grab her and kiss her and then walk away. Heck, he wasn't even going to get to the grabbing part, let alone the kissing part.

Because he had nothing to offer her or any other woman, however much he might want one. Most specifically her. His body might be waking up after the long night of grief, but his brain knew better than to listen. Too much pain down that road.

And he was beginning to sound like a broken record, even to himself. How many times did he need to remind himself? He wondered if he wasn't protesting just a bit too much.

Mary, apparently having decided to truly forgive his churlish behavior, asked him if he wanted any refreshment.

"Water, please," he said. Having a drink would give him an excuse to stay longer. He assured himself it was simply that he didn't want to go home.

She returned with a glass of ice water for each of them and sat down again. "I saw you go into your father's house," she remarked. "Did you get to talk?"

"Not much." He squirmed a little inwardly as he admitted that the brevity of the conversation had more to do with him than Elijah. "I guess I wasn't in a mood to listen."

"You don't make many excuses for yourself, do you?"

"Sure I do."

She shook her head. "I know excuses. You're taking the full blame for the lack of conversation on yourself. You're not even suggesting that the years of misunderstanding between the two of you might be at fault."

"Misunderstanding?" He repeated the word, musing about it a bit. After a few minutes he said, "Maybe it *was* misunderstanding. On both our parts."

"Some, maybe. And some may have been the typical unfortunate result of a father who wanted his son to turn out even better, while following in his footsteps."

Sam arched an eyebrow at her. "That's an interesting spin."

Mary smiled. "I've see a lot of teenagers dealing with a lot of parents. There's a great deal of conflict at that age, as kids are getting ready to break away from the family. Some of it's there in every family, but it's worse in families where one or both parents try to maintain the kind of control they had when their children were small. And a lot worse when a parent wants a child to follow a certain path."

"I can testify to that. Nothing but being a preacher would have been good enough."

"And that's the last thing you wanted to be?"

He gave a quiet snort, almost a laugh. "I got to see the job from the inside. A preacher should be a man of conviction, but when he has a family to feed, he winds up being a man of mainstream conviction, regardless of his private thoughts."

"You're saying your dad sold out?"

"I don't know. Maybe to some extent. I know that he had to be careful which ox he gored, because if he gored the wrong one, he'd have the elders at his door to call him back in line. They were particularly unhappy about sermons on the evil of wealth."

She arched a brow. "Wealth isn't necessarily evil."

"Of course not. Some people do a lot of good with their money. But no matter how he worded it, they'd get their dander up, saying he was implying that simply because they were well-off, there was something wrong with them. He never seemed to know how to answer that one."

"How would you have answered it?"

"That a rich man necessarily has more of an obligation to do good than a poor man."

She smiled. "I like that."

"It's true. But that probably would have been interpreted as Communist."

She laughed then, that beautiful sound that seemed to send sparkles running along his nerve endings. He could listen to her laugh by the hour.

"Basically you're saying you're in trouble no matter what."

"For a preacher, that seems to be the case. Dad tried not to knuckle under too much, I guess. Which is probably why we moved every few years. And I didn't like that, either."

"That's very hard on a child. So you're putting down roots here?"

"You better believe it."

She reached for her glass and took a sip. "Is being a cop better than being a preacher?"

"By a long shot. I still get to help people, but they're not as likely to argue with me." He said that with a smile, and again she laughed, as he'd hoped she would.

Hoping she would laugh again, he added, "I also get to swagger."

She did laugh again, her eyes sparkling. "How do you guys learn that swagger, anyway?"

"They put these gun belts on us. Then you have to hold out your arms when you walk so they don't keep banging on your gun or whatever, and pretty soon you're walking like the king ape."

Her giggle was a delicious sound, every bit as good as her laugh. And right now he felt more at peace than he could remember feeling in a long time.

Which meant it was time to go. If he hung around too long, he would get addicted. But he didn't budge, just smiled back at her.

Then her laughter trailed away, and she reached for the flier. "Do you think fire is going to be a problem around town?"

"I hope not. But the danger is awfully high, and there's no rain in sight."

"Plus," she said quietly, "they can't stop the fire in the valley. It might come over the pass."

"It could. The damn thing's been leaping firebreaks like they don't even exist."

"That's what I've been hearing. People are starting to get frightened."

"Fear's a good thing. Folks really need to gather up anything they can't replace, like photos and family Bibles and important papers, and be ready to run. It's just one huge tinderbox out there now.''

Mary sighed. ''My neighbors were complaining last night that they're not even allowed to grill with charcoal.''

''Not right now.''

''I can see why, but I guess they can't.''

''I hope folks don't ignore the restrictions.''

He liked the fact that she didn't even bother to say they wouldn't. Of course someone would think they knew better. It never failed. A lot of people seemed to live in a world of ''it won't happen to me.''

''I've got the day off tomorrow,'' he said, before he even knew the thought was forming. ''Would you like to go boating on the lake?''

''I'd love to.''

Her acceptance was unhesitating, but it seemed to him that behind the smile in her eyes a shadow lurked.

What the hell had happened to this woman in the past?

14

The following morning, getting the boat ready to take out proved to be an unnerving experience for Sam. He hadn't been out on the lake since Beth's death. Oh, he'd taken it to the lake and put it in the water so he could run the engine and change the gas and keep things in working order, but he hadn't cruised in it.

The idea had hurt too much. Beth had loved to pop out in the boat before dawn and fish, or go out in the twilight of the long summer evenings. The boat and Beth were as inextricably linked in his mind as night and day.

So what had possessed him?

He pulled the cover off and climbed aboard, glad to see that no mice or rats had taken up residence. There was a little dust that had managed to sift through the canvas, but not much.

It wasn't a big boat, but it did have a below-the-deck galley, and a vee-berth that he and Beth had never used. Beth had been into fishing, not spending hours on the water sunning or just enjoying the day. She'd certainly never wanted to spend a night on the boat. It was too confined.

Sam, on the other hand, had often wished they could spend nights on the lake, snuggled up in the small cabin while the waves rocked them to sleep. It had never happened. Now it never would happen.

Oh well.

He checked out the galley, put some ice in the icebox, along with some cold drinks, made sure he had coffee, and hit the store for some sandwich fixings.

He must be out of his mind.

But at least they weren't going out at dawn or dusk. He was taking Mary out at the height of a warm, sunny day. No memories there.

Mary was ready for him. He'd barely gotten out of his SUV before she was locking her front door and coming to join him with a basket in hand. She smiled and held up the basket.

"I made us some lunch," she said.

"Super. Thanks." He smiled, taking her in, and decided she looked good enough to eat herself, in matching emerald-green shorts and a T-shirt. On her head she wore a white ball cap, with her hair spilling out the small hole in the back. The sun seemed to set it on fire. He wanted in the worst way to run his hands through it and feel its warmth.

"I haven't ever been boating before," she confided as they drove up to the lake. "You'll have to tell me what to do."

"Other than wearing a life jacket, you don't have to do anything except enjoy yourself."

"But I can swim."

"Good. That water's really cold, though. Or if you fell over, you could knock your head. So when you're on the deck, wear a life jacket, okay?"

After a moment, she said, "I'm sorry."

"For what?"

"That was a really stupid remark, wasn't it? 'I can swim.'"

He glanced her way and saw her smiling with self-deprecating humor. "You're not the first, and you won't be the last."

"Ah, but I pride myself on my intelligence. And that was a stupid remark."

That was food for thought, but he hadn't quite worked through it by the time he backed the boat down the ramp and set them afloat on the lake. Besides, for a while there, he'd been overwhelmed by his memories. At one point, when he'd been backing the boat down the ramp, he'd looked into his rearview mirror out of habit and been shaken when he didn't see Beth.

He'd hit the brake and wondered if he was going to be able to do this at all. But then, as quickly as it had come, the moment passed. He was once again in the here and now, and he was about to go boating with a truly beautiful woman. And he was entitled to do that.

The last thought surprised him. It was so alien to his way of thinking that it seemed to come from somewhere else. He was *entitled* to enjoy himself? Never in his life had he felt that way.

But that was another thought that had to wait for now, because minutes later he and Mary were motoring out across the lake, the wind in their faces, and Mary looked as if she was having the time of her life. Her head was thrown back, soaking up the sun and the breeze, and her hair tossed wildly behind her. Enjoying her reaction, he stepped up a bit on the power, and soon they were zooming across the water, the boat slapping again and again on the small waves.

He took them on a full circuit of the lake, enjoying the power of the throttle beneath his hand, enjoying the way the boat skimmed over the waves for the first time in forever. Passing other boats, he waved, and their occupants waved back. Some of them he remembered well from times when he and Beth had been out here fishing. Others, most others, were visitors, people enjoying a vacation break.

But he couldn't keep speeding around the lake forever. Which meant he had to find a place to stop.

And stopping meant the two of them would be alone together. For the first time it seriously occurred to him that this invitation had been a dangerous one. A *really* dangerous one. Because they would have nothing to do together except talk. If he really couldn't resist being with her, he should have invited her to a movie. That would have provided two hours of entertainment, followed by another hour of talking about the movie. It would have been safe.

Out here it was silent except for the murmur of the breeze and the slapping of the gentle waves against the boat. And there would be nothing to do except talk.

He was afraid of where that might take them.

He was afraid of the vee-berth below. He was afraid of the paths his thoughts were going to have to follow if all he had to do was look at her.

He was flirting with catastrophe, and he had no one to blame but himself.

Nonetheless, he throttled back and found them a quiet, sunny spot not too far from shore, where they could look into the shadows beneath the pines or stare out over the lake and watch the other boats. It was the most private of public places, and he wondered why he'd ever flapped his jaws.

But Mary seemed comfortable and content. When they stopped, she smiled and leaned back against the cushions on the stern bench, looking as if she wanted nothing more than to soak up the sun. He threw the anchor over the side, then resumed his seat, trying not to stare at her.

She looked like an Irish goddess, he found himself thinking. An Irish goddess wrapped in an international-orange life vest. Her long, slender legs were stretched out, her skin the color of cream, so delicate and soft looking it might have been the petal of an orchid. Her arms were above her head, and for the first time in his life he noticed how vulnerable the soft skin inside the upper arm looked. Her eyes were closed, and she seemed oblivious of his gaze.

Good. Because he needed to drag his gaze away, to stare at the sunlight as it splintered on the water, to stare at the dark depths beneath the trees, to remind himself that reality was reality and dreams were dreams.

And that, as beautiful as dreams were, reality was painful.

Except that this morning it didn't seem painful at all. Not at all. It was as if dreams were bleeding over into reality and making everything misty with yearning.

She spoke, her voice quiet, without stirring a muscle. "This is wonderful," she said. "So peaceful and relaxing. I don't think I've unwound this much in years."

He was unwinding, too, but not into relaxation. Once again he dragged his gaze from her, but the woods and the water stayed in soft focus, as if they'd slipped the bonds of reality.

The boat rocked gently beneath him, making him feel drowsy, but an internal awareness kept him on tenterhooks so that he couldn't have fallen asleep even if he'd been able to stretch out.

She was right; it was peaceful out here. Away from everything. Another world.

Until the wind shifted and the sky began to darken again from the fire in the valley on the other side of the mountains. The smell of smoke seemed to rouse Mary, and she sat up. Reality was back again.

"That's scary," she said, looking up at the graying sky and smudged sun. "No matter how many times I see it, it's still scary."

"The forces of nature are terrifying."

"The hand of God."

"One way to look at it."

She arched her brow at him. "How do *you* look at it?"

"Nature's method of renewal. We just happen to be in the way."

She nodded slowly, seeming to hesitate, then asked, "Sam? Are you a religious man?"

Now it was his turn to hesitate. This wasn't something he thought about often. In fact, for many years he'd tried to avoid thinking about it, because every time religion came up in his head, so did his father.

"I don't know," he said presently. "I don't belong to any particular denomination."

"Because of your father. He gave you quite a distaste for it, didn't he?"

"I guess so. Or maybe I'm just a weird fish, swimming upside down and upstream."

"How so?"

"Well..." Well, how so? Good question. "It's

like…I'm spiritual, I guess. I believe. I've read the Bible more than once, cover to cover. It's just that…I seem to have a different take on it than most people. Or at least a different one than the church I was raised in.''

She nodded encouragingly. ''Tell me?''

That wasn't as easy as it should have been, which told him how little he'd formulated his ideas over the years. He had to search for words, and as he did so, he kept his gaze trained everywhere except on Mary. She was a bigger temptation than the apple in the Garden of Eden.

Finally he said, ''I see the Bible as a romance.''

''Between whom?''

''Between God and his people. The tribes of Israel in the Old Testament, the whole world in the New. It's as if…well, as if God wants our love desperately. And no matter how many times we get wrongheaded or turn our backs, he keeps coming back to us. Keeps calling us to him.''

''I like that.'' Her smile was soft, thoughtful. ''I can see that.''

''And Jesus. Jesus preached to the outcasts. The unwanted. The poor. Did you know that in those times, if you were sick you couldn't enter the Temple? Sickness or birth defect or deformity…all those things were considered a sign of God's judgment against a sinner. And sinners couldn't enter the Temple. Yet time and again Jesus healed the lepers and the lame and the blind, the people who were barred from the Temple, then sent them to the Temple to make an offering. He was speaking up for those people, telling them they were loved by God, too.''

She nodded. ''That's so true. But I never thought of it that way before.''

''Well, I've been thinking of it that way for a long time. And I got a great distaste for churches of any kind that turn their backs on the poor, the outcasts and the sinners. I think they're missing the point.''

''Your dad's church is like that?''

''A lot of them have been. He's been part of it, too. I used to get so angry at that phrase, 'love the sinner but not the sin,' because they used it as an excuse to judge and turn their backs, claiming that if they associated with sinners they were condoning sin.''

''But Jesus associated with sinners.''

''Exactly. Prostitutes, tax collectors, the lame and sick. Seems simple to me. Just like it seems obvious to me that if you're not a sinner, you have no need of a church.''

Mary nodded, and a little laugh escaped her. ''I couldn't agree with you more. It's not the saints among us who need the guidance. But not all churches are like that, Sam.''

''Maybe not. I don't know. I had my fill and hit the road.''

''I can understand that.''

He looked at her. ''Are you religious?''

"Very."

Another problem, he told himself. He wasn't going to get caught up in that morass again. But there was something about the way she'd heard him out, the appearance of a truly open mind, that made him wonder if that would really be a problem at all.

She let the discussion go, as if she had merely wanted to confirm something she had already thought. A bit of uneasiness nibbled at him, because for some reason he didn't at all like the idea that Mary might have found him wanting.

But he didn't know how to pursue the subject, to find out what she was really thinking of him and what he had said, without getting into areas that were apt to make him sound as harsh as his father on a tear in the pulpit.

As the sky darkened with soot haze, the day became chillier. It wasn't exactly cold, but the warmth seemed to have deserted the air, and the lake, which never got truly warm, seemed to suck up everything that was left.

Mary pulled off her life vest and reached into a canvas bag for a sweater. Like everyone who lived hereabouts, she was prepared for the changing mountain weather.

Sam thought about the fishing poles still stowed in the locker below but decided that was a journey too close to old memories. Besides, it wasn't the best time of day to fish, even with the hazy sky. At least that was a good excuse.

After a few more minutes Mary tugged a pair of sweatpants out of her bag and pulled them on over her shorts. The view was diminishing in more ways than one. Maybe he should just head back to the ramp, cut this outing short.

But Mary didn't seem to be impatient. In fact, she leaned over the side and looked down into the water, no longer the deep blue of morning but a steely gray.

"It looks so clear," she said. "Like you could drink it."

"I wouldn't advise it."

She laughed and straightened. "I know. I've been warned about all the parasites in mountain water. What a shame, though. It's hard to believe when we're so close to the tops of the mountains it all comes from."

"From the sublime to the ugly."

She glanced his way in surprise, then laughed delightedly. "You're right. From God to parasites. We *do* cover some territory, don't we?"

It struck him then how different she was from Beth. Beth, God bless her, had been a young man's dream: cute and interested in fishing, camping, hiking and hunting. Like that old joke: Seeking good woman with boat and motor. She'd been a buddy. A pal. A great friend. A great wife.

But he'd changed. He was more contemplative these days, more given to thinking about the issues of life and less given to being a sportsman. And he enjoyed the way Mary seemed to be able to talk about many different things. Beth had been right there in every moment as it turned up. She hadn't given much thought to yesterday or tomorrow.

Mary was different. She was in the here-and-now, too, but she kept a perspective about it, seeming not to lose track of the flow of life.

Beth, for example, had dismissed anything he said about his father with, "Well, he's not here right now." At the time that had seemed a healthy attitude. Now he wasn't so sure.

Because if there was one thing recent days had made him acutely aware of, it was that he needed to deal with his past. To deal with the anger and hurt he had nursed all these years. Otherwise he was never going to get past it.

Not that he wanted to dive into all that right at this moment, but Mary had made him aware of how much a product of his past he was, and just how much he was clinging to it. That wasn't moving on. That was refusing to move on.

So one of these days he was going to have to look it all right in the eye. But that could wait, because right now Mary was turning to him, smiling, and saying, "How about lunch? I'm famished."

He had kind of hoped they could eat on deck, but with the smell of smoke getting thicker, he led the way below.

The galley was small, the little booth table just large enough for two. The vee-berth, which had always looked small to him before, now seemed to loom like the hugest thing in the universe. He looked quickly away from it, trying to ignore the growing weight in his loins and the way Mary's delightful scent seemed to fill the small cabin, all the more acute because of the contrast to the smoke outside.

Even with the curtains over the portholes drawn back, the cabin was dim, so he turned on the light over the table. The battery could keep it going for several hours without any problem. When he and Beth had come out at night, they'd often lit the propane lantern on the gimble overhead, but he didn't want to do that now. They didn't need that much light or heat. Just the little electric light over the table would do.

Mary had packed potato salad, fried chicken and cheese-stuffed celery, a far cry from the cold cuts and loaf of bread he'd stuffed into the cooler. She'd even thought of paper plates and plastic utensils and—this really made him smile—a small red-and-white checked tablecloth. He left his own offering at the bottom of the icebox and brought out frigid cans of soft drinks for them.

They sat facing each other and dug in.

"This chicken is fantastic," Sam told her. It was succulent, crispy and flavorful. "The best I've ever had."

"It was my mother's recipe."

"Are your parents still living?"

She shook her head. "My dad was fifty-five when

I was born, and Mom was in her mid-forties. I was an unexpected blessing, they liked to say.''

"Brothers and sisters?"

"No. I was an only."

"Me, too. But I guess you figured that out." He tasted the potato salad and pronounced it wonderful. "Sometimes I think life would have been easier if I'd had some brothers and sisters."

"It might have spread your father's attention around a little."

"What about you?" he asked.

"I didn't mind being an only child. I had lots of friends. And to be honest, I'm not sure my parents would have been able to cope with more than one kid. They were great, loving, all that. But...they were older."

"There must have been times when that bothered you."

"I suppose. A lot of people thought they were my grandparents. And I can remember a few times when I envied the kids whose parents could play baseball with them. But my dad already had a heart problem by the time I was five. His health had seriously deteriorated by the time I was ten. It wasn't bad, though. It really wasn't."

"How old were you when he passed away?"

"I was a freshman in college."

"I'm sorry."

She nibbled at her chicken for a while, her head turned so she could look out the nearby porthole. He let her be, suspecting that she was thinking about something important. When she spoke, it was about a subject he'd been afraid to broach.

"Sometimes," she said slowly, "I think I married Chet in reaction to my dad's death. And Mom's illness afterward. I was suddenly very much alone in the world. Chet was somebody I could cling to."

"That's understandable."

"Maybe. It still wasn't the right thing to do." Her gaze drifted toward him, and she gave him a pained smile. "He was the wrong choice to lean on, and if I'd been using two brain cells at the time, I would have realized it. He was the last person on earth who could give me the security I was missing. He was too...needy."

"Maybe that's why you picked him. Because he made *you* feel strong."

Her eyebrows lifted, and her gaze drifted back to the porthole. "I never thought of it that way. Maybe you're right. In retrospect, I'd always thought I was just looking for something to cling to. But you might be right. That would explain why I picked him. Because heaven knows there was no way to cling to him."

"He must have had some redeeming qualities."

She gave a little laugh and scooped up some potato salad on her fork. "Sure. He was handsome. He was charming. He had a great sense of humor. And he played on the varsity baseball team. He was a pitcher, and he was going to the majors someday.

Only the majors didn't want him, and he had to take a job selling insurance. And then…'' Her face darkened, and she looked down. ''He didn't handle disappointment or hardship very well. Sad to say.''

Impulsively he put his fork down and reached for her hand. ''I'm sorry.''

She shook her head. ''I'm over it. I just don't like to think how foolish I was.''

But he had a strong feeling there was more to it than that. A lot more. There was something she wasn't telling him, something that kept her bottled up inside in a way no mere divorce from a guy like Chet could do. He tried to find a way to ask her, not because he was curious, although he was, but because he wanted to help her. To make her feel better.

But she squeezed his hand, then let go, and resumed eating. ''How about your marriage?'' she asked presently. ''It was good, wasn't it?''

''It was great.'' Then he added honestly, ''For the person I was then.''

Her head came up sharply. ''How so?''

''Well, I was thinking this morning…. I loved Beth with my whole heart and soul. But I'm a different person in a lot of ways now. If I met her today, I'm not sure it would have worked.''

''But if she'd lived, you would have grown together.''

''That's the idea.'' He shrugged one shoulder. ''It's also something nobody can guarantee.''

Then, realizing how that might have sounded, he hastened to say, "It's not that I didn't love her. It's not that her death didn't leave a gaping hole in my life. It's just that…I'm beginning to feel like a different person."

"Of course you are. Something would be wrong with you if you weren't growing and changing. I've changed a lot, too. I know I'd never give Chet a second look today if he walked into my life as a stranger. Yet I was madly in love with him. Or at least I believed I was." She shook her head abruptly. "That sounds bad. I'm not implying you weren't in love with your wife."

"I know." To his own amazement, he felt himself smile at her. "It's okay. I didn't misunderstand you. I *was* in love with Beth. No question. My situation was different from yours, that's all."

She smiled back at him. It was the most beautiful smile, holding so much warmth that he felt it all the way to his toes. And for once the klaxon in his head didn't start blaring a warning. Instead it remained silent, and a beautiful, almost forgotten kind of peace settled over him.

Maybe the gentle rocking of the boat was soothing him. Or maybe it was being with Mary. He couldn't say for sure, and he damn well wasn't going to question it. Not right now.

"It's getting darker out there," Mary remarked. Apparently she wanted to lighten the conversation for a while. He could handle that. In fact, he wouldn't mind that at all. Except the fire wasn't exactly light subject matter, except by comparison to their personal lives.

He turned to look out the porthole and was surprised to notice that the day had turned dim, a deep gray. "It must be burning worse."

"I hope it's not burning on this side of the mountains."

"Well, I can find out. I never travel without my handy-dandy police radio."

She laughed, as he had hoped she would. Instead of using his handset, however, he used the radio in the galley. Charlene, the part-time dispatcher, answered his call.

"Negative, Sam. It's not burning anywhere around here. The wind's kicking up, though, and from what I gather from eavesdropping on the fire teams, it's blowing up over there. The calls are starting to sound really frantic."

"Thanks, Char. You need me for anything?"

"Hey, it's your day off. Enjoy."

Sam turned off the radio and faced Mary again. Her expression had turned grave.

"Those poor men," she said.

"Yeah." The smoke had cast a pall over them, and he guessed that was just as well. They were in danger of getting too comfy-cozy with each other, and he wasn't sure either one of them wanted that.

They finished eating in relative silence, and Sam knew the outing was over. As soon as they cleaned up, he would head them back to shore. With the air full of gritty ash and the sun all but blocked out, there was no joy to be had on the lake today. Most certainly not when he thought of the men out there fighting that fire.

Cleanup was easy. Everything went into the trash except the leftovers, which he tucked into the icebox. Time to go above and hoist anchor.

But the galley was confined, and the boat was rocking rather strongly—some other boat's wake, he thought—and while he braced himself with practiced ease, Mary was not so fortunate. She fell to one side against the counter and cried out. Without thinking, he reached for her.

And then she was in his arms.

After that nothing else mattered anymore. Not the fire. Not the darkening day. Not the growing rocking of the boat. Not the past. Not even the future.

Just now. Only now.

15

She looked up at him, her green eyes at first startled. Then smoky mists began to swirl in them, and he felt her soften. An instant later his mouth was clamped over hers, drinking from her hot, moist depths almost desperately. When he felt her arms wrap around him, he knew it was all going to be okay.

She kissed him back just as desperately, tongues dueling in an ancient ritual, seeking to learn places where others weren't allowed. The tastes of their lunch mingled, until finally they gave way to the intoxicating scents of musk rising from their eager bodies. Hands grasped, arms clung, and Sam felt there was no way on earth he was ever going to get Mary close enough.

He knew an instant's surprise when he realized he had backed her up against the berth. But then he was reaching for her shirt and she was reaching for his with fingers every bit as impatient and eager. She was meeting him move for move and hunger for hunger, and he was sure he'd never been higher in his life.

The boat rocked again, tumbling them onto the berth. He managed to cushion her fall so she didn't crack herself against anything, and then they were in that most magical of positions, lying side by side, face-to-face, loins to loins. Her shirt was gone. His was gone. He had no idea where they were, and he didn't care.

But he did care about the next minutes. He didn't want them to be a race to the finish line. Drawing a deep shuddering breath, he caught her eager hands in one of his and held them over her head. Instantly she stilled, looking up at him from heavily lidded eyes.

His gaze swept over her, lingering at delicious curves and hollows. Her breasts, cased in simple white, were full and rounded, though not overly large. They seemed to beg for his touch, but he withheld it. Her tummy was flat and her waist narrow at the band of her shorts. The V between her legs was only a hint now, covered by layers of cloth. He toyed with the idea of stripping away the barriers, then decided to wait. His own sense of anticipation was too pleasurable. He wanted to make this last forever.

Her legs were, as he had noted before, perfect. Firm. Shapely. The prettiest ankles he could ever remember seeing. And all of that was offered to him. He must be the luckiest man on earth.

The vinyl covering of the vee-berth was cold and a little sticky against his skin. He thought of going to the locker for a blanket, then decided he didn't want to risk shattering this incredible moment. In fact, he didn't want to think at all.

The boat was rocking them steadily now, the darkening day outside seeming to lock them into a cocoon. Reaching out with his free hand, he traced the line of her ear and jaw, enjoying the little shiver that passed through her, loving the way her eyelids fluttered, then closed.

She was as lost in these moments as he was.

Her skin was soft, smooth, like finest satin. A little down, invisible, sprinkled her upper lip, and he noted it as his finger slid that way, feeling the added softness. Tenderly he traced her cheekbones and the bridge of her nose, then her other ear. She shivered again, and there was a hint, just a hint, of her entire body reaching up to him.

These moments were perfect.

Gently, with greatest care, he dropped little kisses on her eyelids, then brushed another across her lips. Her mouth tried to follow him, but he teased her, instead kissing her chin, then the base of her throat.

A little murmur escaped her, a delicious sound that he felt as much as heard. Lifting his head, he watched as his fingers traced her collarbone, the soft curves of her shoulders, then plunged lower, finding the little gap between her breasts, sliding his finger beneath the material. Teasing. Oh, how he wanted to tease her.

Another murmur escaped her, a little sigh, and a faint smile flickered across her lips. He smiled himself at her response as he slid his finger back and forth, suggesting but not delivering. The clasp was right there, and one little twist would undo it, but he didn't release it, keeping them both suspended in anticipation for just a bit longer.

Considering how much he wanted this woman, considering how hard and insistent the throbbing in his own body was, it amazed him that he felt so patient. So reluctant to hurry. So hungry to linger.

There was, it seemed then, all the time in the world to linger, but much as he wanted to suspend this moment for eternity, he couldn't stay there forever. He wanted her desperately, and his fingers had ideas of their own, anyway.

They strayed over the cups of her bra, causing her to draw a sharp breath, a sound that sent a shaft of delight through him. Even through the fabric he could feel her nipples stiffening in response to his lightest touch. Over and over he brushed them, until finally she whispered his name with exciting impatience.

"Please..." she whispered, and he could no longer deny her.

He popped her bra open with a twist of his finger and spread the white wings of fabric wide, discovering delights that were as beautiful as any dream he might have had. Her nipples, pink and swollen, were like small strawberries on mounds of whipped cream. Moments later, he found they tasted every bit as good.

With his tongue he teased them, loving the way she gasped and arched toward him. Tremors ran through her like shock waves, and his own body responded with a tsunami of desire, a crashing, deafening wave that swept him away.

Lingering became a thing of the past.

"Oh, yes," she whispered as his teeth gently nibbled... "Oh...more..."

With her soft cries and whispers encouraging him, he tried to devour her. As helpless as she, he pressed himself to her thigh, needing the touch, needing so much more.

Downward his mouth trailed, and at some point he let go of her hands. Then she was clutching his head, guiding him, grabbing at her own shorts to get them out of the way.

Exultant and demanding, he rose above her and tugged. Scraps of cloth flew over his shoulder, but he never noticed as her most precious treasure was laid bare: dewy promises amidst silken thickets of red. Awed, he reached out and ran his finger lightly along that moist cleft. She groaned and reared up, now yanking at his shorts.

He got them off somehow. How exactly he would never remember. Then her fingers closed around his silky, swollen staff, and his mind exploded. Then it was he who trembled and was weak. His thigh muscles quivered as he knelt between her legs, and he might have collapsed except that he couldn't bear the thought of this ending.

Nor did it end soon. Her hands touched him, lovingly, tenderly, yet very eagerly. Stroking him as if she knew exactly what pleased him most. Slipping beneath to other secrets until he felt as if she possessed every inch of him.

The boat was rocking more wildly now, but it seemed so much a part of the wild rhythms inside him that he didn't notice.

She was sitting before him, her legs wrapped around his, her hands dancing over his tenderest, hardest flesh. Leaning forward, she dappled kisses on the expanse of his belly until he could bear it no more.

He slipped his hands beneath her bottom and lifted her. Her eyes opened in sleepy surprise, and she clutched at his neck. Moments later, as if they had been made for each other, he settled her onto his manhood, sliding into her slippery depths, filling her and feeling filled all at once.

Their mouths met, lips and tongues almost frantic now. She had no leverage to move, and neither did he. Microscopic little movements of their loins together deepened the ache, increased the demand of their bodies, built the tension until it was almost unbearable.

It was torture. It was exquisite. Her head fell back and a low moan escaped her. He had never seen anything more perfect in his life. Never felt anything more perfect.

But finally, being only human, he could take no more. Lowering her back to the bunk, he stayed within her, propping himself over her on his elbows so he could see her face. Her eyes fluttered open and she smiled. Then she moved, begging him for more.

He moved together with her, not in opposition. The moments drew out and the passion built, their straining bodies reached mindlessly for satisfaction.

Then it happened, a cataclysm so intense that the blood roared in his ears. He jetted into her and heard her own cry of completion join the moan that rose from the depths of his soul.

He dozed briefly, feeling secure in a way he hadn't felt in a long time. She curled trustingly against him, and he held her tight, not wanting to let her go—ever. The rocking of the boat was like a cradle, and the peace that filled him was beyond anything he had ever known.

But eventually reality intruded. The vinyl was sticky and uncomfortable against his skin. He wished he'd spread out the blankets, musty though they probably were after all this time.

But the woman in his arms seemed to make all that irrelevant. He opened his eyes and found her green eyes staring back at him, a faint happy curve on her mouth.

"How are you?" he asked huskily.

Her smile deepened. "Wonderful. You?"

"Better than wonderful." He hugged her with delight, and a laugh escaped her. "This vinyl sucks, though."

"Just slightly."

"Let me get some blankets?"

"It might be better if you checked outside. I've seen some flickers that look like lightning."

"Damn."

She laughed again. "It's okay. We can go back to my place."

Knowing that the day wasn't over made it easier for him to let go of her, though not by much. He climbed out of the berth and pulled his shorts on. That was when he realized they were both still wearing their sneakers. He looked at his feet and laughed. She laughed, too, waggling her foot in the air.

"Don't do that," he cautioned. "I'll leap on you again. Do you have any idea how beautiful you are?"

Dim as the light was, he had the pleasure of seeing her blush. He also saw the teasing glint in her eye as she covered herself with her hands.

He was grinning when he climbed the ladder and looked out. What he saw sobered him immediately.

Ugly-looking thunderclouds blotted out most of the sky, and the day was no longer dark from smoke.

It had a green cast from the clouds. The water was choppy and whitecapped. And there was definitely lightning. Far away yet, without thunder, but probably marching closer.

He backstepped down the ladder and reached for his shirt. "We'd better get to shore. It's going to be bad."

"I can't think of a worse place to be during a storm."

"You got it." But he lingered to watch her rise from the berth, and he picked up her scattered clothes, handing them to her.

"It'd probably be best if you stayed down here," he told her. "No point in being a lightning rod."

"Okay."

Up on deck, he pulled in the anchor, then turned the engine over. Soon they were speeding straight across the lake to the ramp. All the other boats were gone now, their owners having prudently sought shelter.

He felt a little stupid for not realizing how the weather was changing. But he'd been more than a little preoccupied. The memory made him grin into the teeth of the wind.

Mountain storms blew up fast. As a child, he'd lived in places where you could watch the clouds build slowly over the course of a lazy summer afternoon, but here they often seemed to appear almost by magic.

There was still a thin line of blue to the east as

he approached the ramp, but the wind had kicked up, tossing the trees, bending even the big old pines. No rain yet. God, how they needed the rain.

Because of the wind, he needed Mary's help. He had her keep the boat from drifting away while he backed the trailer down the ramp into the water. He was glad when he could bundle her into the SUV while he finished loading and securing the boat, but he had to admit he was feeling a little exposed himself.

Because now the lightning was getting closer, and the last place he wanted to be was standing in knee-deep water. He lashed the boat as quickly as he could, then hurried to climb into the car himself.

Mary was looking at him with pursed lips. "I know I don't have to tell you how stupid that was."

"No, you don't."

"Okay." She smiled.

"It's all your fault, anyway."

"Mine?" She arched a brow.

"Sure. If you hadn't distracted me, I'd have gotten us back sooner."

"Oh." She was trying not to laugh; he could see it. "You're right. I'm a bad influence."

"Absolutely the worst. There oughtta be a law."

"In twenty-nine states, there probably is."

He started laughing. It felt so good to laugh again. To feel free to laugh again. And he had Mary to thank for that.

The trip back was uneventful. The skies continued

to darken and began to growl threateningly, but
there was no rain to make the pavement slick. They
stopped at his house to park the trailer and boat, and
he thought about inviting her in. But somehow he
wasn't ready to do that, so they left immediately for
her house. If she noticed his reluctance, she didn't
betray it.

It bothered *him,* though. After the afternoon he
and Mary had just spent together, he ought to be
willing to invite her into every dusty corner of his
life. Yet something held him back. Something kept
him from taking that step.

And he was no longer sure what that something
was.

They pulled into Mary's driveway, behind her little car. The lightning was flashing wildly overhead
now, and the booms of thunder were almost as sharp
as gun cracks.

They darted to the front door, neither of them
wanting to be out longer than necessary. Once inside, though, Mary opened some of the windows
enough to let the wind blow through, bringing in the
fresh scent of ozone.

It was dark inside, thanks to the storm, and she
was surprisingly reluctant to turn on any lights. As
if casting artificial light over them would somehow
disturb the enchantment she was feeling. The last
thing on earth that she wanted to happen now was
for reality to come barging back.

But she didn't know what to do. Should she offer him something to drink? Turn on music? Only minutes ago she had been feeling secure and safe with him, amazingly comfortable. But now all she could feel was awkward. What if he'd begun to regret their lovemaking? What if all he wanted to do was escape?

Time seemed endless as he stood there just inside the door. Longing to leave? Or feeling just as awkward as she?

But then he sat on the couch and patted the seat beside him. Feeling almost stiff, she sat, then felt everything inside her melt as he wrapped his arm around her and snuggled her to his side. It was okay.

For now. She absolutely refused to think about later until it shoved itself in her face.

Her ear was against Sam's chest, and she could hear his voice rumble deep inside as he spoke. "This has been a wonderful day."

"Yes, it has." Her heart squeezed a little as she wondered if he was working up to ending it now.

"And," he said slowly, "I don't want it to end. How about you?"

She could have laughed from sheer joy. "Me, neither."

"Good."

She felt him brush a kiss on the top of her head, and a thrill raced through her. She wished he would drag her off to bed again right now. And yet...and yet she wanted these quiet, comfortable minutes, too. Minutes that were making it feel as if this could last forever.

Making love with him had been an astounding experience, one that had lived up to her wildest youthful dreams, dreams that had been forgotten when her ex-husband had taught her otherwise. But with Sam it had been beautiful, passionate, almost exuberant. It had been an experience that she would carry as a touchstone for the rest of her days.

Part of her feared that if they made love again she would discover the first time had been a fluke. And part of her feared that if she shattered these peaceful moments in even the slightest way he would disappear like a genie who had granted his last wish.

That she could at once feel so conflicted and so peaceful amazed her. It was as if she were two people in the same body.

So she didn't move, except to snuggle closer. To wrap her arm around Sam's narrow waist and hug him back. How beautiful.

"Do you have any idea how beautiful you are?" he asked, echoing her thought. Lifting his other hand, he stroked her hair gently. "Like fire and mist."

The poetry struck her. She hadn't thought of him as the poetic type. But it also seemed extravagant, and she felt embarrassed. "I'm just your basic Irish-American."

"Really? I don't think there's anything basic about you at all. Not in the least."

She squirmed a little, unaccustomed to such extravagant praise. "Sam..."

"Just say thank you," he chided kindly. "That's all you have to say."

"Thank you," she said meekly.

He chuckled.

Then, feeling inexplicably impish, she added, "You're quite a stud."

"Stud?" His tone held outrage that quickly dissolved into more laughter. "So I'm a stud, am I?"

She dared to steal a look at his face. "Absolutely."

"Hmm. No one's ever said that about me before."

"At least not to your face." He was blushing; she could see it even in the dim light. She liked that.

Lightning suddenly brightened the room, so intense that Mary felt momentarily blinded. The crack of thunder that followed almost immediately made her whole house shudder. For long seconds all she could see was the afterimage of the flash.

"That was close," Sam said, as the rumble died away and along with it the shudder that had passed through her house.

"Yes." She held her breath, anticipating another flash. Or, worse, the sound of a siren that would indicate there was trouble. But all she heard was the rush of the wind and some car alarms.

"That's my alarm," Sam said.

"Don't go out there." Mary tightened her hold

on him. "Sam, that was too close for comfort. The alarm will stop in a few seconds, won't it?"

"A minute or so."

"Then just leave it." She could feel him hesitating, stiffening under her touch, but then he relaxed back into her embrace. "You're right. I tempted fate enough today."

She wondered if he meant his standing in the water while he positioned his boat as lightning flashed overhead, or if he meant something else. Maybe something else. Because she, too, suddenly felt as if she were tempting fate.

Maybe she ought to stand up and call a halt to all of this right now. But she couldn't bring herself to do that. Couldn't tear herself away from the feeling of contentment his arms gave her. The house shook again with another flash and rumble, but not as bright and loud this time. The car alarm stopped as suddenly as it had started.

Then even the wind seemed to hold its breath. The curtains stopped stirring, and for a few minutes the air was as still as a tomb.

The sudden hush was incredible, as if the whole world had stilled, caught between heartbeats.

Then, with a whoosh that blew the curtains straight out from the windows, the wind roared down on them with another blinding flash of lightning and deafening clap of thunder. Moments later Mary heard the occasional plop of large raindrops on her roof.

"Oh, I hope it rains," she said.

"Me, too." But Sam eased away from her, leaving her feeling bereft, and went to look out the window. The day was dark green; the streetlights had even come on, visible over his shoulder. Not wanting to be so far away from him, Mary rose, too, and went to stand beside him.

Raindrops were indeed falling, but only a few, each plop stirring up a little dust as it fell. Lightning crackled across the sky, a fork that left its afterimage imprinted on Mary's retinas. And behind it, the sky glowed green for a long time.

"I've never seen that before," she remarked. "That glow."

"I guess the air is really charged."

"It's going to start another fire, isn't it?"

"I hope not."

"This has been the strangest summer." The wind coming through the windows felt cold now, and Mary wrapped her arms around herself. The temperature drop was huge and sudden, the sign of a truly severe storm.

He wrapped his arm around her, drawing her close to his side, warming her and comforting her all at once as they stood and watched. The trees tossed violently, turning silver. Even a few fresh leaves were ripped away to skitter down the street. Dust was blowing now, clouding the air while the heavens eked out a few paltry drops of water.

"Let it rain," Mary whispered, a prayer.

"Amen," Sam answered. "Let it pour. Let it flood the streets and soak the woods."

"At least the storms are starting to build again," she said, trying to be optimistic. "Maybe the weather will come back to its normal pattern."

"We can hope."

Yes, they could, but she suspected they both knew better. It was going to take more than one good rain to make the world wet enough to be safe again. At this altitude the air was normally so dry anyway that the rain that fell would dry off quickly. At this altitude, water didn't hang around. It would run off quickly in all the brooks and streams that drained to lower elevations.

But her mind wasn't really interested in what the rain would or wouldn't do, nor was the rest of her. Her heart, she realized, had begun a slow heavy beating, and every last bit of her mind was acutely aware of how close Sam was.

Faintly she could smell his scent, and the aroma evoked sharp memories of their coupling on the boat. With those flashes of memory her insides clenched with hunger. With a thrill so deep it was almost painful.

She realized she was holding her breath, afraid even the slightest sound would fracture the spell. Then his arm brushed against hers, an accidental contact. But it reminded her of how good those arms had felt around her and awoke in her the deepest craving she had ever felt.

Common sense and reason fled, leaving her at the mercy of her most basic desires.

She turned to Sam, and in response he turned, too. They were face-to-face, only inches apart. Was she imagining it, or was he holding his breath, too?

Then their eyes met, and she knew she wasn't imagining it. He was feeling it, too. The magic. The spell. The hunger.

Reaching up slowly, she touched his face with her fingertips, tracing its contours with the lightest of touches. He drew a long, shuddery breath and closed his eyes.

Thus encouraged, she continued her exploration. She liked the sensation of his beard stubble beneath her fingertips and remembered it brushing her face when they kissed. His chin was firm, nicely shaped. She traced the fine crow's-feet at the corner of his eyes and found the soft skin of his earlobes.

Then her hands trailed downward, learning his strong neck, feeling the cords there tighten and relax under her touches. Then lower, down the throat of his shirt, to the sides, finding the tiny points of his hard nipples.

He drew a sharp breath, almost a moan. Feeling a bubble of happiness deep inside, she shoved her hands up under his polo shirt and found his naked nipples, brushing them lightly, pinching them gently, until at last a deep moan emerged from him.

Such a sensual man, she thought. Shoving her hands upward, she pulled his shirt over his head, and he raised his arms to help her. Naked now, the expanse of his muscled chest drew her. Feeling deliciously wicked and insatiably curious, she kissed him there, finding his small nipples with her tongue. The shudders that ran through him excited her even more and emboldened her. Gently she nipped him with her teeth.

It was like throwing gasoline on a smoldering fire. Almost before she realized it, he swept her up in his arms and marched with her toward her bedroom.

She had always wanted to drive a man crazy. It seemed she had succeeded.

16

The storm growled outside, rain spattering the windows, and lightning occasionally dispelling the gloom, but Mary hardly noticed. Curled up in Sam's arms, she felt more content than she ever had in her life. Their lovemaking had been spectacular, and now every inch of her body felt languid.

Sam seemed to feel the same way, for he had hardly moved since he had cuddled her close to him. He wasn't sleeping, which surprised her a little. Chet had always slept afterward. But Sam was awake, breathing restfully, his eyes half open. His embrace hadn't slackened at all; indeed, he held her as if he wanted to be sure she didn't try to slip away.

The moment felt so beautifully luxurious, and Mary smiled into Sam's shoulder. Perfect peace. Why couldn't it always be this way?

Because, said a nasty little voice in her head, you haven't been honest with him. You haven't told him

about yourself. And you know when you do he'll
bail out as fast as he can. Just like Chet did.

A sharp pang of fear pierced her, but she forced
it away. Life had given her little enough joy, and
she wasn't going to ruin what she was feeling now
by worrying about the ultimate cost. Not over this.
This was too precious, and it was worth every moment of heartache she was sure to face.

She wasn't often the type who refused to act according to perceived consequences, and it wasn't a
behavior she was likely to indulge often, but when
life handed her a bowl of cherries like this, she was
going to eat as many as time allowed.

Sam stirred, turning toward her so they lay face-
to-face, her head resting on his upper arm. He kissed
her forehead softly, then gave her a gentle squeeze.

"You're beautiful," he murmured. "And so passionate."

Pleased, she wiggled against him. "You bring out
the devil in me."

He gave a throaty chuckle. "In this case, I'd say
that's a good thing."

"I think so." She kissed his chest and looked up
at him, but all she could see was his chin. Her own
cheeks felt pleasantly tender from the rubbing of his
beard stubble, and her body ached in delicious ways.
If only this day would never end.

He spoke. "This is a perfect day for snuggling
like this."

"Cozy," she agreed, listening to the rumble of

thunder and the splatter of rain. Not much rain, just occasional smatters of large drops against her windows. But dark and thundery, and nice to be inside with nowhere to go. Nice to be inside with a lover.

"Much better than being on the boat," he said, a laugh in his voice.

"Oh, definitely. Much better than cleaning the cobwebs out of the garage."

"Was that what you were planning to do?"

She giggled. "Yes. During the school year I'm so busy I fall behind on things. Summer is for catching up."

"With cobwebs."

"Among other things."

"I'm glad I rescued you."

"So am I." Tipping her head up again, she found him looking down at her. Her heart caught, and a little sound escaped her.

"Yeah," he said, as if he could read her mind. For an instant he seemed to go far away, but then, with a little movement of his head, he called himself back and smiled. "I need a shower, ma'am. May I?"

"Help yourself." Even though she didn't want him to be that far away.

Apparently neither did he, because she found herself being drawn from the bed and guided into her bathroom. He didn't turn the light on, though, for which she was grateful. Even though he had touched every part of her body and had kissed many of them, she still wasn't ready to stand nude before him in bright light.

He turned on the water in the tub and let it run to heat up. "You're not supposed to shower in a storm."

"I know."

"I'm feeling invincible right now. How about you?"

She could only laugh. A short time later they were standing under the hot spray together, using a bar of soap as an excuse to touch each other everywhere.

As arousing as it was, Mary also found it to be a tender, caring experience. He washed her hair for her, making her feel special. Loved.

But she warned herself not to go there. That was a dangerous way to start to feel.

Sam, however, was not about to let her run away so easily. He toweled her dry from head to foot, and she realized that she was forever going to think of these moments when a storm rumbled outside. Forever.

He didn't have a change of clothes, so he put on what he had been wearing before. She changed into fresh shorts and a cotton sweater, grieving inside over the apparent end of their day together. Now he would go home, and she would be left alone, wondering if he would ever come back again.

But he didn't leave. Instead he suggested they make a snack. She had some microwave popcorn, and he settled on that. They carried the bowl into the living room and sat side by side on the couch, with the bowl on the coffee table.

It occurred to her that they weren't saying very much. The silence that had fallen between them was almost profound, as if they were both drifting away into their own worlds.

Of course they were, she thought sadly. He was probably thinking about his late wife, and she was thinking about a past that would forever make a future impossible.

He suddenly reached for the small black box that was clipped to his belt and looked at it. "I need to call in to work," he said. "Can I use your phone?"

"Of course." She tried to smile.

The bowl of cherries had just been plucked away.

The wind had carried embers over the top of the mountain into the valley north of Whisper Creek. There the embers had found plenty of dry pine needles to start a fire before the stingy drops of rain could put them out.

The flames skipped along the forest floor and began to climb tree trunks, dining voraciously on tinder that the dry spell had created everywhere. Pine pitch sent clouds of black smoke rising, but the air overhead was so cool from the storm that the cloud sheared and stayed low. For a while, no one saw it.

Then lightning struck a tall lodgepole pine a mile away, and it burst into flames. Squirrels and deer and even a mountain lion began to scatter, many instinctively heading downward to the creek that ran most of the length of the valley and gave the town its name.

In between the two growing rings of fire lay The Little Church in the Woods.

It was Deacon Hasselmyer who discovered the fire. He was on his way out to the church to check the lost-and-found box for his wife's sunglasses. They were very expensive, with three kinds of coatings. Mrs. Hasselmyer was very concerned about the amount of ultraviolet light that reached her eyes, because her mother and father had both had cataracts. Never mind that ordinary glasses could be treated to protect the eyes, the missus claimed that the light was just too bright anyway, especially during the winter, when it bounced off the snow at her from every direction.

The glasses were a minor thing to the deacon. If they made Ina happy, then let her have them. But replacing them was an expense he would rather not have to bear just now, since their twelve-year-old daughter needed braces and they'd just made a big loan to his wife's brother to tide him and his family over until he could find a new job. Not that the deacon had much hope of being repaid. He thought of it more as a gift.

Either way, it would be a great help if he could find those glasses at the church.

He saw the smoke when he was still a mile from

the church, and his stomach lurched. Another fire. He could have turned around right then and gone to town for help, but he was determined to get those glasses. Besides, there was a phone at the church he could use, and he would be there in just a couple of minutes.

It wasn't until he was pulling into the church parking lot that he saw the second fire. And figured out what was going to happen to the church if they couldn't put those fires out. It was enough to make him forget his wife's glasses.

At the door, he fumbled with his keys, his hands starting to shake. His grandfather had helped build this church nail-by-nail. It had been built in the days when small congregations didn't hire the work done but did it themselves from start to finish. It was a simple church, with white clapboard and a steeple, and a bell that had been brought in from Chicago. Each pew had been hand carved, and every one had a family name on it. There was more to be saved here than just a small church and a parish hall.

Finally getting the door unlocked, he stepped inside and hurried to the back office where the phone was. There he dialed 9-1-1.

"We'll get someone right on it," the dispatcher told him. "And you'd better get out of there right away."

Instead of fleeing, though, he dialed the pastor's number. Elijah Canfield wasn't at home, so the deacon left a message about the fire.

That was when he remembered his wife's glasses. He had to look for them first, and he was sure there was plenty of time for that.

He wasn't so sure they would be able to save the church.

The fire engines were already racing out of town before Sam made it to the end of Mary's street. He sped home, ignoring the speed limit so he could change into jeans, work boots and a heavier shirt; then he headed out toward his father's church as fast as he could go. The healing burns on his legs twinged as if in memory.

He was supposed to help organize the volunteers who were expected to show up to build a firebreak around the building. Where these volunteers were going to come from, he didn't know. But he knew one thing about Whisper Creek: for all its human, small-town flaws, when there was an emergency, a good many folks could be counted on to help.

The dispatcher had said something about calling the mine. They could call people who were off work. Or maybe even release some of their on-duty crews to come help. The churches were going to be called. The local businesses. Word would get out soon. He hoped it got out in time.

The forest service was going to be called, too, of course, but he wondered if they had any manpower to spare, what with the fire across the divide.

God. He found himself praying again, praying as

hard as he could. Why? It wasn't just that the town might be in danger now, the homes of a lot of people who had built in the small, wooded subdivisions north of the village. No, it was because he knew his father was going to head straight for the church the instant he heard about the fire.

As he neared the church, he saw what the deacon had seen and felt his chest tighten. The two fires weren't too big yet, but if they didn't control them soon, it was going to be a mess.

The fire trucks were parked in front of the church, and a handful of volunteers had already gathered, people who had most likely followed the trucks from town. The wind was blowing, complicating matters, and the smell of smoke was growing thick. Rain still spattered, as if each drop were reluctantly squeezed out by a resentful cloud.

He recognized Carl Hasselmyer, who owned a small bookstore in town and was deacon at this church. He'd rolled up the sleeves of his shirt and looked as ready as anyone to get to work. The others were miners he knew more by sight than name.

The fire chief came up to greet Sam. "We need to stall this thing where it is now. But the fire service isn't going to be able to get us any tillers quickly. They're using all the ones we have. So I asked Bucky Jones if he could send us some back-loaders and graders. Even some snowplows." Bucky was the manager of the local branch of the state highway department.

"Good. What did he say?"

"He's going to send everything he can. We need to carve our way back to the fire and start clearing."

"We need to clear around this building, too."

The chief nodded. "There are also some homes out that way." He cocked his head to the northwest. "But the wind is blowing to the east. As long as it stays that way, our problem is here. We don't want these fires hooking up."

"Right."

Already more volunteers were arriving, and Sam started organizing them into squads. A few minutes later a pickup arrived carrying spades and shovels from the two hardware stores. Behind it came another carrying chain saws and other assorted equipment that might be useful.

"Okay," the chief said. "For now I'm keeping the trucks here. We might need 'em to save structures. But I need some spotters to get out there and see if they can pinpoint where the fires are."

"What about the fire towers?" Sam asked. "Aren't they reporting?"

The chief shrugged. "I don't know if it's the storm or something else, but we can't get any radio response."

"Hell."

"We're blind, Sam," the chief said. "Blind as a bat. The ceiling's too low to send up a plane."

Sheriff Earl Sanders arrived then, bumping over some ruts as he pulled his car up. He greeted Sam and the fire chief. "I've got my deputies trying to triangulate the fires. We'll see what we come up with."

"Radio contact?" the chief asked.

"Problematic. They're under orders to get out here if they can't get through by radio."

"Good. Okay, here's what we need to do."

The map was spread out on the hood of the truck. Sam went back to organizing the steadily arriving volunteers, handing out shovels and saws, explaining what everyone needed to do.

Then, after what seemed like an interminable wait, the heavy equipment began to arrive. Rumbling up in a long line like bright yellow dinosaurs aboard flatbed trucks, they were greeted with cheers. Behind them, as Sam had feared, came his father.

Elijah climbed out of his car and stood looking at the church, as if he believed it would be the last time he would see it. Deacon Hasselmyer joined him, and the two stood with their heads bowed in prayer, an island of quiet amidst the swirling uproar around them.

After what seemed like forever the deputies began to arrive, sharing what they had seen from various points around the north end of the county. The chief and the sheriff drew pencil lines on the maps until they felt they had the fires triangulated.

Sam, watching, didn't think it looked good at all for the church. With all the trouble they were having controlling the fires in the next valley, he didn't see why they should have any better luck here, especially with no one to help but volunteers. And with radio contact so problematic, coordination was going to be nearly impossible.

"How are we going to coordinate?" he asked the chief.

"Hell. I guess we need runners."

"Clancy," Earl said, referring to one of his deputies. "I'll detail him to run messages." Clancy was older, someone Sam was sure that Earl didn't want doing any heavy physical labor.

A raindrop spattered in the center of the map, darkening one oval. No help at all.

Sam looked up at the sky, thinking what a false promise this storm was. No rain, but a ceiling so low they couldn't even send up the planes to drop fire retardant. No radio contact. Just a sky crackling with dangerous lightning.

The chief started barking orders, sending equipment in two different directions along the road. The crews Sam had organized were also divided up and sent out to follow the heavy equipment.

Sam, ready to depart with one of the crews, was stopped by Earl, however.

"You stay here, Sam."

"We need all the help we can get with the fire."

Earl shook his head. "Stay here. Make sure your father and his people don't do something stupid if the fire gets close. I'm counting on you."

Sam half wished Earl would count on someone

else, but another part of him was relieved. Very relieved. Because the bottom line was, he didn't trust anyone else to be able to deal with his father if the old man got stubborn. And regardless of the hard feelings between them, he didn't want to see Elijah die.

So he stayed behind, leaning against his car, near a pile of shovels and a chain saw that had been left behind so he could pass them out to new volunteers as they arrived.

Elijah and his deacon stayed on the other side of the parking lot, apparently still praying. Sam had never known anyone like Elijah for praying. That man could get into a prayer and totally forget to come out on the other side unless someone disturbed him. Maybe that was a good trait. All Sam knew was that as a child it had driven him crazy. At times he only seemed to get his father's attention when he'd done something wrong.

Elijah had always been busy. If not with his duties as a pastor, then with prayer and Bible study. That had been hard for a child to accept. It wasn't that Sam hadn't understood the importance of God. Hell, if there was one thing in his life he'd known from the cradle, it was that God was Numero Uno. Nor did that bother him. That was the way it was supposed to be.

But in his childhood he'd often felt there was God, there was Elijah, and there was the church—and nobody else existed, least of all little Sam. Even his mother had been bound up in her duties as pastor's wife, but she at least had always made some time for Sam. Elijah, on the other hand, had seemed to look down from his elevated existence only when he was angry.

Sam looked up to the heavens with a sigh and asked himself a tough question: How much of that had been a little boy's perception, born of a child's natural self-centeredness, and how much of it had been real?

He didn't know. Maybe it hadn't been as bad as he remembered it being. Maybe he was remembering a child's emotional reaction, all out of proportion to the truth. If so, did it matter? It had certainly poisoned their relationship.

He had poisoned their relationship. The thought jolted Sam, and he stared at it like a snake. Wait a minute. Wasn't that taking too much responsibility on a child's shoulders?

Maybe it was. But it remained that he unhappily recalled the times he had acted up out of anger and resentment, getting his father's attention no matter what it took. He'd become something of a wild child at times.

Maybe that had been a normal reaction, but he couldn't blame his father's harshness on his father alone. He had to accept some responsibility for it.

They'd been locking horns most of his life. It was hardly to be wondered at that they hardly spoke to each other anymore.

Well, if he ever had a child, he was going to make very sure that his son or daughter knew they were important to him.

And that thought jolted him, too. He'd banished all such thoughts since Beth's death. Where had that one come from?

But he knew. It had come from Mary. From his day with her. Thunder, quiet for so long now, rumbled again, and for an instant he felt he was back in her room, back in her bed with her.

The craving in his body was suddenly intense, but so was the craving in his heart. Oh, man, he couldn't do this again. He couldn't take this risk again.

But it seemed he already had. And for his sake, and hers, he was going to have to figure out soon what he was going to do about it. All he knew for sure right now was that his insides, his heart and mind, felt as if a storm even bigger than the one above his head was ripping them apart.

Just then another vehicle pulled up. Louis and Joe. They stepped out of the car, glancing uncertainly in the direction of Elijah, then came over to Sam.

"We came to help," Louis said. "We heard the church was in danger."

"It may be soon," Sam said. He explained the situation in quick, broad strokes.

"Then we'd better get started," Joe said. "We need to clear-cut, don't we?"

Sam nodded. "The ground needs to be clear eighty feet around the building."

Louis whistled and looked around at the way the forest crowded in on the old church. "That's a lot."

"Then there's no time to waste," Joe said. Ignoring the preacher and the deacon, he went to pick up the chain saw. "I'll cut. You move. Are we gonna get anymore help?"

"I imagine so," Sam said. "I just don't know when."

"Okay," said Joe, "here's how we do it. I'll cut the trees. Do you have a chain so you can drag the trunks away? Or do I need to cut 'em up?"

"I have a tow chain that'll probably work. When we get some more help, we might need to cut them up. I don't know. But let's just worry about what we can do right now." Sam paused. "You *do* know how to cut a tree down?"

"Hell yes," said Joe. "Who do you think cleared the lot for our cabin? And cut all the timber we used to build it?"

Sam felt a smile crease his face. "My man," he said.

Joe laughed and pulled the cord on the saw. It roared to life, and he headed for the first tree.

Sam was in the back of his SUV, pulling out the tow chains, when Elijah came up beside him. "What can we do?" he asked.

"Joe's going to have to cut the limbs off the trees so I can move the trunks. Load them into the back of the deacon's pickup and dump them on the far side of the road.''

He doubted his dad was up to any such thing, but at least it would keep him busy.

Then it struck him: that had been the first time in his life Elijah had ever asked *him* what he should do.

The first tree went over with a crack. Joe started sawing off the limbs, the roar of the chain saw occasionally drowned by a roll of thunder. Sam and Louis helped his dad and the deacon load the limbs into the back of the truck.

While Joe went to work on the second tree, Sam and Louis were chaining the first to the back of his truck. Driving carefully, Sam hauled the cut timber to the far side of the road, more than a hundred feet from the church.

At this rate, Sam thought, they didn't have a chance in hell of finishing a clear-cut.

He drove back across the road and climbed out of his car as Joe started trimming the second tree. Elijah and Deacon Hasselmyer—Carl, that was his name—finished unloading and came back over, too.

"Dad?"

Elijah turned to him, his face tight with worry.

"We need more help, Dad. Is there any way you can get in touch with the folks from your church?"

Elijah turned to Carl Hasselmyer. "Carl?"

"Let me call my wife. She can start the phone tree."

Sam spoke. "We need chain saws, trucks, shovels. Tow chains. Tillers of any kind. Brush cutters. Gasoline for equipment."

Carl nodded. "I'll do what I can."

"Thanks."

The deacon trotted away, leaving Sam and his father to look at each other. Overhead, lightning forked and thunder rumbled. The chain saw whined as Joe cut another limb.

Elijah, for the first time in Sam's memory, looked almost humble. He spoke. "Will you join me in a prayer?"

It was surprisingly easy to say yes. "Sure."

Elijah took his hand, and again Sam was jolted. He couldn't remember the last time his father had taken his hand, and the touch...well, the touch offered a kind of comfort he hadn't felt in a long, long time. Then Elijah shocked him even more. He turned to Louis.

"Will you join us, too?"

Louis's expression echoed Sam's surprise. "Are you sure I'm good enough?"

"The Lord reached out to the outcasts," Elijah said. "It was to the poor, the lame, the sick and the unloved that he came."

Louis reached out hesitantly with both hands and closed the prayer circle. Sam wondered if that had always been his father's viewpoint or if this was some kind of change in attitude. And for the first time it occurred to him that he and his father might really need to talk.

Elijah bowed his head. For a moment it seemed as if he were at a loss for words. He stood there, holding Sam's hand in his right hand, Louis's in his left. They were, Sam thought, two of the people he seemed least likely to pray with, and it was as if his father was reluctant to launch into one of his patented shake-the-rafters-and-yank-the-tears prayers. Instead, after a long pause, he spoke almost too quietly to hear.

"Our Father, who art in heaven..."

Mary watched as Sam tried to bring the spoon of soup to his lips. His hand shook, and soup spilled over the side, splashing back into the bowl and onto the tablecloth. He seemed about to clench his jaw until she reached out and took his hand in hers.

"Nervous?" she asked.

He shook his head. "I've been running a chain saw for hours. I can't stop shaking." He let out a grim chuckle. "I wonder how loggers do this every night."

"I shouldn't have served soup."

His eyes rose to meet hers. "No, Mary. The soup is fine. It's delicious. Really."

He'd shown up at her door an hour earlier, just after ten, covered in dirt and soot, his hair thick with wood chips and sawdust. He'd apologized for his appearance and the unexpected visit, but she'd shushed him and dispatched him to the shower. Looking through the pantry while she listened to the water rushing through the pipes, she'd settled on a family-size can of chicken noodle soup as the fastest hot meal she could prepare. When he'd returned, looking more like a human being and less like a barroom floor, the soup had reached a thorough boil and cooled to serving temperature.

Now, it seemed, she'd prepared exactly the wrong thing. He drew the few drops of soup that were left in the spoon into his mouth, then tried to get another spoonful. Once again, muscles that had spent hours adapting to mechanical vibrations continued to quiver. It was, she realized, much like a sailor who comes ashore and, having grown used to accommodating the roll of a ship's deck, was wobbly on solid ground.

"Don't starve because of manners," she said quietly. "Just drink it from the bowl."

"Duh," he said with an embarrassed smile. "I guess that chain saw shook my brains around, too."

"You're just tired, Sam," she said as he lifted the bowl to his lips. "Will you be able to save the church?"

"I hope so. It's an incredible amount of work to clear an eighty-foot firebreak around a building. When I left, we were maybe a quarter done. The next crew of volunteers left their headlights on so they could work all night."

"Are you sure that's safe? I mean, working with power equipment is hard enough in full sunlight."

He shrugged and took another sip of his soup, sucking a noodle between his lips. "I don't see as how we have a lot of choice. Not unless God wants to dump a pile of rain on us to put that fire out, and He seems to be letting us handle this on our own."

Mary nodded, stirring her own soup absently. "Well, you're not going back tonight. I won't let you."

His eyes fixed on hers. "I have to, Mary. They need every hand we can get out there. We finally got through to the spotters at about six, and they said the lightning had sparked off three other fires. If they get together and start pulling draft before we finish that firebreak, the fire will sweep right down this valley."

"Sam, you're exhausted. You can barely feed yourself. If you go out there, all you'll do is get hurt." She bit off the word again.

"I'll be careful," he said, lifting the bowl to his lips again. As he went to return it to the table, however, his quivering hands betrayed him, and it dropped with a *thud,* splashing the hot liquid onto the tablecloth and into his lap. "Damn!"

Mary was up and moving even before his curse crossed his lips, grabbing a dish towel and running it under cold water. "Here," she said, handing it to him and returning to the sink for another towel to clean off the table. "Use this to wipe yourself off before you burn."

"It's not that hot," he said, dabbing at his trousers.

Mary whirled on him, her eyes flaring. "Damn it, Sam Canfield, stop fighting me when I'm trying to look after you! You may think you have to prove your manhood to your father, but you don't have to prove it to me!"

She regretted the words as soon as she'd said them, knowing they'd cut too close to the quick. And knowing even more that they weren't deserved, not over this incident. Her eyes fell. "I'm sorry, Sam. That was cruel."

"Damn right it was," he said. He rose to his feet, dropping the towel on the table. "I've got to get back."

She stepped between him and the door. "Sam, *no!* You can't even hold a bowl of soup, for God's sake. Let someone else be a hero for tonight."

He drew up short, looking down at her, his eyes steely in his fatigued face. "I've got news for you, Mary. I'm no hero. Not at all. I'm just doing something that needs doing, like a couple hundred other people are doing out there right now. I don't get any special exemption just because I'm Sam Canfield."

"But they're all going to take time off to sleep!"

"They're all going to take time off to go back to work. In the mine."

She looked at him, something inside her shriveling. He was furious with her, she realized. And it was all because she had shot off her mouth. She was fatigued, too, from worry and fear for him, but that still didn't excuse her. "Sam, I said I'm sorry."

"Apology accepted." But nothing about him softened, and he started to pass her on the way to the door.

"Sam?"

He paused.

She bit her lip, fearing the pain she was opening herself up to with the question she was about to speak. "Sam...why did you come here tonight?"

His back was to her, and for endless seconds he didn't move. "I wanted to see you."

Her heart skipped a beat. "Then please don't go."

He shook his head. "Mary, this isn't working. I'm too tired. You're tired."

"Exactly. So crash for an hour or so. I promise to wake you up. I'll even set the alarm if you want. But you need some rest."

Finally he turned to face her. "All right," he said. "I'll crash on the couch. But only for an hour."

"Good." That much at least made her feel better. He couldn't leap right back into firefighting with nothing but a bowl of soup in his belly and no rest. She got him a blanket, then left him alone in the living room. Returning to the kitchen, she decided to use the time to make him something heartier than soup. A couple of thick sandwiches. He was going to need them.

And then she wondered why she hadn't just let him go when he'd been ready to. Because he was just going to go anyway, eventually. Now was as good a time as any.

With an aching heart, she began to make sandwiches.

Sam didn't exactly sleep. He was too wound-up. But he lay in some sort of netherworld, his thoughts running around in circles while his body relaxed bit by bit. With his eyes closed, it was almost as refreshing as sleep.

Or would have been if it hadn't given him so much time to think.

Mary's accusation wouldn't leave him alone. He should have been able to brush it off as words born of fatigue. He'd certainly never felt insecure about his masculinity. Never. It was something he didn't even think about—or hadn't since high school.

But Mary's comment had struck hard, as if she had caught on to something he hadn't recognized himself. Could he feel as if he had something to prove to his father still?

Well, of course he could. In those terms, it wasn't even a surprising comment. He'd never been able to please the man, and with someone like that, you either kept continuously trying or you gave up completely. He thought he'd given up years ago, when he left home.

But maybe Mary was right. Maybe he hadn't really given up, and his father's return to his life had awakened all those old fears and feelings.

It wasn't a thought that made him feel good about himself. After all, he liked to believe that he had matured over the past years.

Cripes, he probably needed a shrink to help him through this. How did you deal with leftover feelings and reactions that went back so far in your life? How did you get past the knee-jerk reactions and responses when you were hardly aware of them? When they seemed so right?

"Sam?"

Mary's voice drew him out of his uncomfortable reverie.

"Sam, it's been an hour. Are you sure you don't want to sleep longer?"

He opened his eyes, knowing he wasn't going to sleep tonight. He had to save that church. Maybe Mary was right. Maybe he just wanted to prove what a man he was to his father. He didn't know anymore, and he was too tired to sort it out right now. All he knew was, he couldn't let that church burn.

"I'm fine," he said, and managed a smile. God, she was beautiful, even with fatigue drawing her face. Beautiful and intelligent and...uncomfortable. What was bugging her? "I'm sorry I got so steamed before."

"It's okay, Sam. I have no business popping off like that. I'm no psychologist."

He sat up and reached for her hand, drawing her

down beside him. Then he gave her a hug and dropped kisses on her cheek. "I'm feeling like a bear. It's my fault. But my arms aren't shaking anymore."

She smiled at him and kissed his cheek back. "Good. And I made you some sandwiches. You can eat them here or take them with you."

"Thanks." He brushed a tendril of her hair back from her cheek, then hugged her again. He couldn't remember that it had ever felt so good to hug anyone. Not ever. He just wanted to sink right into her embrace and forget the rest of the world even existed. But that wouldn't save the church.

"I'm sorry. I have to go."

"Sure. Listen, just stop by here when you take your next break. I don't want to be worrying when you're safe at home, okay?"

"I promise." But he noticed she didn't invite him to stay with her. Maybe his reaction had turned her off for good. The idea pained him, but he didn't know how to pursue it, especially right now. This wasn't a good time for a heart-to-heart. Not with that fire raging.

So he let go of her, hard as it was to do, and accepted the sandwiches and bottled water she offered, and got out of there as fast as he could.

Because he was in danger of forgetting his duty. In danger of forgetting everything. And all for Mary.

It wasn't a happy state of mind.

17

Morning brought dreary skies and worse news. Several of the fires had joined up, creating a wall of flame to the west of the church, and that wall was marching east, toward them. Fire was also spreading toward the subdivisions a few miles north, and most of the fire-fighting effort was being concentrated there.

"Of course it is," Elijah said, when a deputy gave them the news. "People's homes are more important than one church."

Elijah appeared exhausted. He'd caught a few hours of sleep on a church pew during the night, but even in the rosy dawn light he looked ashen.

"Dad," Sam said in his best I'm-the-cop-and-I'm-in-charge voice, "you're not looking good. You need some real rest."

"I can't leave while my people are trying to save the church."

There were about fifty of them now, all members

of the congregation, few sure what to make of Joe and Louis, who were working as hard as ten men. They took their cue from Elijah, though, and were at least civil.

''Then go sit in my car. Roll up the windows and breath some air-conditioned air for a while. This smoke isn't good for anybody.''

And it *was* getting thick. Sam's eyes were burning, not quite as badly as if he were cutting an onion, but badly enough. And every breath he took was making his chest feel raw inside. He'd begun to wear a handkerchief over his nose and mouth, annoying as it was.

Elijah looked as if he were going to argue, but after a moment his shoulders slumped. ''All right. For just a few minutes.''

Sam didn't argue with him about how long. He figured once his dad sat down in the SUV and started breathing air that was relatively smoke-free, exhaustion would probably knock him out.

They had a complete circle around the church cleared now. Men with shovels were digging up dirt to bury stumps. Another man with a small tiller was walking slowly back and forth, turning the dirt and burying the pine needles and dead leaves. They were a long way from an eighty-foot barrier, but it didn't look as hopeless as it had yesterday afternoon.

People were getting tired, though. Dangerously tired. Mary was right; they needed to be extra careful dealing with the chain saws. No building was worth having someone lose a limb, much less his life.

Pulling out a whistle, he blew on it. Break time. They all needed to sit and rest. Have a drink from the fountain and tap inside. He just wished he had some food to offer them.

Reluctantly, it seemed, or maybe just wearily, saws were turned off, tools were dropped, and groups of people straggled toward the church hall.

They needed more helpers. They needed food. And nobody was about to give up, as near as he could tell.

Miraculously, almost as if his thoughts had summoned them, several trucks arrived carrying older women. They climbed out and began toting ice chests and covered bowls into the parish hall.

"The church looks after its own."

Sam turned his head and saw Carl Hasselmyer. "You set this up?"

Carl shook his tired head, a smile lighting his grimy face. "The missus did. Knew she would."

Remembering all the church suppers he had attended as a child, Sam realized he wasn't really surprised. The women had probably been working most of the night to make food. They didn't look as exhausted as the men did, but their eyes were redrimmed and weary.

The food had an energizing effect, though. The hungry and fatigued men began to perk up. To talk a little, to move a bit faster. Sitting at the long picnic

tables in the church hall, they gorged on food and
water and began to sound more like a social meeting
than a fire-fighting team.

Soon the church's urn was full of fresh-perked
coffee, and the women were delivering large foam
cups of coffee to all the people at the tables. Sam
accepted a cup for himself and found it thick and
strong. The caffeine jolt was just what he needed.

Unfortunately the arrival of breakfast had caused
Elijah to abandon Sam's SUV. Now he wandered
around the hall, talking to everyone, expressing his
appreciation at how hard they were working. Joining
in prayer circles one after another. Eating nothing
and drinking nothing.

At first Sam felt irritated: Elijah needed to take
better care of himself. The man was getting up in
years and didn't have the resilience anymore to work
himself nigh unto death.

But as he stood there drinking his coffee and eating a fresh-baked cinnamon roll, he realized something else: Elijah had always been this way. Always
ministering and taking care of his flock, whatever
the self-sacrifice. And for the first time, Sam realized
that it was not selfishness on Elijah's part.

His father felt called to the ministry. Maybe he'd
made some mistakes prioritizing in the past, or
maybe Sam had simply wanted more than he'd had
a right to.

No. He shook his head at that and looked down
into his coffee. Maybe the Catholics had it right, he

thought. Maybe a man who wanted to devote his life to the ministry didn't really have room for a family. Maybe if you were Elijah, and didn't see it as a nine-to-five job, you ought never to marry.

But that didn't make Elijah a bad man. Or did it?

Fatigue was clogging his brain so badly that Sam gave up trying to sort through it. He grabbed another cup of coffee and another roll, and waited for the caffeine to hit his system. All he knew was that Elijah's dedication was real. Apostolic, even. Heck, the Bible never did say what happened to Mrs. Simon-Peter and all the little Simon-Peters. They must have existed, since Peter's mother-in-law was in the Bible.

Imagine what Mrs. Peter's reaction must have been when her husband announced that he was taking up with some itinerant rabbi. Probably something to the effect of, "Simon, how am I supposed to feed the kids? Who's going to pay the tax collector?"

Sam almost laughed at the mental image he got, then sobered as he realized he was getting a little punch-drunk. Not good. Another cup of coffee and maybe a couple of those sausage links.

"Sam?"

At the sound of Mary's voice, he whirled around, nearly spilling his coffee. "Mary? What are you doing here?"

She was dressed in hiking boots, jeans and a

heavy denim shirt. Work gloves peeked out of her front jeans pocket. "I came to help."

He didn't know what to say. Part of him wanted to tell her to go home and be safe. This day was apt to become dangerous if that wall of fire kept marching this way. Yet part of him was touched that she was willing to come out here and help.

"Don't tell me it's not women's work," she said sternly. "We may not have the upper body strength of you guys, but there's plenty we can do anyway."

"The thought never crossed my mind." No, the thought that crossed his mind was, How many of the people he cared deeply about did he want out here risking their necks?

"So tell me what to do," she said.

"Take a break. Everybody's eating right now. We'll go back to work in a few minutes."

"Mary!" Elijah joined them, giving her a smile. "What are you doing here?"

"I came to help. You look like you need some rest, Elijah."

"We all need some. But there's no need for you to—"

Mary shook her head, silencing him. "Every hand can help, mine included. And don't get paternal on me. I'm in better shape than you are."

For an instant Elijah looked stunned; then he gave a weary laugh. "I can't argue with that, my dear."

"In fact, you look about ready to drop. That won't do anyone any good, Elijah."

What the hell?

As soon as he finished gassing up his truck, he went over there.

"What's the holdup?" he asked, his voice cutting over the others'.

"There's a bear cub in the tree," the man holding the chain saw said.

Sam's first thought was to look around and wonder where momma bear was. As far as he knew, they were never more than a few feet from their cubs, and they were fearless about protecting them. "Where's the mom?"

"Haven't seen her," the man answered.

"Sam," Mary said, "we can't cut that tree down with the cub up there. No way."

He suddenly had the worst urge to laugh, to throw up his hands and just roar. Fatigue, he reminded himself. He wasn't thinking clearly or reacting normally. Get a grip, man!

"Mary..." He didn't quite know what to say. "Leaving that tree there would be like leaving a match. It's too close to the church. The fire could leapfrog, no matter how much we manage to clear-cut."

"We've got to get it down."

"How? Only a mother bear can get a scared cub down a tree. Where the hell is she, anyway?"

"Maybe she got hurt. Why else would he be alone?"

Good question. Sam peered up into the tree and,

at a height of about thirty feet, saw the cowering cub. Man, it didn't look like it could be very old.

The man with the chain saw spoke. "We mess with that cub and we might find out where the mother is. Real quick."

There was that possibility, too. But Sam had to admit, he didn't want to hurt the cub, either. Nor did he want to render all their efforts useless by leaving a tower of tinder so close to the church. He sighed and rubbed his weary eyes, trying to think.

"Sam," Mary said, pleading, "we've got to get that cub down."

"I know." He bowed his head a minute, then looked at the men. "Keep clear-cutting, but leave this tree for now. I'm going to get help."

The men shrugged and went off to work on a different tree. Mary tightened her hold on his arm. "What are you going to do?"

"Hell, I don't know. I'll think of something." Looking into her eyes was like drowning, he realized. He could feel everything in the world slip away, leaving him in this tiny bubble of silence as he fell into those green pools.

Danger. "Give me a minute," he said.

He was halfway back to his car when he had a thought. Hurrying inside the hall, he looked for the phone, praying it still worked. A dial tone greeted him when he picked up the receiver.

Thanking God for small mercies, he called the

local vet, Barry Geffen. "Barry," he said when the vet picked up, "I've got a small problem."

"How small?"

"It's about the size of a bear cub. A small bear cub."

"Hmm, that could be a *big* problem."

"Well, it kinda is. It's up in a tree we need to cut down to stop the fire. And its mother is nowhere to be seen."

"Yet," Barry corrected him. "Nowhere to be seen *yet*."

"Well, that thought does cross my mind, when my mind works. But I don't want to cut the tree down with the bear in it."

"No…"

He waited, but Barry didn't say anymore. "Can you come up here and tranquilize the cub? So I can get it down?"

"I was afraid you were going to say that." But Barry laughed. "Sure, I'll leave my waiting room full of dogs and cats and run out there."

"Barry…"

"I'm just kidding. I'll explain to my patients. Or rather, to their parents."

"Thanks. We're at The Little Church in the Woods. Do you know where that's at?"

"I have a passing familiarity. Give me twenty or thirty minutes, okay?"

"Thanks, Barry."

When he stepped outside, everyone was still

working as hard as they could, although he was beginning to see a fatigue lag again. And the tree with the cub now stood in splendid isolation, surrounded by fallen timber. Poor thing must be terrified out of its wits.

The smoke was getting thicker, too. He felt his chest tighten up the instant he stepped outside and pulled the handkerchief back over his nose and mouth, for what little help it offered.

Elijah had finally collapsed, sitting on a stump, head bowed in exhaustion.

"Dad, go home."

Elijah lifted his weary head. "No. I'm waiting to spell Mary."

Sam's eyes sought her out and saw that she was still walking strongly behind the tiller. "Looks like it'll be a while before she needs you. At least go inside and try to nap."

But the stubborn old man wouldn't move, and Sam gave up. It would be easier to move a mountain than to move Elijah.

Barry showed up as promised and got out of his pickup with a rifle. Sam stopped hooking the log up to the chains behind his truck and went over to greet him.

"Thanks for coming, Barry."

"No problem. I don't have any really sick patients at the moment anyway. Take me to the cub."

Together they walked over to the tree. Mary joined them in looking up at the poor little bugger.

"You know," Barry said, "its mother put it up there to be safe. It won't come down until she calls it."

"I doubt she's going to do that in the midst of this crowd," Mary remarked.

"No kidding. Well, you better alert everybody. Because if that cub squalls when I dart it, Big Mamma might not be so worried about all the people and equipment."

"Maybe I should move most everybody inside for a break."

"Might be a good idea. And while you're at it, get out your shotgun, Sam. You never know."

Sam agreed. He blew the whistle and told everyone to go inside for a break. Of course, not everyone listened. There were the requisite number of guys who felt they could help. Or who wanted to see. He gave the most trustworthy of them his shotgun.

Mary, too, refused to go away. She wasn't just curious though. Sam could see the genuine concern in her face and eyes. She was really worried about the cub.

"Okay," Barry said, "I'm going to tranquilize it."

"Not so much that it falls out of the tree," Sam cautioned. "I'll go up and get it."

Barry looked at him over the stock of his rifle, the feathered dart sticking out the end. "This isn't an exact science, Sam. It's not like I know the cub's weight. We'll get what we get. And I might remind you that even a drowsy cub can do a lot of damage with its claws.''

Sam nodded. He'd seen what bear claws could do once when some idiot tourist got too close trying to take a picture. "I don't have any illusions.''

"Are you sure about that?''

There was a crack as Barry fired his rifle. An instant later the bear caterwauled, a heartrending cry. Instinctively everyone looked around for the mother bear. No sign of her.

"Thank God for small favors,'' Barry muttered, lowering his rifle. He kept his eyes fixed on the cub above. "Okay, he's all yours, Sam. By the time you get up there, he should be out, or close to it.''

Sam ran to his truck and got a backpack out, figuring he could use it as a sling to carry the sleepy cub. Then he started climbing. From beneath he heard Mary murmur, "Oh, please...be careful, Sam.''

It had been a long time since he had climbed a tree, but Sam seemed to remember that getting up was easier than getting down by far. Especially if you needed to carry something down. Ah, well. After this was all over, he was going to get his head examined. He wondered if he was going after this cub for its own sake or for Mary's. Mary's, probably. He was beginning to get an idea he couldn't deny that woman anything.

Sam felt the branch break free before he heard the crack. Instincts honed decades ago now reacted before he had time to think. His fingers tightened around the narrowing trunk, and he hooked it with one foot, pulling himself close to it even as the branch gave way beneath his other foot. Immediately he looked down to see where his father was. And that was old instinct, too, he realized.

In that instant he was transported back to the summer of his eighth birthday and the day when he had looked down upon the world from the perspective of a bird, right before a limb had snapped and sent him tumbling, unsure of which way was up but knowing very well which way was down. When he'd hit bottom, it seemed as if his father had been waiting for him, although he later learned that he'd been knocked out by the impact and his father had come dashing across the lawn, roused by his thin cries as he bounced off one branch after another. It had seemed ludicrous at the time that his dad had reached for a switch from the fallen branch and cracked it across Sam's bottom. Hadn't he already been hurt enough? he'd wondered.

But such had been his instruction in right and wrong for as long as he could remember…one sharp whack, not hard enough to leave a mark or bruise, but hard enough to send the message of disapproval, loud and clear. That was the message Sam had grown up hearing most clearly. The few times his father had expressed pride or affirmation paled by comparison to the dozens of times he'd expressed disapproval and criticism.

Sam shook his head as he looked down. His father was nowhere to be seen, of course. He was inside the church with the others. Still, as he recovered his balance and his breath, it was as if he could already feel the snap of the switch across his buttocks. Disapproval.

Anger and a fierce determination flowed into the void left as the fear of the moment passed. He looked up. Only another ten or twelve feet to the cub, which was now looking down at him with vaguely curious eyes clouded by the effect of the tranquilizer. Finding another stable foothold, he shifted his weight from his hands and reached up to grasp another branch. He wasn't eight years old anymore. Lives depended on him now, including the life of this one cub. He hefted himself up and resumed the climb.

As he drew closer, he realized the cub wasn't at all sure what to make of him. Its cries had long since stilled, but its eyes seemed to be focusing better. The tranquilizer was wearing off. Too quickly.

"*Shhhhhh*, it's okay little guy," he half whispered, half grunted, as he pulled himself within arm's reach.

He was, he realized, also within paw's reach. The bear's claws were not yet the four-inch scythes they would be when he was full-grown, but even at two inches they looked plenty sharp and more than plenty dangerous. Animals could sense fear, Sam knew, and tended to react in kind. He kept his voice low and even, as he might speak to a small child.

"Good boy. I'm here to help you. Nobody's gonna hurt you." He reached out, palm up, to trail a hand over the bear's shoulder. "Gonna get you down so you can go find your momma. How does that sound, little guy? You and Momma can hide out from this nasty old fire."

The smoke and heat were denser up here, and he took a moment to glance around. They had less time than he or the people below had realized. Already embers were settling on the tops of trees only a hundred yards away.

"We need to hurry, kiddo. So I'm gonna give you a piggyback ride down this tree."

The bear nuzzled his hand for a moment, then dragged a soft tongue over his wrist. Sam held very still, feeling its hot breath on his skin as it exhaled. Finally it looked at him and let out a low moan, like the sound of metal bending under strain.

"Yeah, I'm scared, too. So we'd better get moving, my little friend."

He found a crotch to wedge himself into for balance, then put his hands under the cub's forelegs at the shoulder and lifted slowly. Its moan rose in pitch, as if it were asking, "Are you sure you know what you're doing?"

"Not especially, little guy. I'm kinda winging it. But we'll get through it together, okay?"

As he drew the cub nearer to him, it reached out

to sniff his face. Its timing could not have been
worse, for he was in the process of ducking his head
forward to maintain his balance. Its nose poked him
right in the eye, causing both bear and man to jerk
away at a time when rapid movements were anything but reassuring. The cub let out another groan,
this one not as quiet as the others. Loud enough for
momma to hear if she were nearby, Sam thought,
regaining his seat in the crotch of the tree.

"Hey there, sport. Let's not do that again, okay?
Momma would be really mad if we fell. And my
daddy wouldn't like it much, either. Or that cute
woman down there. So let's you and I take this slow
and easy, okay?"

By now the cub seemed accustomed to his scent
and his voice. Its broad tongue swept over his face,
and Sam laughed. "Yeah, well, save the thanks for
when we actually get *down*, okay, kiddo?"

Wrestling the cub into the backpack turned out
not to be as difficult as he'd expected. It seemed by
now happy to have warmth and contact, even if that
contact was human rather than ursine. He nestled it
into the bag and shrugged the straps over his shoulders backward, so the cub was snuggled next to his
chest.

"Now comes the hard part, little guy. But you
already knew that, right?" He reached beneath him
with one foot, finding another branch, and held on
to the trunk with both hands as he lifted his other
foot over the branch he'd been sitting on. "Come to

think of it, you must think I'm pretty dumb. You knew the getting up here part was easy, and here I'm feeling so good about getting to you. But we'll find a way down. I promise."

The cub merely let out another of its low moans and nuzzled its bristly nose against his throat.

"Yeah, I know. You'll believe that when you see it."

As if the forest itself were also replying, a hot ember floated on hot updrafts like a cotton ball in a windstorm and settled on the back of his hand. Sam wanted to smother the ember against his leg, but he couldn't yield the handhold. He gritted his teeth as the cherry-red ember sizzled against his skin, finally finding another grip and yanking his hand away. The burning fleck of bark came free as his hand moved, but the damage was already done. Sam groaned through clenched teeth, upsetting the cub, which began to struggle.

Gasping a deep breath, he pulled the cub's head to his shoulder and tried to offer a reassuring coo. But the cub's adrenaline was up, its head turning this way and that as if it were looking for a way out.

Or trying to identify the new danger, Sam realized.

"Here, see?" he said, holding his hand in front of the bear's face. "Just a little burn. That's all."

The bear sniffed the burned flesh, then looked at him.

"Yeah, it hurts like hell. Maybe that woman down there will kiss it and make it better. But first we gotta get down there within kissing range. Okay, kiddo?"

Footholds grew firmer as he descended to the thicker, stronger branches. Trying as best he could to favor the burned hand, Sam felt the cub soften against him, its head on his shoulder, quieter now, and still.

"Just a little more, kiddo. Just a couple more minutes and you can go find momma."

His shoulders and fingers ached from the strain of the descent. The cub wasn't heavy, but it was awkward and forced him to keep his center of gravity farther from the tree. His good hand felt along below him for purchase as the toes of one foot found another sturdy branch to settle on. He lowered himself and repeated the process, again and again, until Mary's voice broke his concentration.

"Sam? Are you okay?"

The cub looked around for the source of the new human sound, rocking Sam off balance.

"I will be once I get out of this tree," he called. "But if y'all would be quiet and not disturb junior here, that'd be a lot easier."

She didn't reply, and he looked down to see if his words had stung. If they had, it didn't show on her face. Instead her hands were clenched together at her mouth, as if she were shushing herself.

"Get Barry over here. I need to lower this little

guy down to him before I jump down. And he seems relaxed, but he's also wide-awake now. So keep everyone away when he gets loose.''

Mary nodded and backed away, then turned and ran to the church. In a moment she and Barry returned. Sam put a finger to his lips, but it was too late. The cub had seen them and moaned again, looking at Sam as if it had been sorely betrayed.

''They're friends, too,'' he said. ''I can't jump out of this tree with you. We'll both get hurt. So you need to trust me on this one, little guy.''

The cub didn't look convinced. Neither did it look disposed to fight the issue.

''I don't like this any more than you do. But that's about the best I can offer, sport.''

It flopped its head on his shoulder again and let out a huff of resignation. Sam pressed a quick kiss to its ear and worked his way the last few feet down to the lowest branch he could find.

''He seems to like you,'' Barry said from beneath him.

Sam looked down and smiled sheepishly. ''Yeah, well. Lemme find my balance here and I'll let you have him.''

Be careful, Mary mouthed silently.

Wedging himself in as best he could, he shifted his arms out of the straps, drawing a groan of consternation from his charge.

''I know, but it's the only way.'' Sam rubbed the bear's scruff and ears. ''I got you this far, didn't I?''

The cub's response was to look down, then back up at him. Another rising groan.

"That's right, kiddo. I'm going to lower you down to Barry there. He's a doctor. He'll check you out to see if you're okay, and then you can go find momma."

The cub looked down again, as if accepting the inevitable. Sam felt a surprising tightness in his chest as he eased the backpack away and down. He leaned down as far as he could, gripping the branch with his good hand as he lowered the bundle toward Barry.

Mary's voice cut the quiet. "Sam. Your hand."

"Not now," he whispered as the cub twisted to look at her, pulling him off balance. Pain tore through his shoulder as he fought to regain his foothold. "We can worry about that once I'm out of this damn tree."

His feet once again set, he lowered the cub again.

"I've got him," Barry said. "Let go, Sam."

It was, Sam realized, easier said than done. He met the cub's eyes. "I'll be down right after you, kiddo. I promise."

And with that he released his charge into Barry's hands. The tightening in his chest grew into a fist as the cub let out a single howl. Sam scrambled to lower himself the last few feet to the ground, then knelt beside the cub as it rolled in Barry's arms.

"*Shhhhhhh...*I'm here, little guy. You're safe now." He looked into the woods as a wind shift swept smoke over the clearing. "As safe as any of us are, in these woods," he added grimly.

"He seems okay," Barry said as his practiced hands examined the cub. "But you need to get that hand looked at. It's blistered, Sam."

"It'll be fine," Sam said. "We don't have as much time as we thought. That fire's closing in fast."

"You'll get yourself to the doctor," Elijah said, having come out of the church. "There's plenty enough of us here to do the work. Get yourself to a doctor, son, and stop acting like a damn fool. You're hurt!"

Sam felt something snap inside, driving him to his feet. A distant part of him realized he was over-reacting. But pain and exhaustion numbed his self-control. He whirled and met his father's eyes.

"Everyone's hurt out here. People are hurting all over this mountain, Dad. Sometimes God or the universe doesn't give a damn whether we're hurt. Sometimes we just have to suck it up and press on." He paused to draw a breath, and his father began to respond, but Sam yelled over him. "That fire isn't going to take a break because I'm hurt, or you're hurt, or anyone else is hurt. There's work to do and too little time to do it. So I'll leave when the work's done and not a minute sooner."

"I always said your sinful pride would be your undoing," Elijah said.

"You always said everything, Dad. But you never

listened worth a damn. Well, I'm not an eight-year-old boy anymore, and you're not the cock of the roost. Mom's dead because you were too busy preaching and praying to notice when she started hurting.''

"Your mother died of cancer," Elijah thundered. "In my arms, Sam. *In my arms!*"

"My mother died of loneliness, Dad. She died of being the pastor's wife, always smiling, always willing, always taking care of everyone else and too afraid of you to speak up when she felt those first cramps inside. She died because everyone else's pain was more important than your own family's. If you'd taken her to a doctor—"

Elijah cut him off with a stinging slap. "Don't you *ever* talk to me like that, boy. If you hadn't been so damn busy carving out your own life as far away as you could get, you'd have known we went to the doctor the first time she felt a lump. It was already too late, Sam. Don't you *dare* blame me for your mother's death. God just took her home, and it ripped my heart out."

"You never had a heart to rip out," Sam said.

"That's enough!" Mary said. "Just shut up, both of you! Shut up. *Shut up!*"

Both of them froze and looked at her. Her fury seemed to be shooting like sparks from her eyes. "You're scaring the cub!"

Sam immediately looked down to see the cub struggling against the backpack straps in which it had entangled. He squatted at once and started talking in a soothing voice.

"Don't worry about it," Barry said. "The more scared he is of people, the more likely he is to live to a ripe old age. Let's just load him up in the cage in the back of my truck. I'll let him go down south, away from the fire."

But Mary had another concern. "Is he old enough to make it on his own?"

"I don't know," Barry admitted. "But he deserves the chance, and it's clear his mother isn't around. The alternative is life in a cage."

Mary nodded, though she didn't look happy about it. "I guess you're right."

"At this time of year," Barry said reassuringly, "they depend mostly on vegetation. I'm sure he knows how to forage."

"Okay."

Sam scooped up the tangled cub and talked soothingly to him as he carried him over to Barry's truck. "You're going to be all right, kiddo. You'll see. Barry will leave you someplace with lots of berries and stuff."

The cub made a mewling sound and struggled against the confinement of the straps and backpack. Whatever was left of the sedative was gone now, and strength was coming back into those limbs. Sam made quick work of putting the cub into the cage and disentangling him from the straps. Those two-inch claws were beginning to pose a real threat.

A minute later, Barry drove off with the cub.

Mary came up beside Sam. "Thanks for saving him."

"It was the right thing to do."

"Let me see your hand."

But he didn't hold it out. "Just a small burn. It's nothing."

"Sure." Her eyes were sparking again as she looked at him. "I can't believe the things you said to your father, Sam. You're every bit as bad as he is."

Sam, suddenly feeling ashamed, agreed. But before he could answer her, she was marching toward his father and poking a finger at the old man. "As for *you*," she said, "you've said some pretty unforgivable things to your son in the past. You two are as alike as peas in a pod."

Then she stormed off to the church hall, even as workers were beginning to reemerge to take up their tools.

Sam, feeling more ashamed of himself than he could remember feeling in his entire life, would have apologized to Elijah, but the old man was already stalking stiffly away to pick up a shovel and start pouring dirt on a tree stump. A chain saw sprang to life with a roar, and the cub's recent treehouse felt its bite.

Later, Sam thought. He would apologize later. Right now they had a fire to worry about.

18

Night had fallen. The clouds to the west glowed a dull orange. Sam was so drunk with fatigue he didn't dare handle anything more dangerous than a shovel. Someone else, a fresher volunteer, was driving his truck to pull the cut timber across the road. The stack was growing, but the clearing still wasn't big enough.

Sam paused, wiping his brow. Was the temperature rising? He didn't want to think about it; there could be only one reason for it to rise at this time of night.

They had a new group of volunteers. After the mine shift let out, people had begun arriving to replace their tired neighbors. Mary had gone home about six, trembling with fatigue. Elijah remained but was slumped on a pew in the church, incapable of doing another thing for a while.

And Sam was getting there. He hadn't had any sleep except for that hour-long doze at Mary's last night. Every muscle in his body was shrieking a protest at every little move.

He'd been trying to get Elijah to go home for a rest most of the day and hadn't succeeded. And all of a sudden, as he stood there almost brain-dead from fatigue, he heard Mary's voice saying, "You two are as alike as peas in a pod."

The thought stung him, but so did the realization that he was no good to anybody in his current state. He went looking for Joe and Louis. The two of them had returned a couple of hours ago, after taking a break most of the day to sleep. They had showed a lot more sense than he had, his numbed mind admitted.

They didn't exactly stand out in the dark, with everyone looking so strange between the dull orange glow of the sky and the harsh glow from headlights. The whole place looked like it had come from an alien planet. He came upon them at last and waited for Joe to finish cutting a tree down.

"I'm taking my dad home," he told them when he got their attention. Everybody knew about the relationship now. How could they not?

"Good," said Louis. "And get some sleep yourself. You're no good to anybody now."

"Yeah. You two take over, okay? Here's the whistle." He pulled it from around his neck and passed it to Louis.

Louis looked at it doubtfully. "Will they listen to us?"

"If they're not fools," Sam said flatly.

"Don't worry, Sam," Joe said. "We'll take care of it."

He was sure they would. "Call me if you need anything." He handed them a card with his pager number. Joe stuffed it into his pocket.

"Now go, go," Louis said, making "go away" motions with his hands. "Before you collapse."

Back in the church, Sam found his father slumped in a pew. He touched the old man's shoulder, trying not to startle him awake, but Elijah wasn't asleep. He looked up slowly and said, "I'm getting too old."

"You're getting too tired, Dad. So am I. Let's go home and get some sleep."

This time Elijah didn't argue. Maybe because Sam was going, too. Or maybe because the fatigue and helplessness had crushed him. Sam hoped not. Lions weren't supposed to get laid low.

They took Elijah's truck so Sam's could still be used to pull timber. Sam drove, and his father slumped beside him, saying nothing.

And the farther they got from the fire, the better Sam could see it. As they rounded one bend, he caught sight of it in the rearview mirror and swore out loud. It looked like the gates of hell had opened.

"What?" Elijah said, rousing himself.

"Look behind you."

Elijah pushed himself around and looked through the rear window. "Oh, my God!"

Sam tried to keep his attention on the road, but all he could see in his mind's eye was the raging wall of fire behind him.

When he'd been at the church, the fire had been hidden by the tall trees, but now that he saw what it really looked like, all he could imagine was the puniness of that building and the puniness of all those people working to save it against the out-of-control monster that was devouring the woods.

And then, at last, it started to rain.

It was still raining by the time he pulled into Elijah's driveway. A steady drizzle. Not enough to put the fire out, not even enough to slow its spread, for the heat of its breath would be enough to keep drying out the fuel it needed to advance. But if the rain got harder, if it kept coming, it might begin to slow the fire down a bit.

Elijah could barely move as he climbed out of the truck and limped toward his front door. Without saying anything, Sam followed him inside.

"Go take a shower, Dad. I'm going to make you something to eat, then you get to bed."

The old man didn't even argue with him, just shuffled down the hall. Sam dragged himself into the kitchen to check out the refrigerator and the cupboards. Apparently Elijah wasn't much of a cook. Finally he settled on a couple of cans of New England clam chowder and started heating them on the stove. He found a box of crackers to go with the soup.

It wasn't much, but it was nourishment. His thoughts kept straying to Mary, just across the street, and he wondered if she would even speak to him again after today. He'd acted like a real ass. Fatigue and pain were poor excuses for what he'd said. She was right. He'd been every bit as cruel as his father had been when Beth died.

It didn't make him feel good at all.

What had he been after? Revenge? A desire to make Elijah feel the same pain Elijah had made him feel? Or maybe—and this was the worst thing— maybe somewhere inside himself he'd really believed those things he'd said.

If so, he was appalled at himself. Because Elijah was right, he hadn't been there when his mother sickened and died. He'd been long gone from home and unwelcome to return. Or so he'd thought.

God, memory was a tricky thing. Looking back now, he didn't know how much of what he remembered was true and how much of it was things he'd imagined to be the case at the time. How much of it was colored by bad feelings and pain.

And if you couldn't trust your memory, how could you know what was true?

Elijah returned just as the soup was beginning to bubble a bit. He'd put on pajamas and looked a lot cleaner, if not less tired.

"Take a seat, Dad. The soup's almost ready."

"Thanks." Elijah sat at the old dinette, the same dinette Sam had eaten at as a boy. Preachers like Elijah didn't make a lot of money. They learned instead to make everything last as long as it possibly could. Sam had sometimes been embarrassed by the hand-me-downs he'd had to wear or the clothes that had been purchased way too large so that he could grow into them, but he'd eventually learned to wear that thriftiness with pride.

He and Beth had furnished their own house with secondhand furniture and had done a pretty good job of it, too. It was amazing how many people discarded items that were barely worn.

And all of this was nothing but sidetracking as he tried not to think of all the times he had sat at this self-same dinette with his mother and father. The vinyl on the chairs was a lot older now, cracking in places, but it was still the same bright white-and-yellow flower pattern that his mother had loved. And the white laminate tabletop was scratched and scarred. He even remembered where some of those scars had come from: the first time he had tried to whittle his knife had slipped, leaving that tiny, deep scar near the edge. And over there was the time he'd gotten impatient and sliced a loaf of his mother's homemade bread without using a cutting board.

He turned away, reaching for bowls to distract himself.

"You need a shower, son," Elijah said. "Feel free."

"I'll go home and do it."

"Have it your way."

Yes, he would have it his way, because he didn't want to go into the bathroom and see the shaving mug and brush his dad probably still used. Or discover that the same lavender towels, however worn, were still on the towel rack. It didn't matter how different the house was. He was used to seeing all these things in different settings. During his childhood, his family had averaged a move every two years.

No, there was no house he thought of as home. Just the items in it. And the occupants.

He filled the bowls and brought them to the table, along with spoons. The same spoons and bowls he'd used all his childhood. They were dime-store blue willow dishes, cracked and stained from thirty years of use. And boy, did they bring back memories. As a child he'd always studied the picture on his plate, imagining stories about the woman on the footbridge and the tall house behind her. It had seemed so exotic, unlike his own life.

They ate in silence for a while, but finally Sam made himself offer the apology he owed. "Dad, I'm sorry about what I said earlier. I shouldn't have said those things."

Elijah looked up, his blue eyes bloodshot with fatigue. "We all say things we don't really mean at times. I hope you didn't mean them."

"I was just trying to hurt you."

"I know. And you did."

"I'm sorry."

Elijah ate a few more spoonfuls of soup before he spoke again. "You always did seem to be able to get my goat. Well, what's past is past."

With that the shutters fell and the conversation ended. And Sam felt the old anger rising in him again. Didn't *he* deserve an apology, too?

Instead Elijah was treating him as he would have treated any stranger. Unfortunately the past wasn't past. It was very much alive between them, a writhing mass of pain that was as impenetrable as any brick wall.

Sam couldn't take anymore. It was as if the careful barricades he'd built to protect himself were bursting wide-open and all the old pain was eating him alive. He had to get out of here now.

He shoved his chair back from the table, leaving his soup uneaten. "I'm going home. I'm tired."

"You do that," Elijah said without looking up.

He didn't give a damn, Sam thought as he went out onto the street. Elijah no more gave a damn about him than he gave a damn about some stranger on the street. He'd opened the door to a conversation with his apology, and all he'd received was a mild rebuke.

Damn him anyway!

Sam stood out on the curb in the gentle rain, looking up the valley toward the orange glow of the fire, and he wanted to swear or kick something. Hell, he'd left his car up there, he had no way to get back up there, and his house was across town, a good half hour walk that he didn't feel much like taking right now. His mind might be alive with fury, but his body was ready to wilt right on the sidewalk. Hell, he should have asked if he could take Elijah's truck.

But right now he would rather walk to the ends of the earth than go back in there and ask that man for anything. Hell's bells.

Mary's lights were still on. They drew his attention inexorably. She was up. Right across the street. He supposed he had some fences to mend there, too. He swore again, thinking that he was too damn tired for any of this, and stomped his way across the street. The night air was getting chilly, and the steady drizzle wasn't helping.

He knocked on her door, trying not to rouse the whole neighborhood. It took a while, but eventually she opened the door. She looked as if she'd been sleeping, and was wrapped in a white terry-cloth robe.

"Sam!"

"You told me to come by when I came down from the fire."

"Yes, yes. Of course. Come in."

But the invitation held little warmth. Not that he could really blame her, after the way he'd acted today. She must be feeling very wary of him now. His own fault.

He stepped inside, aware of how dirty and grungy he was, and without even a change of clothes.

"I wanted to ask if you could drive me home," he said. "But I guess not. You were sleeping."

"No, it's okay. I've been sleeping for hours. Do you need to eat?"

He thought of the bowl of soup he'd abandoned at his father's house and shook his head. "I'll be fine. I just need to shower and clean up and get a few hours of sleep before I go back."

"Well, come sit in the kitchen while I go get dressed." She paused, looking adorably confused. "Uh...did something happen to your car?"

"I brought Elijah home in his. I left mine up there so they could use it to pull timber."

"Oh. Elijah couldn't take you home?"

"He's too tired, and I didn't ask."

Her lips pursed a little, and he saw the disapproval in them. But all she said, coolly, was, "Go have a seat in the kitchen. I'll be dressed in a jiff."

"Thanks."

He sat at her kitchen table and put his head down in his arms. All the warmth was gone, he realized almost stupidly. All the good feeling he'd had with Mary was gone. He'd killed it today by turning on his father.

It seemed like only an instant later that Mary was shaking his shoulder. It was longer, though. He knew it when he moved and realized his arms were numb.

"Sam," she said, "you can't sleep all night like that. I spread an old sheet on the couch. Just go lie down. You can clean up in the morning."

It was almost like a dream. Maybe it was a dream. But somehow he shuffled to her couch and sprawled on it. An instant later, the dream was gone, replaced by another.

In it, he was trying to reach something just out of his grasp.

Mary woke at 4:00 a.m., slept out. Rising, she tiptoed in the dark past Sam and closed the kitchen door behind her so she wouldn't disturb him. She made a pot of coffee and peeked out the window to see if it was still raining. It didn't look like it, unfortunately.

Stepping out her back door, trying to keep the springs on the screen door from squeaking, she went out to look up at the sky. It was clear and full of stars. And to the northwest, she could still see the angry glow of the fire.

Shaking her head she went back inside and wondered how long she should let Sam sleep. He wouldn't be happy if she didn't wake him at a reasonable time.

But why should she care? He was only one man. It wasn't as if he could singlehandedly save the church and the valley. And what was more, after yesterday, she wasn't sure he was a man she could trust. The way he had struck out at his father... Her chest tightened at the memory. She hated to think how he would react if she ever told him the truth about herself.

No, it was best to just pull away now. Keep a safe distance. She couldn't let him get close enough to rip her heart out.

But maybe, she thought miserably, it was already too late. It seemed her heart was going to be in agony no matter what she did. But at least if she distanced herself, she wouldn't have to go through life with a memory of him saying horrible cutting things to her.

The kitchen door hinges creaked, and she turned to see Sam coming into the room. "I smell coffee," he said with a tired smile.

"I'm sorry, I didn't mean to wake you."

He looked rumpled and filthy, and not a whole lot better than when he'd fallen asleep last night. It was evident that five hours of sleep wasn't going to make up for all he'd missed over the last couple of days. But he was moving, albeit stiffly.

"I needed to get up anyway. Did you see how big that fire's grown? And it's getting close to the church."

"It's terrifying," she said simply.

"Yeah." He looked at her almost hesitantly. "Listen, about yesterday...what I said..."

"Forget it," she said, turning her back swiftly.

"No, I'm not going to forget it, and neither are you. Can I have some of that coffee?"

Suddenly embarrassed, she turned swiftly to get a mug from the cupboard for each of them and poured them full. Sam thanked her and sat at her little table, sighing.

"Damn, I think I strained muscles I didn't know I had."

"How long has it been since you climbed a tree?"

"Twenty-five years, maybe."

She managed a smile. "That might have something to do with it."

"Ya think?" But he was smiling a little, too. Just a little. She didn't think she'd seen him look quite as haunted as he did now.

"About yesterday," he said again. "We need to talk."

"Not really, Sam," she said, trying to pull away mentally and emotionally. "What happens between you and your father is none of my business."

"It's your business when it happens right in front of you. Look, it's no excuse, but I was exhausted and in pain from the burn, and my fuse was way too damn short. And it was like years of stuff just all came bubbling out. Worst of all, I didn't even mean what I said."

"You didn't?" She felt herself pulling away even more.

"No, I didn't. And I've never in my life said anything so savage and vicious. I'm downright ashamed of myself."

But he was capable of saying such things, and she would be wise never to forget that, she told herself. Even so, a little voice reminded her that upset, angry, hurting people were all capable of saying terrible things. Her gaze drifted to the back of his hand; it was easier than looking at his face right now. And what she saw made her gasp.

"Oh, Sam, your hand! It's getting infected."

He looked down at it with a shrug. The huge blister had broken sometime yesterday, and the burn was looking angry, as was the skin around it. "I'll get it looked at after we save the church."

"You're not going to wait that long. You might get blood poisoning." Jumping up from the table, she headed for her bathroom. "Pigheaded men," she said, loudly enough for him to hear. "And you're the most pigheaded of all, Sam Canfield."

She returned with hydrogen peroxide and a gauze bandage. "You should at least try to keep it clean."

"Yes, ma'am."

He sipped coffee while she washed the wound over a bowl, pouring the hydrogen peroxide on it and dabbing it gently with a gauze pad to clean away any dirt. Then she rinsed it again with more peroxide and wrapped his hand with a length of gauze. He managed to get through the experience with only a few winces to betray how much it hurt.

"There," she said with satisfaction. "You can still work, and it ought to stay cleaner."

"Thank you. I appreciate it."

She drew back as quickly as she could from the physical contact and saw from the flicker of expression on his face that he had noticed.

Afraid he might say something, she quickly changed the subject. "I'll go get dressed. Do you want some cereal before I take you home?"

"You've been feeding me on a regular basis. My cereal is as good as yours, so why don't we have some at my place?"

So—finally—she was going to see his place. Too bad it was too late.

Sam's house wasn't much bigger than hers, although it did have a second bedroom. It was also as neat as a pin, which surprised her. Somewhere in the back of her mind she must have been expecting a stereotypical bachelor mess. She had a feeling this house would stand up to a white glove inspection. His kitchen was a little bigger than hers, too, and dominated by a round oak pedestal table that showed the scars of many years of use. She wondered if it was some kind of heirloom.

He brought out a jug of milk, a couple of bowls and spoons, and three varieties of cereal. "Help yourself," he said. "I'm going to shower and change before I die from my own stench."

While he was showering, she made herself at home, finding the coffee and starting a fresh pot. She might have had enough sleep, but it was still early enough that her biological clock was making her feel cold. Maybe he had a thermos somewhere so they could take some coffee with them.

When Sam returned, the coffee was ready. And his bandage was gone. Mary looked at his hand and giggled.

"What?" he said.

"I put the bandage on before you showered. Duh."

He looked at his hand and grinned. "Guess so."

"But you have to keep it clean and dry."

"I've probably got some gauze around here I can wrap it with. But let's eat first. All of a sudden I'm feeling like a starving horse."

Thirty minutes later, with Sam's hand freshly wrapped in gauze and an insulated bottle of coffee on the seat between them, Mary drove them up to the church.

It was still dark, and the closer they came to the church, the angrier the orange glow of the fire seemed. "It's almost there," Mary said, her voice tight.

"Looks that way. But you know what? It's not covering as big an area as it was when I left last night. They must be having some luck holding it back from the subdivisions."

"I hope so. All those poor people and their homes... It makes me want to cry when I think about it."

As she spoke, a plane flew low overhead. One of the fire-fighting planes, Mary thought. It was too dark to see much except its navigation lights until it got closer to the fire. Then it became a black shape against the orange, and as they watched, it dumped its load of fire-fighting chemicals.

"Well," Sam remarked, "that's one good thing to come out of the storm's passing."

"Yes." But Mary shrunk in on herself again, realizing she was letting Sam charm her into relaxing in the comfort of his presence.

"Mary?" Sam asked.

"Yes?"

"Are you pissed at me?"

"Why?"

"I keep getting this feeling of...I don't know. It's like you keep closing me out."

Mary bit her lower lip, not knowing how to answer that without revealing too much. "I'm just tired," she finally said lamely.

"No, it's something more. I see it in your eyes. It's about my dad, isn't it?"

At least he was looking in the wrong direction for answers. Sort of. But she still didn't know how to answer. If she explained how his explosion had frightened her, she would have to explain why. And she didn't know if she could bring herself to do that.

Finally she said the only thing she could think of to avoid the subject. "This isn't a good time, Sam. Let's just focus on saving the church. We can talk later." And by the time later came around, maybe he would be ready to move on.

The thought hurt so badly that it was as if her heart was being squeezed by a vicious fist. All she could do was cling to the thought that, whether now or later, Sam was going to leave her.

But Sam wasn't going to let her off so easily. "Pull over, Mary. There's a turnout up ahead."

She wanted to ignore him but couldn't think of any reason that didn't sound unforgivably rude. Okay, she told herself. Let's have it out now. *Now.*

But her hands were shaking and her knees felt weak, and her heart was hammering so hard she could hear it. She hadn't told anyone, *anyone,* what had happened since Chet had dumped her over it. She couldn't even bear to let it cross her mind except in the most indirect way. She had grown so good at diverting her own thoughts that her own mind spoke of what happened the way a kind stranger would. "That incident." "That terrible event." "That awful day."

She managed to brake in the turnout. Sam reached over and switched off the ignition. Then he set the hand-brake.

"Okay," he said. "I have a right to know what's going on. We've been getting pretty close, and if you're going to freeze me out of your life, I think I deserve to know why."

Maybe he did. She stared out the window at the inkiness of the night, then remembered to switch off her headlights. Only the faint, hellish glow from the distant fire illuminated them now. So appropriate, she thought almost wildly, as panic filled her.

"Mary," Sam said kindly. "You can trust me. I promise not to get mad."

The word trust grabbed her, stilling her panic, filling her with an anger that was born more of fright than rage.

"Trust?" she said bitterly. "I haven't trusted any man in six years. What makes you think I'm going to start now?"

"Your husband?"

"Oh, not just him, Sam. How am I supposed to trust *you?* After all those things you said to your father yesterday? Terrible, terrible things. You're just like him, Sam!"

He sat in silence for a minute or so, staring out the window. "I guess I can see your point. Would it make any difference if I told you I'd apologized? That what I said yesterday was the most unforgivable thing I've ever said in my life?"

Mary was gripping the wheel so tightly that her fingers ached. "I don't know."

"I lost it, Mary. But it took a lot of years for that kind of anger to build up in me. And I still wouldn't have said those things if I hadn't been so tired and in so much pain. Something inside me snapped. It happens, Mary. To everyone. But that's the first time since I was a kid that it happened to me."

She wanted to believe him, but she didn't dare. He was talking in generalities, and she had a great big specific to deal with. "I don't know, Sam. I'll have to think about it."

"Okay." His voice was suddenly harsh. "Let's get up to the church."

She realized he thought she was being unforgiving, that she was refusing to understand that he was only human. The problem was, he *was* human. And so was she. And she was very, very frightened.

19

The swath around the church looked as desolate as a moonscape. It still wasn't eighty feet wide—it was about sixty—but the clearing process had become a race against time, mind-numbing fatigue and the advancing inferno. Relatively simple tasks now took longer than ever, because the men performing those tasks were exhausted. Joe and Louis had reorganized the crews, with one man in each crew as the "safety," whose sole job was to make sure the others hadn't overlooked some essential precaution. The men rotated the role of safety, and the crews were rotated from task to task to help prevent the workers from being numbed by routine.

And still there were injuries. Clint Stedman had broken an ankle when someone had forgotten to clamp a tow chain. The chain had snapped loose and whipsawed like a scythe toward a clump of men. The others had heard the *pop* as the chain broke free and jumped out of the way. But Clint's back had been turned, and by the time he realized what was happening the chain had wrapped itself around his ankle and snatched him off his feet. His piercing scream had brought everyone running with an energy they'd thought was long since passed, but Sam knew the adrenaline rush would only be temporary.

"I don't know how much more we can do," Louis told Sam, as Clint was bundled into the back of a pickup and taken to the hospital. "Between cutting, trimming and towing, it's taking us half an hour to clear a tree now, as tired as the men are. We're having to triple-check for safety, and still things happen." Louis nodded toward the smoke hanging like a pall in the forest. "And the fire's getting closer. I just...I don't think we're going to make it."

Sam nodded. "George Patton wrote that a man can only march and fight for sixty hours before he's spent. We're all pushing that now."

"And he was writing about trained, professional soldiers," Louis said. "We're all amateurs, and most of us are out of shape to boot. It's reaching the point where we have to ask whether we're risking more harm than good."

Sam put his hands on his hips and looked down at the ground. Parched ground. More dust than dirt now. "Get the hoses out," he said finally. "Let's make the church as wet as we can get it before an ember sets it off."

"Okay."

"And let's have the freshest men keep cutting. Even if all we do is get the timber down, it might make the fire less threatening if it gets here."

A rising drone drowned him out as another fire-fighting plane swooped low overhead. Sam looked up and watched the mud drop. It wasn't far away at all now.

"Oh, and, Louis?" he said when he could again be heard.

"Yeah?"

"Make sure all the vehicles are gassed up and ready to go. We might have to bail out in a big hurry."

"I'll get somebody to do that."

They were starting to have equipment break-downs, too. A couple of chain saws had given up the ghost; a few shovels had broken. Work gloves were wearing out. And, of course, with each foot outward they expanded their cutting, the total area to clear went up. At sixty feet out from the church, he figured they'd cut only a third of the area they needed to sweep.

Another plane roared overhead and dropped more mud. A garden hose had been hooked up at the faucet inside the church and run out a window. A man was using it to spray the building's roof.

Elijah, who had been staying far away from Sam most of the morning, now approached him.

"Sam?" His voice sounded drained. "Sam, we can't do any more. The equipment is breaking. The people are worn-out. They need to go home before someone gets killed.''

Sam was inclined to agree with him. Much as he didn't want to give up, he could see the signs of hopelessness all around him. And what was more, he could see the ash that was falling from the sky. Sooner or later some of it was going to be hot.

"Just send everyone home," Elijah said. "It's in God's hands now."

Looking at the moonscape they'd worked so hard to create, Sam wondered if even an eighty-foot clear-cut would be enough to save the church if the woods around it went up in flame. "I can't *make* anyone leave, Dad. They're volunteers."

"I know. But if you make the suggestion, they might heed you. No building is worth the price we might pay here if we keep going."

For once he and his father were in agreement. Sam hated to quit, but he knew from experience that his father hated it every bit as much as he did.

Before he could act, however, another plane roared overhead. There was no mistaking that it was dumping the chemicals closer now. Too close.

Sam picked up his whistle and blew it. No one seemed to hear. He walked closer to the edge of the clearing, nearer the workers, and blew it again, sharply. Slowly, as if in a daze, people turned to look at him. One by one, chain saws fell silent.

"Listen up, people. The fire's getting closer. And you're all getting too tired. This would be a good time for everyone to head out. We don't want to lose anybody."

Still no one moved. It was as if they were dazed and couldn't quite comprehend what he said. Or as if they were reluctant to stop.

Just then Mary, who was standing twenty feet away, a shovel in her hands, called out, "Sam!"

At that instant Sam heard a loud crack, and felt a stunning blow to the back of his shoulders. He landed facedown in the dirt, wondering what the hell had hit him.

"Oh, my God," someone said. "Oh, my God!"

Sam rolled over and sat up, then felt his heart stop. His father was lying on the ground nearby, a tree trunk across his legs.

Mary was suddenly there, kneeling beside Sam. "He saved you, Sam. My God, that tree started to tip and he shoved you.... My God!"

Sam scrambled on his hands and knees over to his father. Elijah was lying facedown, the tree across the backs of his legs. "Dad? Dad?"

A groan answered him.

Sam was galvanized. Leaping to his feet, he called out, "Come on, everybody. We've got to get this tree off him."

Hands were suddenly full of more energy than they had been in hours. Men and women gathered together around each side of the tree trunk and put their hands beneath it.

"On the count of three," Sam said, grabbing the

trunk along with everyone else. "And don't anybody let go. Back away down toward his feet until he's clear. Got it?"

A chorus of agreement answered him.

"One, two...three!"

They lifted all at once, thirty pairs of hands making the load lighter. It was still heavy enough, but they didn't have too much trouble lifting the trunk and backing it away from Elijah.

They set it down with equal care, making sure no one got a crushed foot. Then Sam hurried back to his father, kneeling in the dirt beside him.

"Dad? Dad, are you awake?"

"Yeah. Yeah. I think my leg is broken."

Sam wanted to swear, but he didn't swear much around his father. Never had. He was worried sick, though. "We've got to get him to the hospital right away."

"I'll take him," Mary volunteered.

"Not in your car," Sam said. "We'll have to lay him out flat in the back of my SUV."

Joe spoke. "But first we have to move him carefully. Anybody got a tarp or a blanket?"

That turned out to be an easy request to fill. So was coming up with a couple of branches so they could splint Elijah's legs. The whole time they worked on him, Mary held Elijah's hand and talked soothingly to him. Sam felt an ugly little sting of jealousy, wondering why she seemed to like his father more than him.

But it was an ugly thought, and he drove it away swiftly.

With great care, they carried Elijah to the back of Sam's car. He'd long ago removed the rear seat for more cargo space, and now it made a reasonably soft, protected bed for Elijah.

"My truck," Elijah said.

"Don't worry," Joe said. "I'll have Louis drive it to your house. How's that?"

Sam gave Mary his car keys. "I'll be along as soon as I can."

"I know," she said simply. "Don't worry. I'll take good care of him. Here are my keys."

Then, astonishing him, she squeezed his hand before climbing into his truck. He watched them drive off with a terrible sense of foreboding. It seemed the universe hadn't finished playing dirty tricks yet.

Some of the volunteers took off, but some remained, as if they were as reluctant as Sam to write off the church. The wind was picking up, indicating that the fire was coming closer and drawing air to its heart. Maybe, Sam thought, the wind would protect them from hot ash for a while. But even as he had the thought, he knew better. The ash was rising on the updraft from the flames, but it would still drift on the upper air currents and eventually be sucked down by the steady draw of the fire. Some of it would wind up here.

"We've got to get out of here," Sam said to those

who had stayed behind. "Those attack planes are dropping mud two, three hundred yards into the forest."

"Clint gave an ankle and your dad a leg for this church," Billy Miller said. "If we quit now, what do we tell them? That what they did was wasted?"

A few men nodded in agreement, but Sam put up a hand. "Look, guys, here's the deal. We have three, maybe four, hours before the fire reaches that tree line. We're down to what? Three chain saws that are still running? So we'd knock down another half-dozen trees. Maybe a dozen, tops. We won't get enough more done to make any difference over what we've done already."

"So we just give up?" Billy asked. "Some of us grew up here. My kids were baptized in this church."

Sam nodded. "Look, I hate to quit as much as anyone. But we gave it our best shot, and we came up short. The fire's winning here at the church. Now we have to start thinking about saving our homes. And we can't do that if I lose half of you to the hospital with injuries, smoke inhalation, heatstroke and everything else we're risking by staying here. We've done what we can here. It's time to pack it up and get out while we can."

"He's right, Billy," another man said. "How many of us are we gonna lose out here? My house is on the edge of town. This church is a landmark, and we'd all hate to lose her. But dying out here, when our wives and kids need us back in town...I don't think that's what God would want.''

Billy finally shucked off his work gloves. He and the others gathered up their tools and loaded them into the remaining vehicles. Sam was the last to leave. As they drove off, he stepped inside the church one more time and knelt at the altar.

''I haven't done a lot of talking to you lately, so I don't have room to ask for much. But if you could help the doctors take care of my dad, and if you could save his church...well, I'd really like a second chance with him.'' Not knowing how else to end the prayer, he said simply, ''Thank you.'' Then he climbed into his dad's truck and headed back to town.

''He's in surgery right now,'' Mary said as Sam walked into the E.R. ''Compound fracture of the tibia, they said.''

''How long before...?'' His question trailed away as he sank into a chair, resting his forehead in his hands. He hated feeling helpless, and right now he was as helpless as he'd ever been. The fire. His dad. Mary.

''Probably a couple of hours.'' Mary sat beside him and touched his hand. ''Sam, I know how hard this is.''

''We had to quit out at the church, Mary. All that work. Clint got hurt. My dad. For nothing.''

''Not for nothing, Sam.''

He looked up at her. "What, then? Why were we out there? To save one building?"

"You were out there to save a dream. And a lot of memories. Your father's dream. And the memories of a whole lot of people in Whisper Creek."

"Maybe if we hadn't stopped everyone while I climbed up that tree to get the bear cub... Maybe if I'd kept working at night, the way some of them did..."

Mary shook her head. "Don't, Sam. That fire is a force of nature. It's bigger than all of us. We can build this hospital and pack it full of high-tech gizmos, but in the end we're just human beings. And that fire...nature...that's bigger than we are. Don't go beating yourself up over things you couldn't control. Take it from an expert, Sam. There's no percentage in it."

That was one of the most revealing things she had ever said to him. Forgetting his own concerns, he looked over at her, and her eyes fell. "What happened, Mary? What are you beating yourself up over?"

She tried to force a smile. "Oh, we all do it, Sam. That's all I meant."

"No," he said, lifting her chin until their eyes met. "No, that isn't all you meant. You've got such a ball and chain attached to your heart, I can hear it clank. I look at you and I see...an angel. Kind. Tender. Thoughtful. Loving. So beautiful. You look in a mirror and see...I don't know what you see, but it isn't beautiful. What do you see that you won't let me see? What could be *that* bad?''

Her face whitened, but she shook her head. ''Nothing.''

''Nothing? Is that why you're so afraid of me? Afraid I might talk to you the way I talked to my father yesterday? Afraid that you can't trust me?''

Her lips tightened even more. ''Sam...''

''Look,'' he said, ''if you're going to ditch me, I at least deserve to know why. You said something about not being able to trust men. I want to know why. I think I'm entitled to know exactly why I frighten you.''

She looked away from him, and he could see that she was beginning to tremble. He wanted to reach out and tell her that everything would be okay, but he couldn't do that until he knew what the problem was. And she wouldn't believe him, anyway. She'd made that perfectly clear to him.

For a long time she didn't say anything. She seemed lost in some anguished memory that he couldn't help her with until she shared it with him. Then he wondered if he could help her anyway. He was such a mess himself. Maybe he wasn't in any state to help another living soul.

She turned to him slowly, but her eyes wouldn't meet his. ''I had a son,'' she said.

He felt his chest tighten, but he refrained from saying anything. She'd told him she had had a son, but now he sensed there was more to the story. He didn't want her to stop talking.

"He was...he'd just turned six. A cute little boy with red hair and freckles and an adventurous nature. We were out in the yard one day. I'll never forget what a beautiful day it was. Not a cloud in the sky, not too warm... I was gardening. He was playing with our cat.

"It was a funny cat, Sam. It liked to play ball, almost as if it was a dog. And Chuckie would roll it for him, and the cat would chase it and bat it around a little bit, then wait for Chuckie to throw it again."

Sam made a soft sound, just enough to let her know she had his attention. Already he was gearing up for the story to come, his entire body tensing in preparation.

"Anyway, I don't know exactly what happened. It was all so fast. One second Chuckie was giggling and tossing the ball, and I couldn't have looked away for more than two seconds.... I mean, I was kneeling so I could keep an eye on them. I looked down for... I don't know. The next thing I heard was the shriek of brakes."

Sam closed his eyes. Then he reached out for her hand. She shook his touch off.

"The woman who hit him said the cat darted into the street right in front of her and Chuckie was right behind him. He died the next day. He never...he never even woke up again."

"Mary..."

She shook her head. "Don't say anything. I was a rotten mother. I wasn't watching closely enough. I know that. Chuckie's dead because I didn't do my job right. And Chet left me because I killed our son."

"Mary..."

She shook her head again, more vehemently. "So that's why I don't trust you. You'll say all the right things right now. Everybody says all the right things. But later..." She sniffled and blinked away tears. "Forget it, Sam. Just look after your father. You might not get another chance."

He racked his brains trying to find something soothing or kind to say. But he needed time to absorb this. Needed time to think it through and figure out if he could help Mary carry her burden, or if he was such a mess himself that he would be no good to her.

God! Words just wouldn't come. "We...need to talk about this some more," he said finally. "I...don't know what to say."

"Of course not." Suddenly brisk, she rose. "See you around, Sam."

Then she left the hospital before he could summon another word to say.

Sam was good at kicking his own butt. He kicked it pretty thoroughly over the next couple of hours until they let him in to see his father. He should have had some words to offer her. Some compassion. Something. But it was as if his brain had just stuttered to a halt. Mary had as big a wound in her heart as he had in his. And he sure hadn't dealt with his own very well. How in the hell could he help with hers? Maybe it would be better for both of them if he just stayed away.

Elijah was groggy, but alert enough to recognize Sam. "Both legs," he said to his son. "Both legs."

Sam looked at the casts and the weights and felt like hell. "You should've let that damn tree fall on *me*."

Elijah gave him a weak grin. "Better my legs than your head."

"I'm not so sure about that. Are you hurting?"

"Not too bad. They got me so full of drugs I don't know which end is up."

"Did they tell you how bad it is?"

"Not too bad. One's a clean break. The other one they had to put a pin in. I'll be up and around in a couple months."

"I'm sorry, Dad."

Elijah reached out a hand and Sam took it carefully, making sure he didn't bump the IV line. "We need to talk, son."

"Yeah."

But before they could do so, Elijah drifted back to sleep. Sam sat by his bed, waiting, as afternoon turned into night.

* * *

Mary thought about packing. She could just pack up everything she owned in a rental truck and be out of this town tomorrow. Call the school, say she had an emergency and couldn't complete her contract.

The urge almost overwhelmed her. Sam's reaction to her story had told her all she needed to know. He needed to think about it. What was there to think about? Either he accepted her as she was, as a negligent mother, or he wasn't going to accept her at all.

God, she wanted to get out of this town. The same way she had fled Denver. Just run away and start anew somewhere else, a place where no one would know her story. Where she would be smarter and not let anyone at all get close to her, not even a wounded charmer like Sam Canfield.

Had she lost her marbles? What could she have been thinking of? Hadn't she figured out yet that she was no longer entitled to a normal life full of love and happiness? Why did she keep wishing? Why had she ever been so *stupid* as to let that man behind her defenses?

How many times did she have to learn her lesson?

She realized she had packed half a suitcase without even being aware of it. Run again? No. No. She had a good job here. She had friends here. And she didn't have to see Sam Canfield except in passing. Besides, it wasn't as if she had enough money to just pull up stakes without another job waiting for her.

It was time to grow up, she told herself. What was that old saw? *You can run, but you can't hide.* Wasn't that the truth. Everywhere she went, she was going to take herself along. It wouldn't be any better anywhere else.

Hurting and aching and wanting nothing more than a dark cave to hide in, she made herself unpack her suitcase. She would survive the heartbreak. She had survived much worse.

It might take a while, but she and Sam could go back to being virtual strangers the way they had been before.

Sitting in her living room, she started to cry, giving way to tears that had been locked up inside for a long, long time.

20

Sam was dozing in the chair beside his father's bed when a sound disturbed him. Opening his eyes, he saw that Elijah was awake and the nurse was checking his IV.

"Doing good, Reverend Canfield," the nurse said cheerfully. Then she looked critically at Sam. "You need to get home and get some sleep yourself."

"In a little bit."

"Not too long. Visiting hours ended an hour ago."

"I'll be good."

"You do that." She gave him a wink as she walked out.

Sam turned to his father. "How are you feeling?"

"Like a mule gave me a double-barreled kick."

But his color was a lot better, and his eyes were brighter. The surgical sedation had worn off.

"They're giving you something for pain, aren't they?"

"She just gave me a shot," Elijah said. "So let's talk before I drop off to sleep again."

Sam nodded. It was as good a time as any. He didn't know where it would take them, but the place they'd been most of his life was about as bad as it could get.

"So talk," he said.

Elijah sighed. "That's a great starting point. If you're just going to sit there with a chip on your shoulder, we're not going to get anywhere."

"I don't have a chip on my shoulder. And there you go, assuming things about me again."

Elijah's mouth opened, then closed. "You're right," he said presently. "I guess I have a tendency to do that."

Sam nodded but didn't say anything. He wanted to know where his father was heading before he opened up his own heart and left himself vulnerable again. Then he would decide just how much of a risk he wanted to take. He had too many scars from this man to want to garner another bunch.

"I guess," Elijah said slowly, "that I wasn't a good father. At least, not for you. Your mom was always saying you were more sensitive than I gave you credit for. But I'm not the most sensitive person myself sometimes. I didn't realize...." He trailed off and sighed.

"It's obvious," he said after a minute, "that I messed up pretty badly or we wouldn't have gone so many years without talking."

Again Sam nodded but said nothing. His hands were clenching into fists in his lap, though, the only outward sign of how tense he was feeling.

"Maybe," Elijah said, "I was the wrong father for you. Or maybe I made the all-too-common mistake of thinking that the only way to raise a child was the way I'd been raised myself. I hit you, and yelled, and tried to control you too much, because that's what I knew. I was too critical." He hesitated. "I guess I was guilty of the sin of pride."

"Pride?"

"I wanted you to be perfect. You were my only child, and I was the preacher, and I wanted you to be better than everyone else's children."

"Instead I was worse."

Elijah lifted his eyebrows. "Worse? Did I make you feel that way? Because you weren't. Far from it. Believe me, I counseled enough parents to know you were far better than most children. It's my failing that I wanted you to be even better than that."

"You were busy all the time."

"Too busy," Elijah allowed. "Too busy by far. I know that. It's a preacher's life, son, but I should have done some thinking about whether it was fair to you."

Sam couldn't believe he was hearing all this. But it still didn't address the biggest problems. "What about throwing me out when I refused to become a preacher?"

"May God forgive me for that sin," Elijah said wearily, his eyes closing. "Your mother never did."

"But why did you do it, Dad? I never understood it. I wasn't cut out to be a preacher. I hated the very idea. Why were you so set on it that you were prepared to throw me out rather than give in?"

Elijah's eyes popped open, and they were suddenly blazing. "You'd have made a fine preacher. One of the best. And to this day I'm sorry you didn't do it." He closed his eyes again and sighed heavily. "God forgive me, I thought I'd make you see the light. Pride. I've been so prideful. Your mother tried to make me see it, but I was so..."

"Bullheaded?" Sam suggested.

"Bullheaded and sinfully prideful. Oh, I was really a model of Christian love and understanding, wasn't I, son? I was so sure I was right and *you* were the one being bullheaded. I was so sure I could make you see the light. And too much of a fool to realize I didn't have that power. I tried to play God with your life."

"Yes," Sam said quietly. "You did."

"Well, if it's any consolation to you, since your mother died, all I've been able to hear in my head are all the things she said to me about you, all the times she told me I was wrong, that I was treating you badly, that I didn't understand, that I needed to be kinder and gentler with you. It's like wearing a hair shirt. And I'm so ashamed I didn't hear her words until after she was gone. Until I was all alone to ponder them, because they were all I had left.''

A tear crept down Elijah's cheek. ''I have a lot to pay for. I was so full of the fire of righteousness that I forgot how to love.''

Sam felt the shell around his heart beginning to crack and the pain beginning to pervade his entire body. He was astonished to realize that he was actually feeling sorry for his father. But there was one more issue. ''Why did you say that God was punishing me by taking Beth?''

''Oh, God, I did say that, didn't I?''

''Yes.'' Sam felt a burst of icy anger at the memory. ''I was grieving my wife, and you said it was my fault she was dead.''

''Like you did yesterday.''

Sam looked down.

''I don't blame you for wanting to get even. Sam...all I know is, that's how I was feeling about your mother. That God was taking her to punish me. And...'' Elijah shook his head, and another tear trailed down his cheek. ''I'm sorry. I don't know what I was thinking. Except I was angry. So angry. Maybe I was a little out of my mind. Maybe...oh, I don't know. It was unforgivable, whatever I was thinking. And it wasn't true. All I know is...I'm not proud of the man I used to be. Not proud at all.''

Weariness was overtaking Elijah, so Sam didn't say any of the things he had once thought he wanted to say to his father, all the angry, hurting things. Somehow they seemed irrelevant now.

"You get some sleep, Dad. I'll be back tomorrow."

"Promise?" Elijah asked. "Promise me."

"I promise." Then he got up and walked out, wondering if he'd ever known his father at all.

Mary went by the hospital in the morning, bringing a small bag of fruit and some flowers from the supermarket for Elijah. She was relieved that Sam wasn't there.

Elijah's welcome was warm, and he seemed a lot more comfortable than the last time she'd seen him.

"Oh, I'll be right as rain in a few months," he said with a wave of his hand. "Unfortunately they're going to keep me here for a while. Something about the possibility of a bone infection." He pointed to the IV line. "I get my antibiotics direct."

Mary laughed and took the seat beside the bed. For an instant she thought she could almost feel the imprint of Sam's bottom in it.

"They seem to be getting the fire under control from what I heard on the radio this morning," she said.

"The church?"

"I don't know. I haven't been up there yet. I'll go up and see later."

"No, no. I don't want you taking any risks. If the church makes it, we'll know soon enough."

Mary realized he was looking at her rather intently, and she had the uncomfortable feeling that her soul was lying bare before his gaze.

"Sam and I started talking last night," he said.

"Good."

"I thought you'd want to know that. I've had the feeling you didn't approve of our relationship."

"It's none of my business."

"Of course it is. You're in love with my son."

Mary felt her cheeks turn bright red. "Elijah, I wouldn't be saying that."

"Why not? It's as plain as the nose on my face. And he's in love with you. You'd make a good couple."

"No, we wouldn't."

Elijah's brows knitted, and he looked at her in perplexity. Mary couldn't bear his stare for long, so she looked down at her hands. She didn't want to discuss this with him. She didn't want to discuss it with anyone. It hurt too much.

"What happened, Mary?"

"Nothing." She promised herself that if he didn't drop this subject, she was going to get up and leave. She had exposed her soul once already and been met with silence. Telling Elijah could only be worse. From things Sam had said, she expected he would heap damnation on her head. And she didn't need anyone to do that for her. She had already damned herself.

"Mary," said Elijah, "answer me. If you're going to hurt Sam, I think I have a right to know why.''

''I haven't hurt Sam!'' she protested in a teary rush as all her barriers crumbled and the pain of loss washed over her again. ''He hurt *me*.''

Angry at herself, she dashed her tears away and tried to make herself get up and leave. But it was as if she was glued to the chair. Her body simply would not obey the demand of her mind. So she sat there, fighting back tears, her throat so tight it felt as if it were caught in a noose, her chest aching so hard she couldn't even breathe right.

Old pain and new pain commingled, filling her with an unbearable anguish. And from somewhere deep inside came an anguished cry, ''Do I have to lose everyone I love?''

Sam drove up to the church. He'd heard that the fire was now under control, and he wanted to see how much damage there had been.

Tired as he was, he hadn't slept much last night. He'd been running around and around the things his father had said, part of him refusing to believe that Elijah could have changed so much, part of him recognizing that his father was a lot older now. That maybe the pain of his losses had taught him to be a kinder, less judgmental man.

Yeah, said an ugly little voice in his head, *and leopards change their spots and zebras change their stripes.*

But he didn't want to listen to that voice. Besides, he'd been doing a lot of thinking over the past days and had realized that in some respects he'd probably misjudged Elijah with a schoolboy's egocentrism. And he'd certainly added some fuel to the fire himself.

Maybe if they kept poking along at it, they could find some kind of meeting of minds. Because if he were honest, he could admit that it would be nice to have his father back in his life. The only family he had left.

And then there was Mary. He'd handled things poorly last night, and he knew it. But he didn't think telling her that she hadn't done anything wrong was going to change her mind one little bit. He was sure plenty of people had told her that. Why would *his* saying it make any difference?

Hell. Maybe if he eventually caught up on his sleep, he could sort his life out.

He arrived at the church to find it still standing. The fire had reached the edge of the clearing but was merely licking along the ground, consuming pine needles and pine cones and other debris. So far the trees hadn't ignited.

He went inside and turned on the bathroom tap, pumping water out through the garden hose that was still where they'd left it yesterday. Then he went outside and sprayed the church roof, making it as wet as he could.

Thirty minutes later, he turned the garden hose on

the burning ground cover, trying to keep it from climbing up the trees. It was like trying to hold back a flood with a broom, but he felt obliged to do it.

Maybe he could save one thing from ruination.

A short while later two fire trucks showed up to help him. They trained their hoses on the forest edge, doing far more good than the puny garden hose, so Sam turned his attention back to the church roof. Ash was falling almost constantly, and there was no way to know what was still hot.

One of the firemen, Hector Maldonado, took a cigarette break and came over to talk to him. "You hear the good news, Sam?"

"That the fire's under control? It was on the radio this morning."

"Don't mean a little wind couldn't put us right up the creek again, but at the moment we're actually beating it back."

"Which is why you're here?"

"You better believe it. We don't want it to break out here because nobody's paying attention. Right now we're pretty much letting it burn what it already has and putting out little fires as they pop up. *Si Dios quiere,* God willing, it'll burn itself out before we get any bad weather that'll keep the planes from going up."

Sam cracked a smile. "I'm beginning to think we're never going to have any weather again."

"Right now, I'm settling for calm, dry and as still as the good Lord can make it." He ran the cigarette butt through the stream from Sam's hose, putting it out, and popped it into a pocket on his coat. "Back to work."

They spent most of the rest of the day putting out small fires. Since there was no fire hydrant out here, the trucks took turns heading to a nearby lake to refill their pumpers. Three times Sam had to put out burning debris that landed on the roof of the church, but by four o'clock it looked like they were winning. A bit of a breeze stirred up after the sun went behind the mountain, allowing the valley to start cooling, but it wasn't enough to stir up the fire to a voracious rage.

Another crew of firefighters with water trucks arrived to replace the county men. Figuring they weren't any more likely to let the church burn than he was, Sam decided it was time to go home, clean up and visit his dad with what appeared to be good news. Talk some more, maybe, and sort things out. Maybe he would have to take the risk and tell his father just how he'd been hurt, and in what ways.

Or maybe, and this thought grabbed him, maybe he could finally be man enough just to let go of it all.

"Sam, you get over to this hospital right now."

The message was waiting on Sam's answering machine when he got home, and he might have thought something was wrong with his father if he hadn't recognized the tone of voice. The old man had a wild hair, and he was giving orders.

Well, he could damn well wait. Sam was no lackey to be summoned in that fashion. Nor was he a kid any longer, who needed to tremble before that tone.

In fact, now that he thought about it, he hadn't missed that tone of voice once in all these years. Just who did Elijah think he was?

Muttering under his breath, Sam headed for the shower, scattering clothes everywhere and not giving a damn. He felt sixteen again, and spiteful and angry and...

Suddenly he laughed at himself and turned around to pick up his clothes. Acting like a sixteen-year-old wasn't going to annoy anyone but himself. Not anymore.

He indulged in the shower until the last drop of hot water was gone, wanting to soak every last bit of smoke stench out of his hair and pores. And tonight, instead of donning work clothes, he was going to put on a decent shirt and slacks. Maybe hit a restaurant for dinner.

As soon as that thought crossed his mind, so did Mary. He had a feeling that if he called her and asked her to join him, she would hang up on him. Damn, why was she so spooked? Okay, so he hadn't had anything useful to say last night, but what was there useful to say? He couldn't change the way she felt about herself. And he did, to be fair to both of them, actually have to think about whether he could share her load adequately.

He was trying to be smart and intelligent about this.

But smart and intelligent wasn't cutting it, as his heart kept reminding him. Damn.

She'd been cutting herself off from him for the last couple of days, though. As if he'd gotten too close to her and she was a skittish foal. What was he supposed to do about that? He couldn't just barge his way into her life and demand that she let him stay. If she couldn't trust him...

If she couldn't trust him, there was nothing more to be said. Period. You had to have trust in any relationship. And right now, considering how she was withdrawing from him, he wasn't sure he could trust *her*.

What a mess.

Just because his father had insisted he come right away, Sam was stubborn enough to have dinner first. Not at a restaurant, where it would take an hour, but at the burger joint on Main. At least it was food.

"Don't be as blind as I was, Sam."

Elijah's words hit him as soon as he entered the room.

"Well, hello to you, too, Dad," Sam said, with more than a hint of sarcasm in his voice.

"I'm sorry. Hi, son, thanks for stopping by.

Now—'' Elijah paused, his eyes boring into Sam's
''—don't be as blind as I was.''

Sam heaved a sigh and sat in the chair nearest the
window and farthest from his father. He felt resentful, wondering how Elijah could possibly believe he
had any right to interfere in Sam's life or to lecture
Sam about anything. He'd lost that right a long time
ago, when he'd told his son to take a permanent
hike.

Clinging to old wounds. That was what he was
doing. He could imagine Mary—if she were still
talking to him—scowling at him and telling him he
was just like his dad. Maybe he needed to start acting like a grown-up instead of a resentful kid.
Maybe he ought to at least listen. He was certainly
old enough now to pick and choose which bits of
advice would benefit him.

He looked out at a young woman trying to corral
three small kids and herd them toward the hospital
entrance. The kids looked to be excited, which was
odd, Sam thought. A hospital visit didn't strike him
as the kind of event that would send kids into run-
ning-around-the-parking-lot glee. Finally he looked
over at his father, prepared to at least try to listen.

''Do I get to find out the reason for this lecture,
or is it a secret?''

Elijah smiled. ''No secret at all, Sam. You're in
love with Mary. Mary's in love with you. And
you've slammed the door on her like a harried
mother on a door-to-door salesman.''

Sam turned his attention back out the window, trying to conceal the pang in his heart. Mary was in love with him? No way. He didn't need a magnifying glass to read the signs she was sending out. "So now you're the village matchmaker?" he asked, without looking at his father.

"I'm a father, Sam. Not a good one, I'll admit, but I tried. And I'm trying now." Elijah drew a deep breath. "But for the life of me, I can't figure out what that woman could possibly have said or done that would make you act this way."

Keeping a tight leash on his feelings, Sam tipped his head back and looked at the ceiling tiles, then finally met his father's gaze. "What exactly is it that I did? Mary won't tell me, and this flailing about in the dark is getting more than a bit frustrating."

Elijah huffed. "You really *are* blind, aren't you? I don't know what all happened, but I do know she told you something and you've been cold as a stone ever since. The poor woman couldn't even talk about it. She just sat in that chair, crying." He paused to scratch at his IV site. "Maybe you learned compassion and forgiveness from me. Or the lack of same."

"Is that what you think?" Sam asked.

"I don't know *what* to think, son. All I know is that two decent people who love each other are on the outs, and it has something to do with what she told you."

Sam rose. "Yes, Dad, it does. But not the way

you think, or the way Mary may be thinking.'' He took a deep breath and looked out the window again. Whatever the mother and her three hyperkinetic charges had been up to, they were out of sight. Probably bouncing off the corridor walls somewhere, he guessed. He tried to find words. ''Dad...''

Elijah waited for a moment, then drew a breath as if to answer. But he let the reply go unspoken and settled back against the pillow, listening.

''Something really awful happened to Mary a few years ago,'' Sam finally said. Having found a place to begin, he found it easier to continue. ''It was a horrible tragedy. She lost her son, and her husband blamed her. He dumped her, and she's been tormenting herself with guilt ever since.''

''And you shut her out because of that?'' Elijah asked, an accusatorial tone resonant in his voice.

''No,'' Sam said. ''That's just it. I didn't say *anything!* I mean, what is there to say that hasn't been said by countless others already? It wasn't her fault. She didn't do anything wrong. But I realized those words would fall on deaf ears. I can't mend her broken heart, Dad. I would if I could. I wish I had that gift. But I'm just a small-town deputy sheriff, with my own skeletons in the closet and my own wounds to lick. Not a psychotherapist. Not a priest. I can't give her absolution, and I can't peel away the layers of her psyche and heal that wound. I can't be what she needs.''

Sam paused and sat again. His shoulders sagged.

"I can't fix her, Dad. She's torn up inside, and I can't do a damn thing about it. Just like I couldn't save Beth."

He pressed the heels of his palms against his eyes, as if trying to shut out some horrible image. Inside, he was a maelstrom of painful emotions, as if everything with Beth and everything with Mary had all come together to tell him just how helpless he truly was. Every day he helped other people, but the two most important people in his life were beyond his ability to help.

Finally he dropped his hands and looked out the window again. There were things he could do and things he couldn't do, and the things he couldn't do had been tripping him up his entire life.

After a long moment, Elijah spoke. "Sam, do you remember Brother Crauley, who came to stay with us in San Diego? The Navy chaplain?"

Sam shrugged. "I guess. It's been a long time, Dad. And I wasn't paying much attention to the home front when we lived in San Diego."

To Sam's surprise, Elijah smiled. He'd been expecting another of his father's withering glares.

"You were busy with Scouts and soccer, son. You were a kid doing kid things. But Chaplain Crauley was a buddy of mine in seminary. He had a couple months medical leave from Vietnam, and we lived near the base. So he came to stay with us while he was recovering."

Sam turned, the memory now rising from the

ashes of his childhood. "Oh, yeah. He got shot or something, right?"

Elijah nodded and touched his upper arm. "Right through the arm. Shattered the bone. He told me about the night it happened. He was with the Marine Corps, somewhere in a rice paddy. His platoon was pulling back to evacuate, and one of the men stepped on a land mine. Jack Crauley went back for him and was pulling him toward their evac area when an NVA sniper hit him. He said it felt like someone had smashed his arm between a hammer and an anvil."

"I remember now. His right arm was in a sling, so he had to eat left-handed. Mom had to cut his meat for him at dinner."

"That's right," Elijah said, his eyes clouding for a moment. "Your mother was always a sweet woman that way." He drew another breath and continued. "Anyway, he's lying there on a levee between two rice paddies, and the platoon corpsman comes up. Jack said he was screaming to wake the dead. Didn't want to let the corpsman touch his arm. But the medic gave him a shot of morphine, calmed him down and splinted his arm, gentle as a dove. Jack looked up through a grimace and asked how the corpsman could be so tender. And he said the man smiled and said 'I've been wounded, too, padre.' Jack told that story in a sermon one night at our church. He said we're all called to be wounded healers."

"You're saying I should talk to Mary."

Elijah smiled again, a gentle smile. "What I'm saying, son, is that you *especially* should talk to Mary. *Because* you lost Beth. *Because* you've been wounded. She doesn't need absolution or psychotherapy. Or if she does, that's not what she needs most. What she needs most is the tender, gentle touch of someone who's been wounded, too."

Sam turned back to the window. The scene before him made sense now, as the woman and children returned to the car with a man in tow. Bringing Daddy home. That was why the kids had been so excited.

"I don't know what I can do except tell her how I feel," Sam said. "I don't know what else to say."

"Maybe that's all you need to say, Sam. Maybe that's what she needs to hear, more than anything in the world. And maybe…just maybe…that's what you need to hear yourself say, more than anything in the world."

Elijah reached out his hand and waited for his son to take it. Only after Sam's hand rested in his did he speak again. "Beth was a wonderful woman, son. I know I never met her, but if you loved her, there's not a doubt in my mind that she was wonderful. But you need to love again. To honor her memory. To heal Mary. And to heal yourself." He squeezed Sam's hand. "And maybe to help an old man feel like he wasn't such a failure as a father after all."

Sam felt a surprising, totally new, rush of tenderness toward Elijah. Awkwardly he leaned down to kiss his father's forehead. "You're not a failure, Dad. It just took us longer to succeed. I love you, Dad."

"I always loved you, son. Always will. And I'm proud as punch to be your father."

On the way out of the hospital, Sam ran into Joe and Louis. They were coming in through the automatic doors carrying a big spray of flowers. Sam greeted them warmly and asked who they were visiting.

"Your dad," Joe said.

"My dad?" The idea stunned Sam.

"Oh, he's not such a bad old bird," Louis said. "We'll sweeten him up and bring him round. Sometimes you just have to get people to see past the stereotypes to the real human beings behind them. He's starting to see."

The idea of Elijah entertaining a visit from two gay men brought a smile to Sam's face for the first time in two days, at least. Maybe longer. The muscles in his cheeks felt unaccustomed to the expression.

"You grin," Joe said. "But let me tell you, when I stopped in to see him this morning, he said he was going to ask the church to give us all the cut timber so we could rebuild our cabin."

"Really?" Sam felt as if the whole planet had just changed its direction of rotation.

"Really," said Louis. "He really *wants* to be a good guy."

Maybe he did, Sam thought as he headed for his car. Maybe Elijah's main failing had always been trying *too* hard. The idea of perfection could be an unforgiving taskmaster, not only for the person who was trying to be perfect himself, but for those around him who he wanted to be perfect, too.

He hadn't made the decision consciously, but he found himself parking in front of Mary's house. Her living-room lights were on, inviting. Or maybe they looked inviting because he knew she was inside.

He didn't get out of his car immediately but sat there in the dark and tried to figure out what he was going to say to her. It all seemed so jumbled up inside his head and heart that he didn't know how he was going to make sense out of it for himself, let alone for her.

But if what his dad said was true, that she had been crying because she felt he had rejected her... Well, it wouldn't matter much what he said as long as he showed up. As long as he showed up and didn't say the *wrong* thing.

Feeling nervous and uneasy, he climbed out of his truck and headed for her door. He didn't know what he would do if she wouldn't let him in, but he at least had to mend whatever hurt he'd inflicted. At least tell her that he hadn't wanted to hurt her. Even if she wouldn't hear another word from his mouth.

The woman who answered the door looked a lot

older and wearier than the Mary he'd met. Her eyes were hollow and almost expressionless as she looked at him.

"Can we talk?" he said without preamble.

"What's the point?"

He shifted on his feet, fighting the urge to slink away like the cur he was. It hurt to realize he'd put that look on Mary's face. He'd never wanted her to look anything but happy, and instead his bollixed emotional state had made him hurt her.

"The point," he said finally, "is that we need to talk. I think there are some misunderstandings. But I can tell you one thing for sure, Mary. There won't be any point to it if we *don't* talk."

After a few seconds of hesitation, she stepped back and let him into the house. Neither of them seemed to want to sit. In fact, Mary stayed close to the door, as if she wanted to be able to run on a moment's notice.

"This is terrible," he said finally.

"What is?"

"Me. I'm a cop, right? I've got smart ideas and words of advice for most of the world. Call me in on an emergency and I know exactly what to do. I can talk fighting couples into making peace. I can soothe accident victims. I can sort out neighborhood squabbles. Hell, once I even talked a burglar into putting down his gun.

"But it's different when it's somebody I care

about. Suddenly I don't have any smart words or good ideas. Damned if I don't get tongue-tied.''

"You don't sound tongue-tied to me.''

"That's because I'm not talking about the things that hurt yet.'' His heart was beating nervously, and he felt his mouth go dry. This was not going to be easy. In fact, it was probably the hardest thing he'd ever done. And right now he felt like a blindfolded man walking into a minefield.

"I don't talk much about what I really feel, Mary. I'm not good at it. But maybe I need to change that. So here goes. I believe in saving the whales and what's left of our forests. I worry about the ozone layer and world hunger, and I joined one of those organizations where you send in twenty bucks a month to feed a hungry child. I've got five kids right now, and I write to them at least once every two months and send them some little doodad I think they'd like.''

Was he imagining it, or was her face softening just a shade? "I think we ought to pay down the national debt, and I think we ought to pay more for food so that family farms can make a living. And I think we all need to do a much better job of taking care of one another than we do now.''

He thought he saw the slightest nod of her head, but he couldn't be sure. "Which leads me to my next point. I haven't done a very good job of taking care of *you*. Last night…last night I just plain didn't know what to say. And I think, to be honest, I should admit that all I could seem to think of were clichés I figured you'd heard a million times and didn't believe anyway.''

She drew a shaky breath and bit her lower lip.

''I mean, what am I going to tell you, Mary? That it wasn't your fault? I don't think it was. God, I've been around kids enough to know how slippery they are and how fast they move. Not two months ago I was called when a motorist hit a four-year-old who rode down the driveway on his tricycle right in front of her. He was okay, by the way, except for some fractures, because the driver was going really slow. But the woman driving was hysterical. She'd seen him on the driveway. She knew he saw *her,* because he looked right at her. Then zip. He dashed right in front of her. She couldn't believe he'd done that.''

Mary looked down, and he felt suddenly cast adrift now that he couldn't see her eyes anymore. ''The point is, kids are slipperier than eels. And not every accident can be prevented. I know that.''

He waited, but she didn't say anything. No help there. So he plunged on.

''I understand that you probably weren't responsible, Mary. But I also know that me saying that doesn't make you feel any better. You feel guilty. You feel like you should have done something more. I understand that, too, because I feel that way about Beth.

''So none of the things I could say are going to make you feel any better. I knew that last night, and

I was casting about for something, *anything,* useful to say to you, and I guess you thought I was rejecting you. But I wasn't. I was thinking, Mary.''

She still didn't look up, but finally she spoke. Quietly. ''What were you thinking, Sam?''

''I was thinking that you had a deep, deep wound. And I was wondering if there was anything I could possibly say or do to help you with it. I mean, I'm not exactly great myself. You've seen enough of my stupid old scars to know. I was wondering if anybody as messed up as me would be any use to you at all.''

Now she did lift her head, and pain showed in her gaze. ''Sam...''

''Hey,'' he said with mock humor, ''I'm on a roll here. Exposing my soul. Let me get on with it before I chicken out.''

She nodded.

''So it wasn't that I didn't care, or that I was appalled at you or anything. I was feeling helpless. I'm no psychotherapist, Mary. And I wasn't there when your son was killed. Nothing I can say is going to make you feel one whit better. Just like nothing anybody can say is going to make me feel better about Beth.''

''What happened with Beth?''

''We were out skiing. I don't know exactly what happened. I was behind her, and she seemed to lose control, and the next thing I knew, she ran into a tree at about sixty miles per hour. Skull fracture. I sweated a lot afterward. I still sweat about it. What if I'd been able to get the ski patrol there sooner? What if I'd lifted her on my back and carried her down the mountain instead of waiting. What if I'd gone first and found that rough spot? What if...? I mean, you can always try to work out ways that things could have been different. We all seem to spend a lot of time doing that when something terrible happens.''

She nodded. "Yes. We do."

"So I wasn't there that day, and I can't second-guess you. And you can dismiss anything I say because I wasn't there. And that's the kind of thing I was thinking last night.''

She nodded. "I'm sorry."

"Let me finish. Like I said, I'm such an emotional basket case myself, I was worrying whether I'd just be a burden to you rather than a support. But maybe...maybe if two people who seem to have only one emotional leg to stand on lean on each other...maybe they can walk. Maybe...maybe you don't need my support as much as you need my understanding. I can't take away the guilt, Mary. But I can understand it.''

She nodded, and some of the tension seeped out of her face. "Maybe."

"But here's the other kicker. You said you couldn't trust me. And without trust we can't get anywhere together. You've got to trust me to move my leg when it's time, and I've got to trust you to move your leg when it's time, and we've both got to trust each other to hang on. Or we might as well just sit down and give up."

Tears were welling in her eyes, and they caused him to step closer. "Mary," he said huskily, "I'd trust you to raise my child."

Her eyes grew huge. She gasped, and then her tears began to fall in earnest. A moment later she was in his arms, clinging for dear life.

"I'm sorry, Sam," she sobbed. "I'm so sorry. I was just so afraid. I started to care so much for you, and I was sure you were going to dump me when you found out about me. I was afraid of how much it was going to hurt! So I pulled back...."

"It's okay," he murmured, running his fingers through her hair. "Oh, sweetie, it's okay. I'm scared, too. It hurts so much to care. It hurts so much to love."

"Love can kill you."

"Just about. But...you know, it's already too late. For me, anyway. Because I'm in love with you, Mary McKinney. I'm in love with you, and I want to spend the rest of my life with you. I want to get married and have babies and see your smile over the breakfast table every morning. And if that means I have to risk that awful pain again...well, I'm already risking it. Right now. I can't walk away. Unless you tell me to go."

Her fingers were knotted into his shirtsleeves, and her tears were dampening his shirtfront. "I can't tell you to go, Sam. I tried, and I felt like I was going to die inside. It hurt so bad.... Oh, Sam, don't ever go away again. Not even if I tell you to. Promise me?"

"I promise. Sweet Mary, I promise. And I'll tell you right now, we're going to get some therapy together. But first—because I don't want to wait that long—I want to know...Mary, will you marry me and have my children?"

She lifted her tear-streaked face, the most beautiful sight he had ever seen. "Yes, Sam. I will. I love you so much!"

Inside him, Sam felt the last of the old walls and barriers crumble. He had expected it to hurt to feel so vulnerable again, but, much to his amazement, all he felt was joy and relief.

It wouldn't always be easy. But it was going to be a wonderful life anyway.

Epilogue

The rain drummed on the roof, almost blotting out the sound of Elijah Canfield's voice. Not that anyone minded. This was the tenth straight day of rain, sometimes slow, sometimes pounding, as if the heavens were determined not only to douse the few remaining fires but to christen the ground for new growth. Already the barren earth around the church was alive with tiny green sprouts, although Sam had laid a carpet runner from the parking lot to the church door, to protect Mary's gown from the mud.

"Do you, Sam Canfield, take this woman, Mary McKinney, to be your lawfully wedded wife, to have and to hold, for richer or poorer, in sickness and in health, so long as you both shall live?"

Sam looked into Mary's green eyes, brimming with tears. "I do," he said, in a voice that betrayed the depth of his own emotion. As if to make sure

Mary didn't misunderstand the quiver in his voice, he added, ''I sure do.''

Elijah's voice now wavered a bit. ''Now then, these two having exchanged vows in the presence of God and witnesses, and by the power vested in me by the State of Colorado, I now pronounce you man and wife.'' He paused to swallow. ''Son, you may kiss your bride.''

Sam folded her veil back over her gleaming red hair, bespeckled with just a few flecks of silver glitter. ''I want to sparkle for you,'' Mary had said when she'd told him what she planned to wear. Sam had assured her that, whether she wore glitter in her hair or mud on her nose, she would always sparkle in his eyes. He remembered that exchange as he bent forward and met her lips, a kiss as soft as a butterfly's breath, melting into a tight embrace.

''I am yours forever, Sam Canfield,'' she whispered in his ear.

''I will love you until the end of time itself,'' he whispered back.

They linked arms and walked down the aisle, stepping into the lightened drizzle amidst a hail of birdseed. Sam chuckled at the thought.

''What?'' Mary asked, squeezing his hand.

''Oh, some of that seed will take root. Some of the new lawn around this church will be...ours.''

''Then you'll have to mow it,'' Elijah quipped, coming up behind them in his wheelchair. ''After all, this old church is still standing because of you, son. You saved its life.''

''A lot of people worked hard to save this church,'' Sam said. ''No one more than you, Dad. Sometimes a battered, old husk is worth saving.''

''Yes,'' Elijah said, nodding. ''Sometimes it is.''

As if in agreement, the heavens responded with a roll of July thunder.

New York Times *Bestselling Author*

LINDA LAEL MILLER

Sharon and Tony Morelli were never able to control the powerful
chemistry between them. It led first to heart-stopping passion, then
to marriage and children. They thought they had it all, but under
pressure their happy home became an explosive battleground. But
even divorce can't completely separate them. Spending alternate days
in their home with their children, their unorthodox arrangement
keeps them in close contact. And keeps the desire alive...

USED-TO-BE LOVERS

"Sensuality, passion, excitement and drama...
are Ms. Miller's hallmarks."
—*Romantic Times*

*Available the first week of April 2002
wherever paperbacks are sold!*

Visit us at www.mirabooks.com

MLLM896

***New York Times* Bestselling Author**

LINDA HOWARD

Michelle Cabot has inherited her father's Florida cattle ranch—and a mountain of debt. To make matters worse, a huge chunk of that debt is owed to her nemesis, John Rafferty. Nothing shocks Rafferty more than discovering that the pampered rich girl he once despised is trying to run the Cabot ranch herself, desperate to save the only thing she has left. What he doesn't know is that underneath Michelle's cool, polished facade lie heartache, secrets and the raw determination to live life as her own woman. But Rafferty wants her for his own…and he isn't about to take no for an answer.

HEARTBREAKER

"There is nothing quite like a sexy and suspenseful story by the amazing Linda Howard!"
—Romantic Times

Visit us at www.mirabooks.com   MLH887